To John Thornhill,

Mr Disraeli's
"Rattle"

with May thanks

Janet Hilderley

Jane Hilderley
19 / 09 / 05

JHA PUBLICATIONS

© Janet Hilderley 2004
Mr Disraeli's "Rattle"

ISBN 0-9547191-0-7

Published by:
JHA Publications
40 Copse Road
Cobham
Surrey
KT11 2TW
England

A CIP catalogue record for this book is available
from the British Library.

Design & production co-ordinated by:
The *Better Book* Company Ltd
Havant
Hampshire
PO9 2XH

Printed in England.

Cover design by MusicPrint

Mrs Disraeli as a young woman

ACKNOWLEDGEMENTS

I would like to thank the following people and institutes who have helped me enormously in bringing this book to fruition.

Jill Field, Senior Editor: The Better Book Company Ltd

Roy Keane

Dennis Lipton

Bristol City Library

Buckinghamshire Record Office

The Guildford Institute Library

Archivists: The House of Commons and the House of Lords

Mary Evans Picture Library

The National Trust, Hugenden Manor

Dr Michael Walsh

Westminster City Council

CONTENTS

NOTE:

This book is a work of fiction based on a true story.
Letters quoted from authentic sources are printed in *italics*;
a few extra letters have been created by the author
and in order to avoid any confusion are given in ***bold italics.***

1 Beginnings

BRAMPFORD SPEKE

A grateful nation had provided Lieutenant John Evans with a canvas bag and two twenty-four pound round shot to anchor him to the bottom of the sea, but his widow and children had to fend for themselves. On a still June evening in 1794 Eleanor Evans carried her two-year old daughter, Mary Anne, and led her son, Johnny, northwards from Exeter and prayed that it would be the last leg of a journey in search of their nearest kin. It was an all too common sight in the hinterlands of the Royal Navy's main ports. Because he had died so young, nearly all the small amount of prize money that had come to Lieutenant Evans had been spent paying his creditors. His only real legacy to the family was his servant, Sam the One Eye, who now pulled the lightly loaded handcart which bore the family's meagre belongings.

'How much further, Mama?' Johnny asked in a demanding tone as he trotted by his mother's side. It was a tone that was to be irritatingly constant throughout the rest of his life.

'Not very far now,' replied Eleanor. Then she realized that she was definitely looking forward. Only Sam had consciously noticed the way his mistress had frequently looked back and knew that she was thinking of baby James, her firstborn, whose infant body occupied a small square of ground on the north side of St Sidwell's Church in Plymouth. Neither John nor Mary Anne ever knew of his brief existence, but Eleanor was to remember him for the rest of her life.

Skirting the hamlet of Bramford Speke they turned off the road at the sign that pointed to Sowden and Moors Farms and climbed the dirt track. Very soon they found themselves surrounded by quacking ducks, squawking geese and barking dogs and the sound summoned Farmer Evans and his wife from the house. They smiled broadly at the weary group and opened their arms.

'Welcome home. Welcome home, m' dears.'

Mary Anne had at last reached the first place she could call home.

Some three months later, as he was nearing the finish of morning milking, farmer Evans heard a horse approaching at a brisk trot. The dogs barked and the geese squawked as farmer Evans, with Sam in attendance, emerged from the cowshed. Both dogs and geese gave second best to the huge man on an equally huge horse who trotted into the farmyard and reined to a halt. James Evans made a respectful bow of the head while Sam pulled himself to attention and tugged his forelock as never before.

'It's the Admiral,' he hissed out of the side of his mouth.

'My horse man,' bellowed the Admiral, nodding at Sam as he dismounted and strode purposefully through the farmhouse door without further ceremony.

Mary Anne looked up as he entered and stopped playing with her toes. This, she decided, was a fine moment to practise her 'man smiles'. The Senior Service in its entirety would have held its breath in shock had it seen the severest disciplinarian it had ever known squat down on his haunches and play "piggy toes" with an infant girl. After a while the Admiral, noting the look of astonishment on the faces of those around him, rose and adopted a more dignified composure. He looked directly at Eleanor.

'Sir John Jervis,' he announced. 'May we speak, ma'am?'

'Of course, Sir John,' she replied. Picking up Mary Anne for comfort, she led him into the parlour, blushing as she saw his gaze fall on the furnishings, for the family was so poor they belonged to "old Queen Elizabeth's" day.

'Forgive me for asking ma'am,' enquired the Admiral. 'Are you able to manage? I remember when I was but a midshipman my father gave me not a penny piece, even though he knew that I must be close to starving.'

'We manage, sir,' replied Eleanor with dignity.

'Of course, ma'am,' responded Sir John, in a near apologetic tone. 'I should have expected nothing less.' He paused. 'I was sorry I had to write such a letter to you, ma'am.'

'I ... do understand,' she replied softly. In the bodice of her dress, not quite in the newer fashion of brocade, she carried next to her heart, her husband's last letter to her. She saw the opening line once again in her mind's eye: *When I hold my adorable wife in these fond arms.*

'Death from the malarias is a common enough an occurrence on the West Indies station, ma'am.' Seeing the pain enter the young woman's eyes, he added gently, 'No comfort I know, ma'am. Lieutenant Evans was an outstanding officer, ma'am.'

'That I am sure of,' replied Eleanor. 'But please, sir, do not feel that you have to address me as ma'am quite so often,' she continued in an effort to put the Admiral more at ease, yet surprised at her own temerity.

'Of course not, ma'am,' responded Sir John. 'Most kind.' He was now warming to his subject. 'Indeed, ma'am, when I first set eyes on young Evans he was then but eleven years of age, damn it. Beg pardon, ma'am. He came on board through the gun port of my own cabin, bold as brass. Did Evans ever tell you about Her Majesty's frigate *Alarm*?' The Navy's first copper-sheathed warship. Carries thirty-two guns. Imagine, ma'am when they all fire at once ...'

'Yes,' answered Eleanor with unaccustomed asperity, 'John did mention his ship.' She was tempted to add, 'He kept me up half our wedding night drawing diagrams of the thing.'

'Aye, the moment young John set foot on my deck I knew the lad possessed quality,' went on Jervis, failing to notice the tinge of bad humour in Eleanor's voice. His gaze was on an imaginary distant horizon and he could have been talking to himself. 'I made him my servant and had him trained along with the midshipmen. I always kept a special eye on him. We parted company for a while when I was promoted to a larger command. But, as luck would have it, I was a member of the examining board when he was up for lieutenant. Passed with flying colours. Trounced the rest of the bunch. I was so impressed that I had him drafted to my own ship, the *Ceres*. He served with distinction in the West Indies, until the damned malaria got him ...' He paused awhile, gazing at some scene in his imagination, then his eyes focused on Eleanor once more.

'With Evans's death, ma'am, the Royal Navy has lost an officer beyond price, you a husband and your children a father. It does not make sense to a simple seaman like myself, ma'am, but the ways of the Almighty are strange and not to be questioned.' Having picked up his hat and tickled Mary Anne's toes on the way out, Sir John Jervis rode out of their lives to take command of the Mediterranean Fleet and become the first Earl St Vincent.

Each Christmas Eve, however, a hamper of food, of the luxuries a small farmer could not afford, was delivered to the Evans's farm, compliments of the Admiral.

After the excitement of the Admiral's visit life for Mary Anne and her brother, Johnny, now a puny schoolboy, settled into a routine. On their occasional visits to Exeter they liked to walk along the quay and listen to old sailors observing the weather and making prophecies about the fate of ships they knew, like, 'The *Nightingale* will go down in this.' At times sailors would come ashore with terrible tales from Paris of "Madame Guillotine's" rapacious appetite for heads, which plopped into baskets, blood spluttering from the decapitated bodies onto the crowd; of old women continuing to knit baby clothes and muttering, 'Knit one, purl one,' as the carnage continued.

Mary Anne did not like the way Johnny cut off flower heads with his toy guillotine, saying, 'une, deux, trois.'

'You are cruel, Johnny.'

'I'm counting in French. The sailors say one day Madame Guillotine will reign here too so I am practising to be the executioner. I would enjoy that.' And another flower head fell to the ground.

A favourite time of all for the children was when they stood before the Church of St Mary steps and looked up and up, so high they felt their eyes would fall out, to the tower which seemed to touch the sky. They felt a tingle of excitement as the three mechanical figures, known as the miller and his sons, emerged to strike the hour. The figures disappeared from sight and the children had to wait an hour if they wished to see them again.

Just before that dreadful day when John was sent away to school an election was called. Mary Anne stood watching a number of prosperous tradesmen and farmers getting drunk on free beer while being addressed from a hay cart by Mr Baring, one of the sitting members. By his side she saw a grave-eyed swarthy young man in his late twenties. He looked gloomily down at her. Mary Anne grinned back at him.

'Come away, Mary Anne,' said Eleanor, pulling her gently by the hand.

'Who is he?'

'A Jewish gentleman from London recovering from the melancholies. They say it runs in his family.'

Isaac D'Israeli went one way and Mary Anne the other, forgetting each other immediately. The thought that they might meet again never entered the mind of either of them.

Mary Anne was lonely without Johnny so she was boarded in Exeter four days a week where she attended school and enjoyed the company of other children. Returning home for a school break, she found Eleanor absent.

'Your mother's away cultivating your great-aunt Mary Anne,' grandmother Evans told her. In her dreadful scrawl, which was to so annoy Disraeli, Mary Anne wrote:

Tuesday 5ᵗʰ June

My Dear Mama,

Our school is broke up and I am very comfortable with three pleasant companions with whom and my brother I shall spend the holidays very agreeable. He unites with me in duty

to you and all kind friends and in wishing they may enjoy the
pleasures of the season.
I am my dear Mama your Dutiful daughter
Mary Anne Evans'

GLOUCESTER

When Mary Anne was fifteen years old her grandparents died. Eleanor was discussing with the vicar who should help her manage the farm when she learned that her late husband's parents had only been tenant farmers. It was a further shock to her as she was still recovering from the letter from Mr Scrope, the family solicitor who was also a cousin, telling her that great-aunt Mary Anne had left a pearl necklace to Mary Anne and nothing to her or to Johnny because she believed that Eleanor possessed a fortune of £5,300, which she certainly had had at the time of her marriage.

There was nothing for it but to travel to Gloucester and hope that her uncle, Captain James Viney would take them in. She had received no reply to her letter to him so if he did not oblige then it was the workhouse for all of them. Eleanor tucked her few remaining pounds into the bodice of her dress along with a yellowing letter.

If you had travelled the road south to Exeter in 1807 you would have seen the same family with the same lightly loaded cart, still pushed by Sam the One Eye, that you would have seen travelling northward thirteen years before. They did not look back and they knew that uncle Captain James Viney would not cry out, 'Welcome home m' dears,' on their arrival.

Eleanor took the letter from her bodice and once again read: 'W*hen I hold my adorable wife in these fond arms* ...' then she tore it up and tossed it into the air where the breeze scattered it like confetti into the brook running by the side of the road.

'Why did you do that, Mama?' asked Mary Anne.

'It belonged to yesterday and we are going to tomorrow,' explained Eleanor.

They arrived at the Ship Inn, close to the city walls, where Eleanor spent some of her dwindling money so that they could spend the night in warmth and comfort.

At seven o'clock in the morning the yard clattered into life. Horses came out of their stables snorting and shaking in anticipation of action and submitted themselves to harnessing. Those left within the stables shifted around and banged the doors as if in sympathy. Valets called out, 'Boots' as ostlers bustled around with harness. Johnny shrank back against the wall frightened by it all but Mary Anne, wide-eyed with excitement, took it all in as she clutched her good luck charm, a doll which had come out of a Christmas hamper given by a sailor called Jervis when she was a baby girl.

'Johnny, you and Sam must travel on top. I cannot afford to pay the extra for you to travel inside. Tuck a blanket over your legs and you'll be fine.' Johnny did as he was told and sat white-faced and gripped the rail for over a mile before realizing that he was not going to fall off. When the call of the horn announced their emergence onto the road Mary Anne leaned out of the window. She watched the horses walking, somewhat stiffly at first, and then, warmed up, urged into a steady mile-consuming trot, pulling them into the future.

Two days later they arrived in Gloucester and were put down near the cathedral, tired, dirty, hungry and frightened. Some of the clergy stopped and stared as the family made its way to James Viney's home, Cathedral House, which adjoined the close. The bell rang and uncle Captain James Viney came out to meet them. As always, he wore a full braided red-coated military uniform. 'Good journey?' he asked brusquely, only to be met with a volubility second to none. He was engulfed by a torrent of words.

'We travelled along the Bristol road, uncle … wind, dust, horses … boats in the Channel … could see Wales … not one highwayman … why is the Prince of Wales like a cloudy day? Because he's likely to reign.'

He drew back. He had seen military action, had been under fire. He was to go on to win medals at the battles of Corunna,

Rolera and Vimiera and become a Knight Companion of the Bath. Officers, gentlemen and soldiers treated him with respect. Now he wished he had never asked the question. Between words he managed to stutter, 'For you, miss, the pin factory girls. Teach 'em their letters on Sundays.' If they can ever come up for air, he added to himself.

Eleanor flung her arms around the starched figure of her brother and kissed him over and over again. The poor man shook Johnny's hand firmly. At least there was a sensible male in the family. But then Johnny burst into tears.

The following morning Mary Anne got dressed and took breakfast with her uncle. He muttered something about, 'It's a pity you're not the boy.' He went on to tell her about the pin factory girls and said he would arrange for her to start teaching them to read and write the following Sunday.

Mary Anne was soon getting to know a group of twelve to fourteen-year old white-faced, ill fed, squinting girls, meeting every Sunday in a non-conformist chapel. Through them she learned that she was a fortunate young woman. She now belonged in the close and was therefore destined to a genteel middle-class life.

Two years after the Evans family arrived in Gloucester, on a bright sunny evening, one of the girls waited after class to speak to her.

'Millie, won't your mother be waiting for you?' asked Mary Anne. The girl stood looking down and rubbing the back of one hand with the other. Mary Anne saw that the fingernails were bitten to the quick. 'What's worrying you, Millie?'

'I've missed, Miss. The child's hair fell into her eyes as she looked up. 'I'm expecting.'

'You can't mean … You're not fourteen yet …'

'I'm twelve, Miss.' She paused. 'It happens to girls like us, Miss. Not to your sort. They grab us when they're drunk.' She paused again. 'I can't have it, Miss … and I can't go to old Ma Grist's on my own.' A few days later Mary Anne placed a half crown into Ma Grist's dirty, claw-like hand.

'It's against the law, this. So a guinea if you please.'

'Too much,' said Mary Anne.

'Too much? The likes of you can afford it. Anyway, that's my rate.'

Mary Anne placed another half crown into the woman's hand. 'That's my rate. There may be another one in a month's time if the girl survives,' she said in a tone of finality. 'If you don't want the deal I'll find someone else. And you can expect a visit from the Watch.'

'You drive a hard bargain,' said Ma Grist, obviously taken aback. 'Typical of your sort to take advantage of us poor people. But think on it. One day you might have to come to old Ma Grist yourself, my fine lady.'

'Not with those dirty hands, I won't,' snapped Mary Anne. 'Wash 'em.'

Ma Grist nodded to Millie. 'Take your drawers off, girl,' she said before going out into the back yard, muttering.

The room was lit by a single candle, while filthy floral curtains kept prying eyes at bay. Incongruously a silver bowl, filled with roses, sat in the middle of a table on a crumb-covered cloth which it shared with an elderly, sleeping cat. Millie stood there, seemingly unable to move.

'Do as she says,' said Mary Anne, softly.

The old woman came back with a bottle of gin, mixed with a little water, which she proceeded to pour down Millie's throat.

'Be careful. You'll choke the girl,' warned Mary Anne. Ma Grist slowed up her administration of anaesthetic and noticed Mary Anne's expression of puzzlement as she looked at the bowl of roses.

'It belonged to my family. Once I was your sort. I can talk proper when I want to. My father was one of the gentry, but he was ill advised in his investments and lost his money. I was pretty but I fell for the son of a friend of my father. He used me, then cast me off.' The old woman suddenly softened. 'Remember, my dear, men destroy women's lives.'

Adroitly and showing no emotion, she strapped the semi-comatose Millie to the table, lifted up her skirts and began her dreadful task. Mary Anne held the child's hand and smoothed her brow, and in that terrible moment lost her faith in the stained glass Jesus of her Devon days. She wondered if there was a god, and if there was why He allowed this sort of thing to go on. Perhaps He was only the god of the wealthy, or the god of men. He was always referred to as 'He', never as 'She'. She felt that she should pray, but now she doubted if there was anybody, or anything to listen to her.

'Wet her lips. Keep her quiet,' said Ma Grist. 'We can't afford nosy neighbours.'

Something came away from the child and was thrown into a chamber pot. Millie was left moaning, perhaps for her baby, perhaps simply because of the pain.

'Give her this,' said Ma Grist, 'and don't look so horrified. It's the lot of women to suffer. We're the playthings of men and while we cannot control our bodies we shall always be so. The pain would have been worse if she had borne it. Go on. Give it to her.' Millie took the rag doll and hugged it to her breast.

Overcome with curiosity, Mary Anne lifted the crochet mat covering the chamber pot and was immediately sick over the contents. Right then, however, Ma Grist wanted Millie gone as she had "another one" coming in. Mary Anne was able to bribe a passing sailor to carry Millie to her home. Having listened to the story, however, her mother promptly said, 'Get her out of here. I told her that if she ever got in the family way that there'd be no home for her here.'

'But she has nowhere to go,' protested Mary Anne.

'That's her problem,' said the woman firmly. 'I've got ten others and without her wages I can't afford to keep her. Go to the foundling hospital and ask them.'

Mary Anne knew of a Mrs Rooke, a kindly Christian woman who kept a boarding house. It was she and her daughter, Norah, who cared for Millie. When, two weeks later, Millie died from an infection caused by the operation Mary Anne laid the doll beside her. To avoid a pauper's funeral she paid for the grave and the funeral expenses herself.

'How much do I owe you for your services, Mrs Rooke?' asked Mary Anne.

'Nothing, Miss Evans,' replied Mrs Rooke with a firm but polite shake of her head.

When Mary Anne's fortunes improved Norah Rooke became her lady's maid and her closest friend.

Returning to Cathedral House one afternoon from her walk around the cathedral gardens Mary Anne found a large, well-featured man making her mother both laugh and blush. Captain Viney stepped forward.

'Mr Yate, let me present my niece, Miss Mary Anne Evans. Mary Anne, this is a very particular friend of mine, Mr Thomas Yate. We met in his army days when he was a surgeon with my regiment of artillery.'

Thomas Yate looked up at Mary Anne. Her eyes took in the once handsome but now coarse and bloated features, the food stains on the velvet waistcoat and the cheap, dark stockings which failed to conceal the hairy legs. He did not bother to stand up. He was aware of her sharp nose, down which her gaze seemed to penetrate his outer layer of bonhomie, and unsmiling lips. There and then the two of them decided that they would never be friends.

From then on, however, Thomas Yate was a regular visitor to Cathedral House. Equally, regular letters arrived from Johnny, stamped with the emblem of the 29th Regular of Foot.

The young ensign's ambitions grew with each letter and Mary Anne became concerned to read of the growing debt: '*I have bought my man ... my mess bills are enclosed ... my new horse.*'

Mary Anne wrote to her brother:

'*Johnny, you are a selfish little creature. We have just enough money for ourselves. Rents have fallen for our properties here and uncle Captain is dependent on Mama and I looking after the house while he is away at the wars....Johnny you must understand.'*

Mary Anne was becoming increasingly concerned at the growing intimacy between Thomas Yate and her mother. They exchanged glances whenever she entered the room. She took to knocking before entering and often found her mother pink-flushed when she entered. One day Eleanor took her daughter to one side.

'Mr Yate and I plan to marry. Do not look so horrified Mary Anne. You do not know what it is like to be a widow. Left on the shelf with precious little money. Pitied by the men and a threat to every woman.'

'But, Mama,' protested Mary Anne, 'not Mr Yate. He is coarse, ill-mannered …'

'He is an officer, a gentleman and your uncle's closest friend,' broke in her mother, turning away to signify the end of the matter.

'He is a drunk, Mama. He will drink what little income you have.'

Eleanor turned, her hand raised to strike her, but Mary Anne had gone. Shortly afterwards Eleanor and Thomas Yate married. Mary Anne did not attend the wedding. She was unable to live alone in her uncle's house. Mr Yate made the necessary arrangements for maintenance whilst his friend was away with his regiment in the Peninsula. Mary Anne had no option but to move with them to Bristol.

BRISTOL

Here, in very modest accommodation at 50 Park Street, the distance between Eleanor and her daughter grew. Mary Anne decided to take positive steps to gain more control over her life. She did not consult the Yates, or even Johnny, but apprenticed herself to a milliner close to the merchant wives of Redcliffe. Buried in the basement, with only half candles to light the room and a dust-covered window to show the life going on outside, Mary Anne and half a dozen other girls sewed. Madam saw that the new girl watched things carefully, learned quickly and had a good eye for design. Mary Anne noted that Madam kept every piece of leftover embroidery silk, button and straw chip.

'These cost good money and can always be found a use,' she would say. 'None of them will go to waste.' Mary Anne appreciated the wisdom of her frugality. Having been taught by her grandmother, she helped Madam keep the accounts. Slowly the older woman felt affection for the young girl.

'Could you find fifty pounds to become my partner?' she said out of the blue one day. Having already been saving assiduously and with the assistance of her solicitor cousin Scrope, who handled the Viney affairs, Mary Anne raised the money. In a short time, taking the gamble of pawning great-aunt Mary Anne's pearls, she bought out a very willing Madam completely. She did not renew the lease in Redcliffe but took a new lease on premises in Culver Street which ran parallel to Park Street. She found the premises better for her girls to work in and she had an eye to attracting custom from neighbouring Clifton.

Eleanor was pleasantly surprised to find that her daughter had become a fully-fledged businesswoman. Mr Yate protested that it was rather downgrading to have a stepdaughter "in trade" but could not suppress a grudging respect for her.

In the bow-fronted new "Bonnets and Bows" in Culver Street, Bristol, the year before Waterloo, women of all shapes and sizes competed to buy a small bonnet, white-chipped, trimmed with pink satin and minute blush pink roses which was displayed in the window. There was no price on it. The small, neatly dressed milliner in her navy serge took orders but continually repeated, 'No, the bonnet is not for sale. It is unique. There will be no copies. A bonnet shall be designed especially for you … at a price.'

Some of them noted that her dress was neither long-waisted, in the English style, nor worn over stiff corsets. Her skirt was straight and she wore no ornaments. It was relieved only by a white lace collar. But then, few knew that Miss Evans had a French dressmaker, a friend of her Mama from the "old days".

The little bonnet was never sold but was always displayed somewhere in the bow window, a constant enticement to all the ladies who wanted something just beyond the ordinary. Miss Evans continued to take orders and on certain afternoons was to be seen making her deliveries, wearing neat kid slippers, hidden by high wooden clogs, to protect against the muck of the Bristol streets. At odd moments a glimpse could be caught of ribbed stockings with lace clocks climbing up the sides.

Mary Anne took no apparent notice of anyone. She walked hurriedly towards College Green, where she paused for a while to watch the workmen on the cathedral nave continuing work begun over five hundred years before by Augustinian monks. Then she continued on until her clogs clanked over the busy narrow drawbridge. The sight of the large merchant ships alongside the quay with their sails billowing gently as they dried in a light breeze, overshadowing the small figure passing them by, reminded Mary Anne of her childhood in Exeter. She would not send her girls into this area. She could not afford to employ a man to protect them. She shuddered as girls much younger than her disappeared down alleyways with a swaggering sailor or two. At times an old woman would be carted off to the workhouse, crying out the name of a deceased husband. Occasionally a bier with a covered corpse emerged from a rundown house.

'Time, time, God give me time,' she prayed to herself.

It was while she was knocking at the tradesmen's entrance of an imposing house in Bath Street that she became aware of a shadow. A tall young man was lolling against the iron railings around the property. He was eyeing her coldly up and down with the nonchalance only the hereditary wealthy could possess. His long, thin manicured forefinger pushed back the tall hat from his eyes. Mary Anne stared back challengingly.

He adjusted his cravat, tied in the Byronic mode and moved his weight from one riding boot covered leg to the other. And those, sir, thought Mary Anne, have never bestrode a horse. She was used to such behaviour, though not from such an attractive source. But I must not encourage it, she told herself. The door opened and the footman, having noticed the presence of the young man, smirked. The interest of a "gent" gave him the opportunity to make passes at her. Word would then get back to "Mistress" who would then find fault with the bonnet and refuse to pay for it.

When Mary Anne left the house nearly an hour later he was waiting for her. She walked straight past him, tossing her head in disdain. She had shown clearly that she did not welcome his attentions, but he ignored her signals. He moved swiftly to stand directly in front of her, stopping her further progress, pushed his top hat back, pulled her to him and kissed her on the lips. Taken aback, she raised her hand to strike him, but he picked up her empty basket and, without invitation, escorted her decorously back to the shop and her wide-eyed assistant, Molly. Following this event, the lady of the house cancelled further orders, but each morning Mary Anne's shop was filled with silk red roses and scented cards of adoration – all bearing the inscription, 'from Augustus Fitzhardinge Berkeley'.

Enquiries to Thomas Yate revealed that Augustus and his brother William had long records of profligacy and seduction. They were related to the Earl of Berkeley, a member of the dubious Worcester set and Augustus was a particular friend of the courtesan Harriette Wilson. When they met, as if by accident, Berkeley flirted. He sent notes, but he made no direct approach. Mary Anne became confused and worried. 'What does he want? Will he or won't he declare himself?' she asked Molly.

Her polite, amused interest in Berkeley changed. She tried to find out who, if anyone, he was having an affair with. Did he have a wife? Did he have a mistress? If he did then why was he dancing around her?

One delivery day as she was passing the Llandoger Trow, an inn on the dockside, there came the sounds of men singing a popular sea shanty. As the song ended two men emerged from the shadows and Mary Anne saw that they were carrying knives. A light rain began and the men laughed and chattered at one another. They stopped when they noticed Mary Anne looking at them and then, with drunken gait started to run towards her. Stimulated by fear, she kicked off her clogs and ran. But her pale green kid shoes slipped on the wet cobbles and her arms flailed desperately as she lost her balance. Suddenly strong arms seized her firmly and she found herself looking up into Berkeley's eyes. Quickly he pushed her behind him, grabbed one of her baskets of bonnets and hurled it at the large black man running at him. The man instinctively tried to duck, slipped and fell, cracking his head on the cobbles. The other man approached more cautiously, a long, slim knife, already smeared with blood poised to thrust. Berkeley parried his clumsy lunge with his arm and, as the man slipped, pushed him nonchalantly into the water. Mary Anne, half-fainting, heard a splash and a cry for help which mingled with the screech of the gulls. She felt very, very cold and submitted without a struggle as Berkeley picked her up and carried her into the inn.

'Out of our way,' called Berkeley as he carried his burden through the door, and such was his tone of command that all, drunk or sober, made way. He entered the room the landlord led them to and laid her gently on the bed. 'Hot toddy if you please, landlord. Then privacy,' he commanded.

When warmed and comforted by the toddy, he looked at her appraisingly.

'Well now, Rose?'

'My name is Mary Anne.'

'To me, all of you are Rose.'

Although she knew she should resist, virginity was becoming wearisome to her. Her instinct to submit was stronger than she could have known. She looked up into Berkeley's eyes. The intensity of desire she saw there drained what little resistance remained.

'Rose, Rose,' he whispered, 'let me.' She folded her arms around him and against the noisy background she let him have his way.

Despite the sound of drunken laughter and the combined smell of gin and urine, she clung to him, murmuring only, 'But I've taken no precautions. I should have a sponge soaked in vinegar inside me.' Berkeley ignored her remark.

Later, as they lay naked together, Mary Anne said to Berkeley, 'I will treasure this moment for as long as I live.' But she did not know that she would have to wait over twenty years before another man would give her the delight which Berkeley had so casually given her.

As Master of Ceremonies at the Clifton Assembly Rooms, it was Mr Yate's job to notice who was having an affair with whom. He noticed Mary Anne growing prettier by the day.

'Who's after you Miss High and Mighty?' he enquired. 'Nobody who will marry you I warrant.'

The next morning when Berkeley called in at the shop Mary Anne looked him firmly in the eye.

'What is our future, Berkeley?'

'Our future?' he queried. Seeing Mary Anne's expression he continued, 'My dear little girl, you don't expect me to marry you, do you? A little milliner? Have some sense, Rose. Whatever would my family say?'

Mary Anne carefully removed the locket which Berkeley had given her as a keepsake and tossed it to him in a contemptuous gesture. She opened the door and politely and quietly said, 'Get out, Berkeley.'

'But Rose, you cannot live without me. You won't get an offer of marriage from my sort. Be sensible. You've cost me forty thousand pounds already.'

'Have I Berkeley? Good. So, you've turned down a rich widow whose dowry was not enough to compensate for your taste. But soon you will find somebody and leave me to a comfortless poverty stricken old age. I'm nearly twenty-four and a woman of twenty-five has little chance of marrying. I cannot afford to be sentimental over you. Now, do go away.'

The door slammed shut and Mary Anne went back to her sewing.

Berkeley walked down the street, throwing a coin to Molly who he passed going the other way. At the corner he stopped and waved as he called out, 'We will see who will win this duel.' He could never have envisaged the day when he would write a letter to Mary Anne begging her to save him from starving in the gutter.

2 Marriage

Rain slashed against Mary Anne's shop window. Bonnets, in baskets close to the door, lay cuddling up together like disgruntled kittens. Mary Anne kicked them out of the way and set off on foot for Clifton's Mall where Mangeon's Hotel cringed beside the Assembly Rooms, which dominated Clifton from the top of the hill. Her heel-less shoes squelched with water. Hackney cab drivers called 'Whoa boy' as they drew up beside the gentry, who were happy to pay to get out of the rain. Few paid any attention to the small woman splashing her determined way, for good or ill, into her future.

'Want a lift up the hill, Missy?' said a voice. Mary Anne looked up into the weathered face of hackney cab driver Joe Grinlings. Never know, thought Joe. Some gent might be grateful for this little dolly being looked after by a kind old fellow like me. 'Get aboard quick now, Miss.' The horse was slightly taken aback to be stopped somewhat short of the porticoed hotel entrance. Joe did not want his reputation sullied by bringing in the "wrong type", but he was too obvious about it. A sharp rap on the window of the cab startled him and forced the fat boy snoozing in the porch to rush forward to open the door, only to be disappointed when his open palm was ignored. Oh well, thought Joe. If she wants to act like the gentry she can pay like the gentry. 'Sixpence if you please, young lady.'

'One penny,' snapped Mary Anne.

Pink-flushed, Mary Anne entered the dark oak wooded hallway. Gliding down gilded staircases came ladies of the county's lesser gentry, sniffing as they observed an unescorted young woman. Aristocratic young London gentlemen imagined the pretty wench in the nude. Professional men assessed the prize, preparing themselves for a night's sport with the little vixen. The clerk behind the desk grinned at Mary Anne. His coat was only a little shiny, his hair only a little over-oiled.

'Ticket for the Waterloo Ball,' said Mary Anne, looking him straight in the eyes.

'I'm afraid, madam, that ladies will have to be escorted into the ballroom.'

'Ticket for the ball, if you please,' repeated Mary Anne firmly.

Nonplussed, the clerk looked around for inspiration or support. Retired army and navy officers stopped their reminiscing. A kindly looking clergyman bumbled up to the desk.

'This is a place of respectability, my dear,' he said gently. Mary Anne turned a basilisk gaze on him. He looked disconcerted and bumbled away again.

At that moment Major Vernon-Graham, the portly chairman of the Wellington Ball committee, bounced into the hall, patting his balding head. He was followed by tall, thin, Mrs Vernon-Graham in green taffeta. Their four plain daughters trailed behind mama in the manner of a family of ducklings.

Vernon-Graham assessed the situation immediately. Apart from knowing Mary Anne's mother he had a natural sense of gallantry. Moreover, nothing was going to upset the ball he had spent so much time organising to raise money for the widows of Waterloo.

'Come, come, young man. Snap to it. This young lady is one of my party.'

'Thank you, Major,' said Mary Anne. With a radiant smile she inclined her head slightly to the right and made a half-curtsy. Vernon-Graham's chest swelled with pleasure as he smiled in return. Mrs Vernon-Graham glared fiercely at him and the taffeta rustled a warning. He did not notice either.

So the following evening Mary Anne went to the ball – alone. Mrs Vernon-Graham drew the line at having her "gals" in the company of a mere milliner, even if her dear mother had been a Miss Viney.

On seeing Mary Anne enter the Clifton Assembly ballroom Mr Yate needed more than his usual four brandies to steady himself. Mary Anne stood quite still in the middle of the entrance, her bright turquoise dress drawing attention to the blue of her eyes and enhancing the whiteness of her skin, though somewhat offset by the ageing effect of great-aunt Mary Anne's pearls. The Bristol Mercury reported the following day that the Crichton-Stuarts were there, the Smythe-Joneses, the Osmands: in fact the cream of Welsh and Bristol society were at the ball. The newspaper did not, apparently, notice Miss Mary Anne Evans. But the assembled company did. Most of them stood riveted at her entrance.

'I must not shake. I must not let them see how frightened I am,' said Mary Anne under her breath.

Fans were lowered mockingly, 'Oh my dear. What a sight.'

Fiddles stopped playing.

Mr Yate began praying, 'Good Lord, do not desert me.'

There was silence.

I may as well be hanged for a sheep as a lamb, thought Mary Anne. With a poise that surprised herself she curtsied very low. Great-aunt Mary Anne's pearls swung out from the low-cut dress, drawing attention to the sight of two pretty little pert breasts. Looking up, eyes sparkling, lips thinned, she proudly returned the stare of the crowd. I am the winner, she thought. In every man's eyes she saw lust, and in every woman's spite.

A long, thin, white-gloved hand extended towards her. She did not want to take it but she knew she had no alternative. Berkeley, tall, gallant, black velvet-jacketed, was helping her to her feet. As she stood up she noticed how tight were his white breeches. And he noticed her glance. Inclining his torso toward her he spoke in a sarcastic tone.

'Madam, I congratulate you. A magnificent performance; worthy of a pompadour.' Her moment of triumph seemed to have vanished. He had made her into no more than a courtesan. Suddenly she was surrounded by a host of young men, all flourishing their dance cards. I must not faint, she told herself. I must not. How they would all laugh. In that one moment Berkeley had made her into a cheap little milliner, to be auctioned to the highest bidder.

'If only my Papa had lived,' she murmured.

Relief was at hand, however. Once more Major Vernon-Graham plucked her out of the mire of despond and placed her at the portal of opportunity. With cavalier disregard for his wife's displeasure, he led her gallantly away from the admiring throng to his own party of guests.

'May I introduce to you, Miss Evans, Mr John Wyndham Lewis.'

Wyndham Lewis was taller than Berkeley. His hair was dark and ruggedly cut. His shot silk waistcoat seemed intent on escaping his muscular body and his breeches were a shade too large for his frame. He stood five feet and ten inches of tongue-tied fright.

'Pleased to meet you, ma'am. I gather your Mama is a friend of …'

'Get on with it Tony. The dance is starting,' encouraged Vernon-Graham.

Mary Anne grabbed Wyndham Lewis's hand and before he knew where he was he was cavorting up and down between clapping hands and laughing faces.

'Dancing, ma'am, is not one of my … more used to hunting, ma'am.'

'Never mind,' Mary Anne assured him as she whirled him on and on. Berkeley never perspired. Wydham Lewis sweated.

Mary Anne had never seen so many diamonds sparkling, so many flowers, or tables piled high with food. She danced on and on, through bowls of Waterloo scarlet geraniums. Round and round she went, accompanied by a clodhopping Wyndham Lewis, watched from the ceiling by chubby gilt cherubs set amongst glittering crystal chandeliers whose thousand candles lit up the fountains directly beneath them, splashing away as background to the music.

'Mr Wyndham Lewis, I believe we have gone to heaven,' said Mary Anne archly.

'To my friends, ma'am, I am Tony,' he responded, promptly sitting down exhausted.

'Oh,' said Mary Anne, 'then Tony you will be to me, Mr Wyndham Lewis.'

There was whispering among the fans.

'If that young woman plays her cards well, she will capture £11,000 a year, from the Dowlais ironworks.

'Sound money,' they agreed in chorus.

'A man of thirty-seven years; reasonably attractive for a husband.'

'Intelligent enough to become a barrister.'

'Thankfully lacking the confidence to practise at the Bar.'

'Respectable enough to become Glamorgan's Deputy Lieutenant … but her?'

It was before dawn when Mary Anne awoke after the ball. Her gown, made by herself, lay on the floor. Little gold shoes sat disconsolately on the dressing table and great-aunt Mary Anne's pearls hung disapprovingly on the door handle. No birds seemed to sing that morning as she stumbled out of bed. Seeing Mr Yate snoring and grunting in his wine-stained waistcoat before the kitchen range she set out without breakfast into a deserted Park Street. Things seemed bleak as she walked wearily towards her little business in Culver Street, back to the dreary life stretching on and on before her.

Berkeley has destroyed me, she thought. The business will go downhill now. Perhaps I should try to become a governess with a kind family … but I have no references … besides the gentlemen of the household would be too interested in me for the mistress's comfort. No. I would not employ me if I were her.

On her arrival at the little milliner's shop she found waiting for her … Berkeley.

'Do you know what you have become now? You would be wise, my dear, to consider returning to our original arrangement.' Mary Anne thought of Ma Grist's wise words and shuddered.

'There was no "arrangement", sir,' she said firmly as she shouldered the illegitimate third son of the Earl of Berkeley out of her way.

As Mary Anne was getting ready for the business of the day a note arrived.

'You call yourself my friend, and say
You glory in the name;
But tell me, will you, on the day
When Poverty, in drear array,
With sorrow drives each smile away
Preserve the sacred flame?
Berkeley'

A few hours later a messenger delivered a second note.

'I can assure you from my heart that it will afford me most unfeigned pleasure to enjoy your charming company.'

John Wyndham Lewis'

Mary Anne recalled the riddle she had copied out in her Occasional Book: *'What is the best way to keep a man's love? – Not to return it.'* Under the circumstances, she decided not to stick too rigidly to this adage.

Wyndham Lewis proved a dull suitor, ever considerate of her "virgin status". He was, however, also considerate of her mother. He noticed that whenever he visited their modest home in Park Street that Mrs Yate would withdraw from the sitting room to leave them alone, probably at Mary Anne's request. He realised that the only other fire in the house was in the kitchen. Although he had no respect for the inebriate Thomas Yate, he warmed to Mrs Yate. Consequently, probably the only demand he made on Mary Anne was, 'I must beg of you that when your mother is at hand that we will not drive her from her fireside.' Mrs Yate received gifts of hare and woodcock, which he brought from Glamorgan, with gratitude and pleasure, kissing him daintily on the cheek. She was more comfortable with the ironmaster than she would ever be with her daughter's second husband.

Such was Wyndham Lewis's ardour that he even allowed his business affairs to slip, staying for days at a time at Mangeon's Hotel. When at home in Wales he sent endless love poems and notes to Mary Anne who quickly realized that Lewis was the best catch she was likely to find. He was kind, intelligent, rich and, importantly in her view, very manageable. She looked forward to seeing their children playing on the lawn.

In early October 1815, whilst Mrs Yate was politicly overseeing some affairs in the kitchen, Wyndham Lewis paced up and down the carpeted floor of the parlour. Mary Anne's eyes followed him knowingly. Eventually he spoke.

'There is something I have been meaning to ask you, Mary Anne, my dear.'

'Please feel to ask, dearest,' replied Mary Anne. 'But please do it on your feet. A real man looks ridiculous on one knee.' Wyndham Lewis stopped pacing and the rigidity of his shoulders disappeared.

'How do you know what it is?'

'Let's call it intuition. Or to put it another way, your body sends out messages more eloquently than your words.'

'Hmmm,' said Wyndham Lewis. He sat down beside her and took both of her hands into his own. 'Will you then?'

'Will I what?'

'Be my wife of course. Marry me.'

'You haven't asked me yet.'

'But you said ...'

'I know, but you've still got to say it.'

'Marry me.'

Mary Anne looked at him soulfully. She had decided to make sure that he really wanted to before she said yes.

'Am I not a little on the old side? I shall be twenty-four next month. Most men prefer a lady to be younger.'

'Certainly not. I do not want a wife who has yet to grow up. And you've still got plenty of child-bearing years ahead.'

'And what about my social standing, Wyndham? How will your county friends, not to say your family, think of you marrying a milliner?'

'There are plenty of distressed gentlewomen about, Mary Anne. But there're damn few, forgive me, who have had the character to take their own lives into their hands to avoid destitution. That's one of the qualities I love you for. Besides, your mother, and through her you, are still well regarded. The Viney name still has reputation throughout Gloucestershire.'

'You know well, my darling, that I can bring no dowry.'

'I do not care about a dowry. It's you I want. Your wit, your humour, your intelligence, your courage and ability to get things done. I do not want a simpering maid. I need someone who can manage Greenmeadow while I am away. And someone I can look forward to coming home to. I love you. I want you. I need you.'

'Oh, Wyndham, Wyndham. Yes,' said Mary Anne softly as she wrapped her arms around him.

On 22 October 1815 Mary Anne received a letter from Wyndham Lewis regretting the absence of his "most charming darling". He was in Plymouth where he had gone to visit her uncle, James Viney, the senior member of the family for his consent to marry his niece. Mary Anne congratulated herself on her balanced campaign.

Brother John, now a captain, wrote:

'*I must congratulate you on your approaching nuptials to a gentleman you seem to have a particular regard for, as he is the finest out of so many admirers ... You will be obliged in many things to be responsible. The charge of a house and perhaps a family ... I need not tell you to be always uncommonly regular in your devotions to God, as from Him all blessings flow ... I hope one of these days, when resting from the fatigues of my Campaigning (or our holiday as we soldiers call it) I shall have the honour of being introduced to Mr Lewis ...*'

Ignoring the sanctimonious content of this letter, Mary Anne enigmatically replied:

'You know I never wish you to marry – if you will only keep single you may call yourself one of the Saints not withstanding all your wicked ways.' Do anything but fall in love, my dearest, she whispered to herself.

Mary Anne knew, so did Johnny, so did Wyndham Lewis, that she loved her brother more deeply than any other living being. She would do so until she met her second husband, who ironically, loved his sister, Sarah, in the same way.

In the little church at Clifton Mary Anne married John Wyndham Lewis. It was just before Christmas and she wore a bright red cape touched with fur. As she walked up the aisle, on the arm of her uncle Colonel James Viney, she saw a bride's bouquet lying before the altar. As was the custom when a young girl died before her wedding day her wedding bouquet was carried on her coffin. On catching sight of the wilting flowers Mary Anne immediately thought of Berkeley. John Wyndham Lewis may not be the man I want, but I am alive. Johnny can go on being an officer and a gentleman taking part in grand reviews and saluting Wellington.

At the sight of her daughter Mrs Yate burst into tears. Mr Yate took a swig from a hip flask. The numerous Wyndham Lewises who attended welcomed Mary Anne into the family without reserve. After the ceremony all the guests 'ummed and oohed' at the magnificent plate given by the great Glamorgan landowners, the Butes. Wyndham Lewis stood proudly before the gift telling all who would listen that his choice of wife was 'an acknowledgement of the family's approval of Mary Anne,' who did not dimple with pleasure as she should have done.

3 Greenmeadow

It took the newly-weds several days to reach Mary Anne's new home north of Cardiff, in the Dowlais Valley. In the gathering darkness of a short winter's day the horses walked wearily up the driveway towards the fine, large, whitewashed house surrounded by water meadows. Behind the hills the sun crept away, leaving its reds and oranges dancing on the waters of the River Taff which ran by the house, murmuring tales of long ago.

'I'm sorry about the noise,' said Wyndham Lewis. 'You only hear the mine workings when the wind is blowing in this direction.' But it was the sound of chanting that Mary Anne heard, echoes of long dead Cistercian monks, whose place Greenmeadow had once been. As the carriage cleared the dark trees which lined the drive and approached the entrance of the house, Wyndham Lewis clasped Mary Anne's hands in his saying, 'Welcome home, my dear. Welcome home at last.'

The new Mrs Wyndham Lewis walked into the entrance hall and straightened her back as the line of household servants curtsied to her.

'Mrs Jones,' she told the housekeeper, 'I shall come to your kitchens at eleven tomorrow morning. Please have the books ready for my inspection.' Mary Anne saw by the old woman's face that she was as straight as anyone and patted her wrinkled, ring-less hand. Then she looked into the butler's face. 'I shall inspect the wine cellar at two o'clock. And the account books.' That, she thought, should give him time to sort things out and find the money's shortfall, one way or another.

The old woman smiled. She was going to be a friend. Mary Anne looked at the butler again and saw the contempt in his eyes. She realized that he was a younger son of distressed gentry and could not conceal the dislike of the lower gentry for the newly arrived. He was going to be an enemy.

That night, in a large bed bought by Wyndham Lewis's grandfather for his new wife, Wyndham Lewis made love to his bride. His gentle, clumsy consideration made her spirit pray for the expertise of Berkeley and her body longed for a goose feather mattress.

The next day Mary Anne learned that, honeymoon or not, Wyndham Lewis kept to a routine which he seldom broke. Twice a month, he went on business to London. Once a month he journeyed to Swansea for days at a time. The servants were used to the master being away so much and being on their own.

Mary Anne worked out her own routine. While her husband was away she breakfasted in bed, entering the kitchen promptly at eleven o'clock. In the evening, following her grandmother's example, she summarized the day's activities and expenses:

'... buns 2d, bunch of violets ½d, milk 7½d, etc, etc ...'

In her Occasional Book Mary Anne jotted down useful notes:

'A strengthening recipe:

Take a bottle of port wine, and an ounce of isinglass, a small piece of cinnamon and sugar to your taste, put all the ingredients together on the fire, and when half is gone, it will be sufficiently done. Take every morning at eleven o'clock, the quantity about the size of a nutmeg.'

She needed the recipe. The servants giggled behind her back.

'Only a farmer's daughter.'

'She called herself a milliner.'

Nevertheless, Mary Anne noticed every spice that vanished from the kitchen, or a shortage of flour, and commented, 'Surely, cook, you made twelve pies. Why are there only ten?'

The long husbandless days had to be filled, not always to Wyndham Lewis's convenience. He called for his carriage only to find that it was on route to Bristol to pick up "Mama". Mary Anne somehow developed an unforeseen gift as a marriage broker. He found himself paying for elaborate wedding presents. On the drawing room wall by the fireplace hung a satin ribbon entwined with rows of small dried flowers. On this, in clear gothic script, Mary Anne had painted the names of the girls for whom she had found suitable husbands:

Susannah, Jane, Emma, Daisy, Mary, Eleanor and Lucy. One "strong-minded" girl who insisted on remaining a spinster had, under Mary Anne's reluctant patronage, become the village schoolmistress. But when Mary Anne went to live in London the young woman married a widowed farmer whom she had been in love with for over ten years.

Mary Anne bought herself French and Italian grammars and taught herself to speak both languages competently. This proved to be a great asset to her second husband who spoke no language other than his own except perversely, the dead language of Latin. Other young ladies recited poetry, played the harpsichord and sung like canaries. Mary Anne looked at the faces of those she was entertaining and found a Spanish musician who taught her to play the guitar. She soon found herself the centre of attention for such an unusual accomplishment and complained to friends and family alike, 'I have a fine voice. Why has nobody told me so before?'

On pleasant afternoons between three and six o'clock the ladies of Cardiff could be seen handing calling cards to footmen who delivered them to the front doors of great houses. Etiquette demanded that a young wife left her card and it was up to the receiver to call first on the young couple. Mary Anne, however, simply drove by in her black four-in-hand, lined with cherry pink satin, with her maid, Norah Rooke and Charles the footman in attendance. Servants in kitchens whispered about Mrs Wyndham Lewis. Some ladies said they would bring her down.

'Do you think she does not know the etiquette?' they asked one another.

One hidebound old lady said, 'If she left her card then I could refuse to call on a former milliner. But I cannot if she does not.'

'Most provoking,' said another elderly lady with a wry smile. Mary Anne's carriage continued to drive through Cardiff, often going to the races.

Benjy, her lopsided greyhound ran beside her. He was a present from Wyndham Lewis's irascible brother, the Reverend William Price Lewis. Benjy's wandering ways caused much embarrassment. He sniffed at gentry with the same casual attitude as he sniffed around gamblers, gypsies, prostitutes, wrestlers and fortune tellers, and joined in the rough and tumble of the acrobats, much to his mistress's amusement.

The "Governor", as Price Lewis was known throughout the locality, was more often to be found in the shooting or hunting field than in the pulpit. His introduction to Mary Anne had been when he married her to his nephew. He was obviously taken with her. Over a glass of champagne, and with a twinkle in his eye, he had invited her to, 'Come hunt with me and my nice little pack of harriers when you're settled in at Greenmeadow.'

'He's an incorrigible old devil,' said Wyndham Lewis when Mary Anne told him. 'He holds the livings of seventeen parishes, so he's got seventeen sets of tithes coming in to pay his curates and feed his numerous illegitimate children.'

'At least he acknowledges and cares for his offspring,' replied Mary Anne. She was intrigued. This was an invitation not to turn down.

'You do not propose to hunt with the Governor?' exclaimed Price Lewis's huntsman when Mary Anne appeared for her first hunt. He had heard of hunts in which women rode, often as well as or better than many of the men. But this had always been a man's hunt. He felt that certain social graces which he lacked would be needed with a lady in the field.

'B...b...but should you fall off your horse, ma'am, I should see your under things.'

'Sir, if you have not seen a woman's under things at your age then it's time you did.' And up went Mary Anne's skirts.

Mrs Yate benefited from the Governor's hunting prowess, receiving many gifts of game sent to her by her daughter. On one occasion Mary Anne wrote:

'Not been very successful in killing many partridges, only three brace a day, but woodcock were more plentiful and yesterday the dogs caught many hares.'

After one of Mary Anne's escapades some of the servants waited to tell Wyndham Lewis of his wife's misdemeanours in the hopes that he would divorce her and they would be rid of her. On that day he entered her room, closed the door quietly and looked directly at her. She had learned to be wary of such quietness.

'How have you spent your day?' he asked. Mary Anne sensed danger. She knew that she had been foolhardy and now saw the carriage, the clothes and the whole lifestyle in the balance. Despite being aware of giggling the other side of the servants' door, she answered honestly.

'I too have made a journey,' she said, 'with my nieces, Catherine and Mary Williams. I took them into your mines in a tram wagon. We went a mile and a half underground. It was such fun in the blackness that we screamed and laughed all the way back.'

Wyndham Lewis's lips tightened. There was silence for a while then he got up and walked out of the room. He never mentioned the matter again. Mary Anne put down her embroidery, walked quietly to the door, swung it open and boxed the ears of the crouching servants.

'That's how we treat key-holers in Devon. Pack your bags and leave. Without a reference.'

'But master …' they squealed.

'I am mistress here. Now be off.'

Mary Anne never entered the mine again.

As winter fogs crept through the Glamorgan valleys, Mary Anne in her bright, shiny carriage rode through Dowlais, which became increasingly drear. From her carriage window the wife of the fine ironmaster looked down into bleak cottages, some little more than hovels. At least the availability of coal, arduously picked from the spoil heaps, meant that they had fires. Screaming children ran from door to door. Women, some thin with hunger, begged for food. Then the snows came. Mary Anne went alone into the valley with blankets and warm clothing. Many women kissed her. Many men spat and sneered.

Mr Disraeli's "Rattle"

'Tell your man to pay proper wages. Not send his missus as an angel of mercy. We earn less than a shilling a day.'

'And drink most of it,' cried the women.

She found some of the cottages sparkling clean. Crisp white linen hung around the room to dry. 'We can't put it out. Black specks from the ironworks see. Never stop.' Such a cottage was managed by a strong-minded wife who saw to the needs of her husband. He in turn would be a diligent workman who saw that his wife had sufficient money to care for the family before he went to quench his thirst at the inn.

But other cottages housed a half-hearted fire, on which the small dark folk who crowded round, managed somehow to keep a pot simmering, into which all the food was put. This shared the hearth with a metal teapot, filled on waking and emptied at bedtime. Here the woman of the house had either chosen a husband unwisely or had not been able to cope with one of a weak or a bullying nature. After a wearying day in either the mine or the ironworks he had succumbed to the transient escape of the alehouse at a cost to his wife and children. Mary Anne enquired carefully into the needs of each family. As Christmas approached she prepared two hundred and fifty hampers with her own hands and wrote the names on tickets of those most in need. Each ticket bore instructions of the type and quality of food each person was to have.

Wyndham Lewis, seeing his wife growing thin and wan, and wondering why so many of his work people inquired after her, asked her why she spent so much effort on them. Her answer shocked him.

'We are rich. We are fortunate. It is merely the throw of the dice that has made us so.'

'No,' replied Wyndham Lewis firmly. 'It is the will of God. He has ordered things so. He has created these people as a lesser sort.' It was Mary Anne's turn to be shocked.

As a first wedding anniversary present Wyndham Lewis had extensive alterations made to Greenmeadow, transforming it into Pantgwynlais Castle.

'You now live in the most fashionable residence in Glamorgan, my darling,' announced Wyndham Lewis when the workmen left their newly fashioned home. That night Mary Anne made love to her husband with an ardour he had not experienced from her before. At dawn she crept out of the house and through the dew-covered grass to the river to hear the monks singing, but she heard only the whispering of the spring breeze. Mary Anne knew that the magic of Greenmeadow, which may have been her first youth as well, had vanished for ever.

On a swirling foggy morning in November 1819 Mrs Wyndham Lewis was, at last, seen leaving cards. When the gentry looked at them they found invitations to a grand ball at Pantgwynlais Castle. It all cost Wyndham Lewis, who was cautious with his money, rather a lot. Most of the guests agreed with Mrs Yate that the geranium red and Wellington blue corridors were rather vulgar.

Mary Anne wrote notes in her journal:

Everybody congratulated me on the beautiful manner in which the place was ornamented. The artificial flowers and the profusion of lights evoked admiration. We served eight courses and everybody drank quantities of champagne.'

In 1818 Thomas Yate, back in Bristol, stumbled down the back steps into death. A few days after they buried him Mrs Yate, writing to friends, heard the sound of a large carriage rumbling up Park Street. To her surprise it stopped outside her small, rented, unattractive house. As the "quality" rarely appeared in this street, lace curtains began to twitch. Mrs Yate, adhering to her own standards, did not follow suit. Consequently, she was shaken by the fierceness of the rap on her front door. On opening it she was even more startled to see Mary Anne standing there. Her daughter was fingering a set of cameos.

'Worth four hundred pounds, Mama. A present from Wyndham,' she said with a cheerful smile.

'I would rather my daughter wore a chemise under her gown and was the chairman of the Cardiff Ladies Society,' replied Mrs Yate tartly.

Mary Anne entered the house giggling, but when she arrived in the parlour her manner changed.

'Mama, I am here to draw up a statement of the bills you have paid on behalf of Mr Yate. I have talked to Wyndham's solicitor ...'

'But Cousin Scropes is advising,' put in Mrs Yate.

'Cousin Scropes, Mama, is in Devon. I suspect that you are still paying amounts which even Mr Yate did not manage to sustain.'

After three hours Mary Anne took a sip of water and put down the quill.

'You cannot go on like this living in serious debt, Mama. I have recently had to write to Johnny on the same matter.'

I think it now proper to tell you that it was not my Uncle who gave you the £500 but your own little Whizz. I have at last determined to tell you, to convince you, of the impossibility of my supplying you with money for some years. I have borrowed the money from two people and I must pay it off.

'Perhaps, Mama, you would be so good as to write to Johnny about it. He will never listen to me but ... well it's worth a try.'

As requested, or, as she felt, instructed, Mrs Yate duly wrote her son solemn advice about living within his means, but blunted the impact of the message by finishing:

'...follow my example in a steady example of public and private worship; having ever found through the vicissitudes of this mortal state religion and a firm truth in the Almighty has ever been my greatest comfort, which I earnestly recommend to my dearest son.'

Johnny wrote back thanking his mother then promptly penned another begging letter to his sister.

On occasions Mary Anne would report on the progress of her life to Johnny, "the delight and torment of my life."

'*I was so pleased at your having a party to drink our healths – I fancy how well you did it all. How different my journal is to yours. I rise at eleven ... answer notes and take a lesson on the guitar and eat luncheon, go out in the carriage, pay visits and shop.*'

Mary Anne enjoyed being a hostess, running a home and, to stave off the boredom – as many wives did – flirting discreetly. In the current society verses were a popular and amusing means of communication. She wrote to a family friend, Sir Charles Morgan of Tredegar:

The lady will try her utmost to please,
Your bed shall be warm and made to your ease,
But of nightcaps I own I have now got another
To keep it and wear it and prize it for ever.
Were I but a mouse I'd venture to peep,
To look at my pet when he is asleep ...
Rose.'

Sir Charles remains a shadowy figure soon vanishing from the scene but his reply leaves an unanswered question. How far did Mary Anne go with bachelor Sir Charles? He replied:

'*To describe the great comforts I found at Green Meadow,*
I commence with the pleasure of dear little bed, oh.
Such dreams I have had I shall ever remember ... '

Another adorer, known only as H.L.B. wrote:

'*Farewell to Green Meadow, one ling'ring farewell,*
To Wales where Elysium and Harmony dwell ...
Where happiness reigns in the zenith of power,
And the Rose of enjoyment is Lewis's flower.'

In August 1819 Mary Anne read in *The Times* that a "vast mob" of some sixty thousand men and women had rallied in St Peter's Fields in Manchester. There were many family groups. Parents had taken their children with them to listen to the popular orator, Henry Hunt, talk about parliamentary reform. The authorities, members of the landed gentry, ever fearful of revolution following events in France, over-reacted. Local yeomanry, ordered to arrest Hunt, charged the crowd. There were casualties. Eleven died and hundreds were injured, many with sabre cuts. Perhaps, thought Mary Anne, it was just one officer, a Johnny, who panicked and caused the whole army to charge.

Norah Rooke entered the room with some lace for a new dress. Mary Anne held the newspaper up to her.

'Have they heard of Peterloo in the town, Norah?'

'Oh yes, ma'am. Someone just down from London said that gentlemen there have had billboards hurled at them. They have pictures painted on them of cavalry hacking shrieking, blood-soaked women and children with their sabres. They say there will be riots, ma'am.'

Mary Anne was aware of the discontent amongst many of Wyndham's workers and hoped that it was not strong enough to drive them to any extreme action. As it was, things stayed calm and the outrage began to fade in importance. Then at the end of January 1820 there was further excitement. The newspapers announced the death of King George III.

'How old was he?' asked Mary Anne when Wyndham read her the newspaper's headline.

'Eighty-one. He would have been eighty-two this year.'

'Will it actually make any difference, dear? I mean, Prinny has been standing in for him for so long, I cannot imagine any great change.'

'Well, if you want some excitement then London will be the place to be.'

'Why is that, dear?'

'The coronation of course,' said Wyndham Lewis. 'Though I don't suppose that it will take place until next year. Just think, Mary Anne, the majority of people in the country, including you and me, have never lived through a coronation. King George has ruled for nearly sixty years.

'Of course,' went on Wyndham Lewis, now that the Regent has become George IV, there will be a general election. But Cardiff is in Lord Bute's pocket, so there will be no change here.'

As it happened, Wyndham Lewis was wrong about there being no change in Cardiff. A few days later Norah Rooke returned from an errand to the town in an excited state.

'The news in the town, Mrs Lewis, is that Lord William Crichton-Stuart, the Earl's son, has decided not to stand in this election. Does that mean that Cardiff will not be represented?'

'Certainly not,' replied Mary Anne curtly. 'Call my carriage will you Norah. I have to go out.'

Unknown to her husband, Mary Anne called on Lord Bute.

'My Lord, do not concern yourself. We have a candidate. He will prove excellent.'

Mary Anne donned her "Welshness" and rode into Cardiff, canvassed with handshakes and even kisses and gave a goose dinner for a hundred and nine worthy voting burgesses. She wrote to Johnny:

'They cheer me wherever I go. They are all quite charmed by my heroism. Wyndham is popular beyond what I can describe … The lower orders are mad for him.'

'I promise you, my dear, if I win I will pay off all your brother's debts,' said Wyndham Lewis in gratitude.

Wyndham Lewis could hardly speak. He had beaten his opponent, Ludlow, the Whig, comfortably. Mary Anne stood on the Angel Inn balcony acknowledging the calls of the crowds for the "Good Lady". Her mother and Wyndham Lewis stood in silent shock as Mary Anne threw down baskets full of rich plumb cake, ribbons and cards and blew kisses to all and sundry.

'They must remember your name,' she explained. 'Especially Lord William's tenants. Many of them nearly voted for Ludlow by mistake. We don't want to have to work so hard for votes next time.'

A few days later Major John Viney Evans received a very large cheque. Wyndham Lewis told Mary Anne, 'From now on, my dear, John Viney Evans can be disgraced and damned.'

Overnight Mary Anne had become a woman of some importance. As the Member of Parliament's wife she entertained all the great people of the Principality – High Sheriffs, judges, businessmen, professional men of standing. She even became the patroness of the Cardiff Grand Ball and the Swansea Daffodil Ball She wore a superb and brilliant tiara which Wyndham Lewis had paid a thousand guineas for, together with five hundred pounds for the matching bracelet. Mary Anne had pleasure in conveying this information to Mrs Vernon-Graham.

In April it took the Wyndham Lewises five days and numerous changes of horses to travel through the slush of winter from South Wales to London. They entered the metropolis, the horses picking their way along the high street of the pretty little village of Kensington, then into the residential part of London which lay between Charing Cross and Hyde Park Corner.

The carriage jostled its way along Piccadilly to number 13 Burlington Street, which they would rent until August when parliament rose. Wyndham Lewis complained bitterly that the place cost twenty-five guineas a week 'for a mere hovel without even a proper water closet'. Subsequently they rented 12, Welbeck Street, 1, Cumberland Place and 8, Hertford Street. When Wyndham Lewis paid a thousand guineas for eighteen months for number 24 Portman Square Mary Anne nagged him, with encouragements of a private nature, to purchase a London house.

Mary Anne's organizational abilities soon had the Wyndham Lewises settled into Burlington Street. With the ever-reliable Norah Rooke at her side, servants were hired and, where necessary, chivvied into their duties. She insisted that Wyndham should have a suitable place to call home whilst in London and that she was the only person who could provide it. Her first taste of London life was, of course, some compensation for her wifely devotion. Teething problems were barely over when a new wave of excitement hit London. Wyndham Lewis brought the news home with him on 6 June.

'Well, Mary Anne, it seems that our new King's past is catching up with him.'

'Come now, Wyndham,' said Mary Anne, 'don't talk in riddles. Let's hear the news.'

'Queen Caroline arrived in London today. She's calling herself Queen-Consort and insists that she will be by her husband's side at the coronation.'

'Queen Caroline!' repeated Mary Anne, calling back memories. 'I remember hearing gossip about her from time to time. Didn't she leave Prince George and go off to the continent? I vaguely remember tales about the strange company she kept. And illegitimate children? But really, Wyndham, I've no idea how old she is even. I couldn't have said if she was still alive. Are the stories true?'

'How can we really know, my dear,' replied Wyndham. There were terrible stories told about her at the beginning of the century. But who started them is anyone's guess. Apparently in 1806 Prince George himself virtually compelled the Government to investigate her behaviour. He wanted an act of Parliament to nullify the marriage. But the Committee of the Privy Council cleared her of all accusations.'

'Oh. But how old is she now?'

'Just turned fifty so I understand.'

'What does she look like then?'

'Well, I've not seen her myself, but those who have say she looks quite grotesque. They say she wears white make-up like a Pierrot clown. Then she has a poorly fitting wig, topped by an enormous wide-brimmed hat.'

Mary Anne giggled.

'She had quite a retinue with her,' went on Wyndham. Apparently there's an Italian count and a former Lord Mayor of London among them. God knows if it's true. But they certainly say that she has a personal attendant who wears a turban.'

Mary Anne laughed out loud at the mental picture she conjured up.

'But Wyndham, why on earth did she leave her husband?'

'Oh, she didn't. He left her.'

'Really? Why?'

'He didn't really want to marry her in the first place. He was quite happy with Mrs Fitzherbert. But that was totally unofficial, of course. As next in line to the throne there was pressure on him to produce an heir. So he married Caroline. She's a first cousin of his from Brunswick. They married in 1795.'

'Good heavens. I was only three then,' said Mary Anne. 'When did he leave her?'

'The very next year. Just after she had produced a daughter for him; Princess Charlotte.'

'But why, Wyndham, dear?' asked Mary Anne plaintively, no longer finding anything funny in the whole affair.

'Apparently he said that she was as boring as she was ugly. Then producing a daughter instead of a son was just too much.'

'Where is Princess Charlotte now, Wyndham?'

'She died three years ago. Sad I know, but she would have been in for a hard time if she had lived to succeed her father. There're precious few in government who think that a woman makes an acceptable monarch.'

'Wyndham,' asked Mary Anne in an unusually serious tone, 'do you think that out new king has acted correctly or honourably regarding his lawful wife?'

'No, my dear,' replied Wyndham gently, with a sad shake of his head.

Mary Anne could imagine Queen Caroline's feelings on being abandoned. She remembered Berkeley. She remembered the words of Ma Grist: 'Remember my dear, men destroy women's lives.' In the following year, when Queen Caroline died just nineteen days after being turned away from her husband's coronation, Mary Anne mourned her sad life and gave thanks for the husband she had.

4 A Home in London

In 1820, seven years before she came into possession of a fine mansion opposite Hyde Park, Mary Anne had written to Johnny:

'Wyndham has promised me a beautiful house in town and this is to be made very pretty ... it will be so much more comfortable to have a regular town house and country house.'
She was aware that Cardiff society had been shocked when their new Member of Parliament's wife had laughed in the face of Lady Fitzby Jones.

'Me!' she exclaimed. 'Me! Chairman of the Cardiff Bible Society.' She laughed all the way back to Pantgwynlais Castle. Cardiff society was not, however, outraged at the way Mrs Wyndham Lewis took over the role of chairman of various committees. She even took control of the ladies organising the Swansea Daffodil Ball. Each woman was allocated a job with a smile from Mary Anne and received a sharp retort if she did not complete the allotted task satisfactorily.

Mary Anne found that Mayfair society was neither shocked nor impressed by her. In short, it did not notice her. The smart, dark barouche belonging to Mrs Wyndham Lewis was only one of many weaving its way through the stench of Piccadilly. The diamonds she wore daily drew no comment. Mary Anne, looking in her mirror, saw reflected back at her just one of the multitude of wealthy women who had town houses in the west end of London.

'How can one be part of society if one stays for the season in rented accommodation, however expensive?' she asked Wyndham Lewis, who saw London life as being of only a few years' duration before returning to Wales.

From the moment Mary Anne arrived in the capital, however, she began her search for a London house. Unfortunately, the places she found were all too expensive for Wyndham Lewis's taste. He felt that the London housing bubble could not continue.

On a light summer day, when sprigged muslins were in fashion, Mary Anne walked past Tyburn and on into the former Tyburn Lane, now called Park Lane.

'Old Q, you know, the Duke of Queensbury, lives here,' she said to Norah Rooke. 'All the great and the good have their place in this street, even Byron. And down there,' she said pointing to the corner of Hyde Park in the middle distance, 'that's Apsley House. The Duke of Wellington lives there. It's Number 1, London. Rather fitting, don't you think, Norah?'

Just then Mary Anne noticed the sign on Number 1, Grosvenor Gate. It read: "For Sale this magnificent mansion" followed by the name and address of the agent. She looked across the roadway to the park. Right opposite was the Grosvenor Gate, by which, until recently, a cowshed had stood. Beyond that cows were grazing.

A gentleman passing by paused, looked thoughtfully at the house for some time, then raised his tall hat to Mary Anne and said, 'My dear madam, the house will need a great deal of renovation.'

She went immediately to the agents. £13,000 freehold was the asking price she was told. She almost skipped her way back to Portman Square, despite a despondent Norah Rooke desperately trying to make realistic protestations.

'However parsimonious Mr Wyndham Lewis is with his money, he cannot refuse such a bargain,' Mary Anne told her.

That evening Wyndham Lewis was pleasantly surprised. He had spent the afternoon in his favourite club, the House of Commons. When supper was served he found placed before him pheasant, champagne, his favourite dessert, Charlotte Russe, as well as little extras being offered by Mary Anne. The meal completed, he sank back in his armchair, innocently loosening his stock. Mary Anne handed him a cigar and a glass of port.

'Wyndham, darling. Darling Wyndham. Do you think £13,000 is too much to pay for a mansion in Park Lane?'

'It depends if it is freehold,' replied Wyndham Lewis, a slight frown of suspicion beginning to form.

'It is,' said Mary Anne, a note of excitement coming into her voice. 'Just think, darling, we are paying fifty guineas a week to rent here. And before that it was twenty-five guineas for little more than a hovel in Burlington Street. Work it out yourself, dear. In less that five years we could recoup our losses.' Mary Anne gabbled on. Wyndham Lewis dozed.

A few days later a horse trotted up to the Grosvenor Gate where its rider, his dark cape dripping with rain, reined him in. The Duke of Wellington looked down his large, hooked nose at the mansion opposite. With a well-practised movement he produced his pocket telescope and held it to his eye.

'Good gad. There's a pretty little miss sheltering with her maid in the porch of that old house,' he observed softly to the horse and an appreciative smile broke across his craggy features. It was one of the Duke's great pleasures in life to enjoy the sight of a pretty lady and he recognized with delight Mary Anne's obvious country character. 'Nobody has looked at that crumbly old mansion for years. She looks a sharp little thing though.' He stared in disbelief as Mary Anne, with Norah Rooke, followed the vendor's agent into the building. 'Hasn't she noticed that even the green shutters are hanging at half mast?' He looked forward to seeing what might develop.

Mary Anne had, of course, noticed. She also saw the flaking paint on the woodwork and the rusting balustrades. As she pushed the front door open wider she found herself in a peeling brown-painted entrance hall with a brass chandelier hanging menacingly above her.

'I think Mr Wyndham Lewis must not see this place — until after it is a little restored,' she said to Norah, her voice echoing up the stairway. A startled mouse disappeared somewhere in a corner.

'This is the entrance hall,' began the agent, with a noticeable lack of enthusiasm.

'Surely, ma'am,' said Norah Rooke in shocked tones, 'you're not serious about buying this?' The agent looked at Mary Anne.

'I've done my best to persuade the vendor to have at least a modicum of repair and refurbishment carried out,' he said.

'Cats,' said Mary Anne. 'Many of them. The door must be opened by a huge black footman, dressed in Wyndham's livery. When that's polished up,' she said gesturing at the chandelier, 'it will look quite impressive. An aspidistra against that wall. That's the fashionable thing today. In fact, Wyndham's meanness must not stop me from turning this place into one of the prettiest houses in London.'

The agent's jaw dropped, but he did not say anything as he led the way upstairs. This was a moment matched only by dreams. Mary Anne stepped from the landing into a large, elegant room, obviously the library, and opened the windows to reduce the musty smell.

'The tired gilt must be re-gilded and, to show that we are not country bumpkins, olive green fleur-de-lys paper must cover the walls. I will not have Wyndham considered a dolt because he has not even given his maiden speech in the House. And I will buy proper books, not thirty yards of leather-bound book covers. Mary Anne moved on.

'This must be the drawing room … A cheerful but imposing colour scheme of red, gold and white is needed here … Now this special room which gives such a clear view of the Park … my blue drawing room … It is large enough to hold a great ball … and will do so. No one will know the furnishings come from Brick Lane. I can negotiate with the Jew merchants as well as anybody.' Norah Rooke nodded her head sagely.

Standing on the balcony, Mary Anne declared to the air, 'House, you and I will make each other.' And stepping into the little breakfast room she added, 'And you will be my private parlour.' Climbing more stairs she found two boudoirs, four guest rooms and, high in the attic, six rooms for servants. Her mind whirled with ideas for colour schemes, curtains and furniture.

Shortly after the visit Mary Anne called on the agent with a proposal. But Wyndham Lewis had already seen Number 1 Grosvenor Gate and declared, 'Never, Mary Anne. Never.'

'Number 1 Grosvenor Gate will never go,' sighed the agent.

'Oh yes it will,' replied Mary Anne firmly. 'I will produce costings for a full restoration of the property and present them to my husband. Meanwhile you will find workmen to paint and tidy the place up. In a fortnight's time, on a sunny evening, you will sell the place to Mr Wyndham Lewis for £13,000 freehold, which, of course, includes the repairs.

The agent muttered about his starving children and times being hard, but fourteen days later Wyndham Lewis told his wife, 'You are now mistress of Number 1 Grosvenor Gate.'

Once in residence Mary Anne set about establishing, and constantly refining, the running of the household. Servants were easy to come by, but not good ones. These tended to be cosseted by masters and mistresses who recognised and valued their good qualities. Mary Anne, whilst appreciating the few who displayed proficiency and loyalty, was undoubtedly a harsh mistress. Consequently there was a rather high turnover of staff. In the autumn Mrs Yate arrived to assist her daughter and son-in-law to become "gentlefolk". She and Mary Anne, much to the annoyance of the cook, continued to keep strict accounts, as they had always done. Servants either came up to standard or departed as Mary Anne constantly chivvied them in their duties. She was working up to making her entry into London society with her first grand ball.

Mary Anne knew that nobody would attend unless someone of high social importance came. Without hesitation she settled on the Duke of Wellington. She realized that he would be most unlikely to respond to a formal invitation and that she stood little chance of gaining access to him at Apsley House. Although they had never actually met she had been aware of his gaze on her on more than one occasion. She instinctively felt that a soldier would appreciate a bold, frontal approach. Consequently, she threw all caution to the wind and accosted him during his morning ride in the Park.

'Good God, madam, this is most irregular,' exclaimed Wellington, reining in his trotting horse when Mary Anne stepped calmly and deliberately into its path. Norah Rooke, he noticed, had remained circumspectly by the trees.

'Good morning, Your Grace,' said Mary Anne brightly. 'I do apologise for stopping you in such an irregular manner. It is, although you may not at first agree, for a very important reason. My name is Mary Anne Wyndham Lewis. My husband is …'

'You're the young miss just moved into Grosvenor House,' broke in Wellington, looking admiringly at the oval face centred on a long, slim nose and framed beneath the bonnet by dark brown curls. 'Your husband has made a brave purchase if I may say so.'

Mary Anne, seeing the shy, unattractive boy whose mother had thought him good enough only for the army, who, by his endeavours, had become the nation's hero, gave him a broad, un-London like grin. Wellington's stern features relaxed in response.

'Well, m'dear,' he said, resting both hands on the cantle of the saddle and leaning towards her, 'what is this matter of such importance?'

'Why, I wish to invite Your Grace, as my most distinguished neighbour, to be the guest of honour at my first London ball.'

'And why me pray?' Wellington inquired, a smile of amusement beginning.

'Because then all the others will come,' replied Mary Anne with a smile of beguilement.

'Hmm. Devil take the others, Mrs Wyndham Lewis. I shall be delighted to attend.'

When the ball was over Mary Anne wrote to Johnny.

'My company were most of the first people in London. The Duke of Wellington said it was like fairy land, the best ball he had been at this season, but are you not dazzled at your little Whizzy having received the Noble Hero at her house, the Duchess appears so very kind and amiable and expressed

so much admiration at all she saw ... the balustrades of the staircases were entwined with wreaths of flowers, the whole of the balcony (which goes all round the house) was enclosed as if making part of it, a crimson carpet at the bottom, the whole lined with lampshades all the way round.'

Mary Anne stopped writing and smiled. How Johnny would have loved to see the dancing open with a quadrille and his own little Mary Anne dancing the waltz much to the dismay of Wyndham.

Johnny, now a captain, whistled aloud as he read the letter. I hope she will not forget my debts in the excitement of it all, he thought.

When Grosvenor Gate was at last deserted, servants removed the wreaths twined round the balustrades and lamps were blown out. Maids looked in fireplace nooks and crannies, removing the greenhouse plants which had seemed to grow out of the walls. The white and rose muslin hangings, the blue silks, the amber damask draperies disappeared. The rooms became once more just rooms.

At the end of 1827 Mary Anne summed up her year.

'What a lucky house this has been for me – all in the year 1827.

A beautiful new house and furniture.

A seat in Parliament.

A living for (nephew) John.

A grand ball.

My brother's promotion to a majority.

The lawsuit with (illegible) ended.

A proposal from Mr Gibson Graham to our Catherine, which she has accepted.'

This was a definite improvement on 1826, when a general election had been called. Wyndham Lewis had served his constituency of Cardiff with unstinted devotion for the previous six years. Mary Anne re-donned her "Welshness" and began to campaign once more on his behalf. An even more triumphant result than 1820 was expected. Then, virtually on the eve of the election, Lord William Crichton-Stuart demanded the return of "his" seat. Wyndham Lewis had no choice but to accede to his demand. There would have been no point in trying to oppose Glamorgan's greatest landowner.

With difficulty Wyndham Lewis eventually found himself another seat, Aldeburgh in Suffolk, which was trying not to be washed away by the North Sea. Mary Anne never forgot or forgave the Butes the hurt they had inflicted on her husband. By holding the ball and inviting every prominent member of society except the powerful Butes she had shown, as much as she dared, the contempt she felt for them. From the moment of that success, Welsh society became of little interest or importance to Mrs Wyndham Lewis, and none at all to Mrs Disraeli.

Mary Anne's new place in society meant that she met more interesting people. She did not know Disraeli when she was introduced to the plump little publisher, Henry Colbourne.

'Books sell not on merit but on puffery,' he told her. 'Hints of naughtiness, that's what sells books. For instance, I have a capital book coming out now, *Vivian Grey*. The authorship is a great secret – a man of high fashion.'

On 22 April 1826 the "silver fork" novel, *Vivian Grey*, appeared in the bookshops. The genre was the work of certain members of society and gave those who aspired to become members an insight into the semi-aristocratic life. Mary Anne suspected that Edward Bulwer, an impoverished aristocrat who successfully wrote novels to finance his extravagant lifestyle, was the author. She did not at this time know him, but she was beginning to become friendly with his beautiful but wilful and amusing Irish wife, Rosina. Like her, Rosina had achieved entry into high society from humble beginnings. No one, it seemed, suspected Disraeli as being the author as it was said to be written by a gentleman belonging to the highest society.

While society looked for the spy in their midst, Mary Anne continued her romancing. Her life was far from dull. A letter remains which Mary Anne did not send to a Charles Shanklin, esquire, c/o No. 1 Waterloo Place, Regent Street, dated 22 August 1836.

'Your letter reached me in safety – your dear, dear letter. Need I say how it has been treasur'd ... Will you accept and believe a heart which is yours and yours only ... As you are a man of honour I implore you, I charge you, not to try to discover my name – or you will bring down certain destruction on me ...'

It would seem that a discreet go-between was used in this case.

That was her final romance before the Duke of Wellington observed Mary Anne walking, once a week, the short distance from Number 1 Grosvenor Gate to Number 23a Grosvenor Gate West. 'Where,' the Duke told his latest mistress, 'that Irish officer, George Beauclerk, who serves in the Royal Welsh Fusiliers lives – alone – and unmarried. They say his tastes are quite perverted.'

Despite many inquiries, the Duke never found out what had happened between Mary Anne and her lover, who told her:

'I am attracted to you by your kindness with an air of romantic feeling. You know the end of all love with me is gratification.'

Mary Anne would stand trembling with excitement at such words, but waiting for what to happen we shall never know. She told Rosina Bulwer:

'I do not find George physically attractive, but I learn the arts of the brothel from him.' The affair became public knowledge and lasted three years, during which time "whisperers behind fans" wondered who did what to whom.

Mary Anne played the good wife and Wyndham Lewis the innocent husband. Beauclerk was descended from the Duke of St Albans, a child of Charles II and Nell Gwyn. When Mary Anne married Disraeli a drunken Rosina baited him, 'You follow in good company, Dizzy. I hope you enjoy the fruits of the games of a King and a courtesan.'

Disraeli fixed his great dark eyes on her and, taking his wife's hand, replied: 'Yes, I believe I follow in distinguished company, that of King Charles and Nell Gwyn. Tell me madam, who boasts of following you into your bed?'

Towards the end of 1828 the tenor of life changed for the Wyndham Lewises. The price of pig iron crashed and Wyndham Lewis found himself close to bankruptcy. He applied for the Chiltern Hundreds and planned to re-establish himself back in Wales. His health was declining and perhaps this was why he lost any real sexual interest in Mary Anne. He initiated arrangements to sell Grosvenor Gate, but Mary Anne persuaded him to sell Pantgwynlais Castle instead. Eventually, it seems to have been let. The struggle to remain financially sound affected Wyndham Lewis more than Mary Anne who had already in her life experienced some degree of poverty. She made stringent economies. Perhaps the whole business contributed to the appeal of Beauclerk.

Johnny wrote to his sister that he was in serious financial trouble once again.

'I have forwarded thirteen hundred pounds to that young gentleman. No more,' snapped Wyndham Lewis. Mary Anne wrote to her brother:

'Johnny you are a selfish little oaf. Why do you keep horses and purchase gigs and guns when your tailor's bills are unpaid ... We are in desperate straits too.'

Very slowly the price of pig iron improved and their financial situation recovered. Mary Anne wanted to both celebrate and to re-establish their social situation.

'We should take the Grand Tour,' she said to Wyndham Lewis in the spring of 1830.

'Whatever for, my dear. That's not for the likes of us. We are now a comfortable middle-class couple.'

'We are not,' replied Mary Anne firmly. 'We have to re-establish ourselves as society folk.'

They went first to Paris, an interesting, not to say dangerous, place just after the July Revolution which had seen the autocratic, repressive Charles X overthrown and replaced by the more conciliatory Orleanist, Louis Philippe, the Citizen King. From there they proceeded to Switzerland, where they admired the Alps, and Italy for the usual tour of historic cities. Although she enjoyed the gaiety of Florence, Mary Anne got little pleasure out of antique ruins. '*I found Pompeii very melancholy*,' she wrote to her mother. Having surfeited on culture, they returned to London in May 1831.

One June morning Mary Anne stood on her balcony with Rosina Bulwer watching the people walking or driving through the park, many of them admiring the towering figure of Achilles, made of thirty-six tons of metal from melted down canons captured at Salamanca, Vitoria, Toulouse and Waterloo. In one carriage passing by a young man driving with a young lady caught her eye. It was the paleness of his complexion which first caught her attention. His hair, however, was a thick, heavy mass of black curls, rippling down over his shoulders. He wore a plain black silk scarf and a coat of bottle green which was lined with satin. Around his cuffs gathered a mass of long lace ruffles, reaching nearly to the tips of his fingers. His hands were covered with white gloves with rings sparkling on the fingers. The waistcoat was canary yellow and glittered with chains, contrasting vividly with the purple velvet trousers with gold running down the outside seams. His shoes were adorned with silver buckles and rosettes.

'Who … is that?' inquired Mary Anne, turning to Rosina.

'Benjamin Disraeli.'

5 Enter Disraeli

**A soireé
to be held
at 36 Hertford Street, Mayfair
on the 28 April 1832**

The talented Edward Bulwer, later to assume the surname Lytton after his mother and to become a baron, and his beautiful wife, Rosina were hosting yet another gathering including the brightest young talent in London. Sheridan's granddaughter, the writer Caroline Norton, wandered from her small flat along Birdcage Walk, humming to herself. She was looking forward to meeting her lover and had bought a nosegay of daffodils to give him. Benjamin Disraeli, strolling along Piccadilly having left friends in Regent Street, caught sight of himself in the window of Fortnum and Mason. The shop always encouraged him. If two mere footmen, over a hundred years before, could become part of London life what could a "genuine genius" such as himself not achieve in this society of opportunity. He turned up his collar so that it covered his ears and loosened his cravat.

'At twenty-eight sir, you are indeed a pretty fellow still,' he said to his reflection. He continued along the edge of Green Park, crossed the road, dodging the carriages, and turned into Down Street walking briskly towards Hertford Street. Disraeli was ready to go on stage.

As Disraeli made his entrance his host and close friend, Edward Bulwer, came forward with arms outstretched. He was enjoying the attention which his latest novel, *Eugene Aram*, brought him. With a smirk he said, 'Dizzy, I have a particular desire to introduce you to ...'

'Mrs Wyndham Lewis.' Rosina Bulwer, unable to resist the opportunity for a bit of mischief, stepped forward. 'Mr Benjamin Disraeli,' she announced, 'the author of *Vivian Grey.*' She knew full well that not only had Mary Anne been trying to find out the identity of the author of the best seller, but also that Disraeli wanted it kept secret.

Disraeli judged Mary Anne to be in her late twenties. (She was in her fortieth year.) He noted that her dress was cut a shade too low, her accent peculiar and her diamonds too many and too large. He guessed that she was a bored provincial wife come to town to have an adventure. Yes, my dear, he thought, I might be willing to play – for a while.

Mary Anne noted the summing up look and interpreted it accurately. Disraeli made her feel like an over-painted doll wearing the wrong clothes.

'Oh, Mr Disraeli,' she gushed, 'you must be so clever to write books. I could never write books. I never remember who came first, the Romans or the Greeks.'

Disraeli smiled down at her. This one could be fun. Again, Mary Anne interpreted the look accurately and gave him her best "man smile". He offered her his arm and escorted her into supper. He attempted a witticism.

'Are not guests like Noah's animals going into …' But Mary Anne's nerves overcame her. And she overcame Disraeli with a spate of words which gushed on and on, drowning any effort to interject the merest comment. Just when both were beginning to recover from her onslaught, Rosina, glass in hand, clutched Disraeli by his coat collar.

'Tell me, Dizzy, do all you young literary gentlemen imitate Lord Byron in dress and morals? Do you have a little lamb in your bed too?'

The gibe was fortuitous for at that moment the tall world-weary figure of the Home Secretary, Lord Melbourne, entered the room. It was a cruel reminder of his wife, Lady Caroline Lamb, who had had an affair with Byron and from whom he was now separated. Having suffered mental instability since she was a child, she became quite unhinged when she met the funeral cortege of her lover. It seemed to her as if he was going to take her into hell with him. But, always the master of any situation, the urbane Melbourne simply looked towards his

Mr Disraeli's "Rattle"

mistress, Caroline Norton. She blushed sweetly and handed him the nosegay. He kissed her and the company relaxed.

'She expects her husband to divorce her and Melbourne to marry her,' whispered Rosina to Disraeli and Mary Anne. Disraeli smiled knowingly as Rosina stepped forward to greet her distinguished guest. Mary Anne, whose friendship with Rosina was growing, watched and listened avidly to the goings-on.

'Is it true?' asked a voice close by her. 'Did Byron make love to the Bulwers simultaneously?'

Mary Anne giggled. 'I don't know, Mr Disraeli, but they spend £30,000 a year on entertaining and his income is a mere £500 a year.'

'Who are his bankers? They must be sympathetic.'

Mary Anne looked at Disraeli and wondered about his curiosity regarding money matters. Was it true that he was in trouble from borrowing too heavily from Lombards?

Disraeli was one of the last to leave the Bulwer's party. He wandered down the street with a friend, Benjamin Austen, a solicitor whose wife was also a writer. Placing his thumbs in his waistcoat arms, he bemoaned his luck to his friend.

'My evening was completely ruined, for I escorted into supper that pretty little woman – a Mrs Wyndham Lewis, a flirt and a *"rattle"* with a volubility second to none. She told me, "I like silent, melancholy men." I answered, 'I have no doubt of it, ma'am.'

As she climbed into her barouche, Mary Anne heard the elegant Lord Lyndhurst mutter, 'A useful young fool, that Disraeli.' A breeze ran its fingers through her hair, reminding her briefly of Berkeley. I could not make anything of that wastrel, she mused – but Disraeli …

The Wyndham Lewises and Disraeli continued to meet on the social circuit. Especially popular were the Sheridan sisters, beautiful Helen who Disraeli had once fallen in love with and Caroline Norton. She looked something like Caroline Lamb and shared a touch of her instability. Whenever Melbourne upset her she would remove her hat and kick it into the air. The most popular venue for the literary set, however, was the Bulwer's. Lord Lyndhurst, the Tory Lord Chancellor, was often a guest, amusing the company with naughty stories told in his American accent. The thin elegant dandy Count D'Orsay, son-in-law of Countess Blessington and reputedly her lover, was always welcome for his sparkling wit. Lady Blessington at Gore House, Kensington, hosted writers, artists and musicians and was noted for the quality of the food to be had at her table.

'We are frightened that our dear Dizzy will become a nasty Tory,' the Sheridan sisters, staunch Whigs, said to Mary Anne one evening.

'Ladies, in order for me to avoid such a terrible fate I must become a member of a St James's club. But, sadly, I have no connections,' replied Disraeli connivingly. Neither had Mary Anne, but her friend Lady Tankerville had.

The Atheneum, the club of which his father was a founding member, shuddered at the thought of Disraeli as a member and pronounced a firm 'No'. The Garrick and the Travellers' clubs both returned an equally resounding 'No'.

'Dizzy, the ninnies are frightened you will fit them into a book,' joked Bulwer.

Finally Lady Tankerville's reputation as a leader in society was sufficient influence to bully Almacks into accepting him. But then, it was she who had faced Wellington on the steps of Almacks with the challenge, 'Sir, you wear trousers. Breeches only here, sir.' The mighty Wellington had walked quietly away.

Another house to be seen in was Lord Eliot's. He invited to one of his dinners a north country man of industrial stock and his beautiful wife. Disraeli annoyed the guest by flirting with his wife. He later observed to Mary Anne that the gentleman was, altogether quite unpleasant: 'When I asked him to lend me some of his private papers for the next book I am preparing, he buried his chin into his neckcloth. In my view, Mrs Wyndham Lewis, the gentleman is not a gentleman by the manner in which he attacks his turbot with a knife.'

The gentleman, Sir Robert Peel, filed Disraeli into his formidable first class honours brain as an arrogant young puppy.

While good John Wyndham Lewis, with neither looks nor charm to speak of, and with only one alleged illegitimate daughter to his name, split his time between London and South Wales, his wife flirted with Disraeli, who sent her little notes. He, however, attended a number of mistresses, telling himself that he was seeking a wife. Society, on the other hand, named him "Gigolo".

One young lady Disraeli was serious about was bespectacled Lady Charlotte Bertie, though not for her predilection for collecting pincushions. On 18 May 1833 he escorted her to the Italian opera at the invitation of Lady Henrietta Sykes. Although married and having borne four children, Henrietta was still a captivating beauty. As the candles fluttered, Lady Henrietta directed a devastating smile at Disraeli. Charlotte, seeing how things were going to be, sat down next to Wyndham Lewis's business partner, the middle-aged John Guest. She later married him and bore him ten children. Henrietta continued to hold Disraeli's gaze as she encouragingly lowered the chiffon from around her shoulders.

'I shall wear you like a jewel,' Mary Anne heard Disraeli murmur.

And if you do, she thought, it will not be me that makes a man of you.

When the violins began playing *Cosi Fan Tutte*, Mozart's tale of two immoral lovers, Disraeli still held Henriettas's gaze.

'Do sit down, Dizzy,' said Mary Anne sharply. 'Nobody can see a thing.'

The affair gathered momentum. Mary Anne was shaken to learn that Disraeli had taken Henrietta to meet his family at their country home at Bradenham in Buckinghamshire. Years later she found a letter from Henrietta to Disraeli.

'12 o'clock Thursday Night

It is the night Dearest the night that we used to pass so happily together. I cannot sleep and the sad reality that we are parted presses heavily upon me ...

Good Angels guard my dearest. A thousand and a thousand kisses. Good night. Sleep and dream of – your mother.'

If Lady Sykes had not been such a fool ... mused Mary Anne as she carefully replaced the letter. Why worry. Henrietta is long dead. But, she thought as she left the room, is her ghost?

One day during the affair as Mary Anne was passing the offices of the eminent solicitor, Sir Philip Rose, she saw Henrietta coming out of the building. She was heavily veiled.

'Will she divorce?' was the question asked by all society and which Mary Anne now put to Wyndham Lewis.

'It is all ended for Disraeli if she does,' he told her.

The world waited, but matters came naturally to a head. At a house in Southend rented by Sir Francis, Disraeli and Henrietta twined around one another in front of the fire. Out on the damp Scottish moors Henrietta's husband, Sir Francis, shot grouse. Then Henrietta returned to London and found Clara Bolton, a doctor's wife and former lover of Disraeli, waiting for her. A bitter exchange, fuelled by jealousy and rage ensued, about which Rosina was only able to give Mary Anne a rough outline. Then Sir Francis returned home, having been appraised of the general situation. He demanded an explanation of what she had been up to with Disraeli, attempted to castigate his wife verbally and concluded by forbidding her to ever see him again.

'You'll never believe this, Mary Anne,' said Rosina, obviously enjoying telling the tale. 'Henrietta drove up King Street to renew the matter with Clara and what should she find parked outside Clara's house but Sir Francis's carriage. She stormed in and up to the bedroom where, apparently, she tugged the bedclothes off so violently that they both lay writhing naked on the floor.'

Mary Anne asked Disraeli about the incident.

'Henrietta said the fracas did some good,' he said simply, implying that it was none of her business. She later heard that a *ménage à quatre* had been formed, consisting of Disraeli, Henrietta, Sir Francis and Clara, with the occasional guest. Eventually, Sir Francis disappeared to undertake a European tour – alone. Disraeli returned to work on his *Revolutionary Epick* poem.

While all this was going on the Wyndham Lewises still met Disraeli socially, but kept their distance as he was living openly with Henrietta in her house nearby in Upper Grosvenor Street. On one occasion during the very hot summer of 1834 Disraeli was dining with a perspiring Wyndham Lewis and a glowing Mary Anne.

'I have at last met, at Henrietta's, the man who will push me up the greasy pole of politics, Lord Lyndhurst,' he confided to them.

'What is your opinion of the Tory Lord Chancellor, the noble Lord Lyndhurst?' Mary Anne asked Norah Rooke as she undressed that evening.

'He is a married man without principle.'

'That is my view also.' At the time of this alliance Lyndhurst was sixty-two years old, thirty-two years older than Disraeli. The political commentator, Walter Bagehot, wrote of him:

'Few men led a laxer life, few men, to the end of their life, were looser in their conversation; but there was no laxity in his intellectual life.'

The hot summer was followed by a glorious autumn. Henrietta Sykes joined some friends to travel on the Continent. Lyndhurst was one of the party. Rosina Bulwer, whose teasing all too often had a spiteful streak in it, could not resist the opportunity.

'Did you not know, Dizzy? Henrietta has been Lyndhurst's mistress for some time.'

Mary Anne, attending a reception at Lady Blessington's, saw a thin, despairing Disraeli, suddenly aged twenty years.

'The change of life is too sad. I am quite at a loss how ... to manage affairs in future. I find separation more irksome than ... even my bitterest imagination predicted,' he told Mary Anne.

Disraeli went back to Bradenham to recover from his nervous breakdown and began writing *Henrietta Temple*. When the book was published Mary Anne read:

'There is no love but love at first sight. This is the transcendent and surpassing offspring of sheer and unpolluted sympathy. All other is the illegitimate result of observation, of reflection, of compromise, of comparison, of expediency. The passions that endure like the lightning: they search the soul, but it is warmed for ever.'

She knew that Disraeli would never love like that again and she cried, not knowing why.

Henrietta returned to Disraeli with Lyndhurst hovering in the background. Shortly afterwards a young Irish painter, Daniel Maclise, joined the group. His portrait of Henrietta shows a woman in her sexual prime, a sensual body waiting for the diamonds and furs covering it to be removed. She is smiling, a secret, serene, fulfilled smile. It is the work of a lover. During the summer of 1837 society enjoyed a drama worthy of the music hall stage. Sir Francis, seemingly always fated to be unfortunate, caught Henrietta and Maclise lying on top of the bed, stark naked, sipping coffee and kissing each other all over. He immediately began legal proceedings against Henrietta. She was utterly disgraced and dropped out of society.

Cook informed Mary Anne that Nanny had gathered Lady Sykes's four children around her and told them, 'You must forget your Mama now.'

'I have parted from Henrietta,' Disraeli told her casually. One day he would say to her, 'Oh, the terrible catastrophe of Henrietta!' On his death it was found that Disraeli, who otherwise destroyed all correspondence, had kept every one of Henrietta's letters.

Nine years later Henrietta Sykes lay dead. Mary Anne had learned one great lesson from her – discretion. At the end of Disraeli's affair she looked at her own indiscretion. She promptly asked Charles Beauclerk to persuade his brother, George, to return all the letters she had sent him. He replied:

'Dear Mrs Wyndham Lewis,

I return you the letters all safe – they entirely remove from your intimacy with my Brother all grounds for any ill-natured scandal that the world may have cast upon it …

Very truly yrs

Charles Beauclerk'

Mary Anne felt relieved. Rumour was one thing, but written evidence was another.

6 Changes

As Disraeli's affair with Henrietta finally drew to an end another chapter began to open for the whole nation. In June 1837 William IV, the old sailor King, died and a lonely, rather plain girl of eighteen, who had lived a quiet life with her widowed mother, became Queen. Many older people still mourned Caroline of Brunswick's daughter by George IV, Princess Charlotte, who had died in childbirth. She was clever and beautiful and so much had been expected of her. Little was known about the new Queen, Alexandrina Victoria.

On 20 June, Lyndhurst, as a Privy Councillor, was commanded to pay homage to the young woman. He had been delighted with the acclaim given to *A Vindication of the English Constitution* (in a letter to a noble and learned lord) by Disraeli, the Younger. This political tract had enabled Lyndhurst to promote the interests of the Tory Party and consequently, he invited Disraeli to accompany him to Kensington Palace.

After the ceremony Disraeli took a cab directly to Grosvenor Gate. When the door was opened he ignored all formalities. He simply barged past Charles, the footman, and ran directly upstairs, bursting uninvited into Mary Anne's sitting room.

'Mary Anne, Mary Anne, Oh I do wish you could have been there. It was a wonderful sight. Lyndhurst left me to wait in the Cupola Room, just outside the Council Chamber. What an array they had in there. There were bishops, admirals, generals, secretaries of state ...'

'Have you eaten?' asked Mary Anne.

Disraeli did not notice the question.

'As the clock struck half past eleven this short, slim girl in plain mourning came into the room – alone. She moved forward – with extraordinary dignity and grace – and sat down. Her uncles, the Duke of Cumberland and the Duke of Sussex, sat close by and Lord Melbourne addressed her.

'I take it that we are talking about the Queen,' said Mary Anne, as she pushed towards him the plate of sandwiches which a servant had just brought into the room.

'Yes, yes. Of course. She has such a clear, silvery voice. Even standing in the antechamber I could hear every word.'

'My lords, this awful responsibility which has been imposed upon me so suddenly and at so early a period of my life … I wish to be known as Queen Victoria.'

'I thought that her name was Alexandrina Victoria and she was expected to be called Queen Alexandra,' said Mary Anne.

'Yes,' said Disraeli, 'but before anyone had a chance to say anything the little figure – with her consummate grace and amazing dignity – was up and gone.'

The next day Mary Anne saw Disraeli and Lyndhurst vanishing into Madame de Prée's house in Cleveland Street.

'Madame,' Rosina had told Mary Anne, 'knows the nature of her clientele. When the gentlemen have enjoyed themselves with a French maid they can then cross the road to Mr Hammond's house at number 19 to be whipped by a stable lad.'

Bulwer happened to be in the brothel at the same time and he and others were waiting to take a turn with a "little Vicky". Whilst waiting the men discussed the new Queen. Disraeli reported the conversation to Mary Anne, although he omitted mention of the venue.

'I'll tell you, we'll have to get her a sound English husband,' said one.

'Already she has banished her mother to her own bedroom.'

'Her Uncle Leopold has been put in his place …'

'And to tell such an eminent gentleman what she wished to be called!'

'One can only admire a young woman who commands the respect of men old enough to be her grandfather,' commented Disraeli.

A new Monarch meant a new election and whilst at dinner with the Wyndham Lewises one evening Disraeli regaled his hosts with the tale of his unsuccessful attempts to gain a seat in Parliament.

'I have long felt that it is my destiny to hold high office in the government of England,' he said.

Wyndham Lewis looked unimpressed. Mary Anne was about to giggle at such a pretentious statement, but somehow a strange sincerity in Disraeli's voice checked the impulse.

'Trouble is,' he went on, 'it's nigh impossible to win a seat in the House without the backing of one or other of the behemoths who dominate our political system. So many of the members simply follow the dictates of their leaders, without giving matters under discussion even cursory consideration.' He stared thoughtfully at his plate.

'I understand you have stood at High Wycombe, Mr Disraeli,' said Mary Anne.

'I have indeed, Mrs Wyndham Lewis. Three times.'

'And what did you stand as?' inquired Mary Anne.

'As an Independent. Although on the last occasion the Tories actually contributed five hundred pounds towards my expenses. Hoped I'd be able to oust one of the Whigs. Made little difference I'm sorry to say. I recalled Lord Melbourne's words to me the first time I met him. I told him that I intended to be Prime Minister one day. What do you think he said?'

'I've no idea,' said Mary Anne. Wyndham Lewis raised his eyebrows slightly and shook his head.

'He said, "First, young man, it is necessary to win an election." So, with Lyndhurst's help, I joined the Tories. Stood as their candidate at Taunton two years ago. Busy little place, but no social life.'

'Yes,' said Wyndham Lewis, 'I remember the talk about your spat with Mr O'Connell, our papist member for County Clare. How did that start?'

'The Press. Misquotation. I was simply dishing the Whigs by observing that they had allied themselves with O'Connell, whom they themselves had denounced as a traitor. But according to the Press it was I who denounced him as such. O'Connell read the report in Dublin. Didn't bother to check. Just made a savage and totally defamatory attack on me. Said I was descended from the impenitent thief on the cross at the Crucifixion. Of course I challenged him to a duel, but he wormed his way out. Said he'd killed a man before in a duel and had vowed never to fight another. So I challenged his son, Morgan. He tried to slip out of it too, but I insisted. It was all arranged. Young Henry Baillie was my second. But the Peelers intervened.'

'Oh, Dizzy, how romantic,' murmured the enraptured Mary Anne.

'Well,' responded Disraeli with as much modesty as he could muster, 'I did feel that I greatly distinguished myself.'

'Darling,' said Mary Anne, looking beguilingly at Wyndham Lewis. 'Since Mr Roberts, the Whig member, is retiring, why don't you take Mr Disraeli to stand with you at Maidstone? Then, hopefully, they will have two Tory members.'

Disraeli startled Maidstone, wearing blue and turquoise, tossing his ringlets about him and with gold chains straddling his chest. He spoke vehemently against all and any of the recently passed Whig legislation, especially the Poor Law Act. Wyndham Lewis was obviously impressed.

'Disraeli, my dear, is on his legs more than an hour at a time; he is a splendid orator and astonishes people.'

Again, Mary Anne fought the canvas fiercely, but for some reason decided to remain in London with her mother during the election.

Wyndham Lewis received 706 votes and Disraeli 616, a clear lead over the only other candidate, the radical editor of the *Westminster Review*, Colonel Perronet Thompson, with 412. On hearing the news, Mary Anne rushed from London with her mother to join in the celebrations. She wrote to Johnny:

I cannot explain to you the tumult of joy we have all been in, Wyndham's great popularity in giving so largely to the poor and Mr Disraeli being so fine a speaker joined to my humble worth carried everything before us ... My head is so dizzy with the noise I have been in and I am so tired, cannot you fancy me driving about Town? Some of the women fell down to me in the streets. Many of them clasped Wyndham in their arms and kissed him again and again in spite of his struggles, which sent Mr Disraeli and your Whizzy into fits of laughter, our colours all purple ...Mark what I say – mark what I prophesy, Mr Disraeli will in a very few years be one of the greatest men of his day. His great talents, backed by his friends Lord Lyndhurst and Lord Chandos, with Wyndham's power to keep him in Parliament, will insure his success. They call him my Parliamentary protégé.'

Disraeli wrote a formal note of thanks to Mr and Mrs Wyndham Lewis and invited them to spend some time at his parents' Buckinghamshire home at Bradenham amongst the beech groves and enjoy simple pleasures of a sylvan scene and an affectionate hearth. He made no mention of the £500 he had offered Wyndham Lewis to defray the £5,000 he had paid for Disraeli to fight the election. Needless to say, the amount was never paid.

Before the Wyndham Lewises visited Bradenham Disraeli dined with them at Grosvenor Gate. He told Mrs Wyndham Lewis, as he always called her in public, 'This is, Mrs Wyndham Lewis, a fine dinner well cooked and a gorgeous service.' In a year's time he would remember that Mrs Wyndham Lewis ran an excellent household. Meanwhile, Mary Anne prepared for the Bradenham visit.

The Wyndham Lewises travelled in the barouche, stopping overnight at the ancient New Inn at Ealing. They avoided travelling after dark for fear of highwaymen lurking in the extensive woodland. Next day they continued through Beaconsfield and High Wycombe then up the picturesque valleys to the hamlet of Bradenham. They approached the manor by the green and through the wrought iron gates. Mary Anne exclaimed at the beauty of the large gardens hidden from the neighbouring churchyard by a high brick wall. As she descended from the carriage, marvelling at the slender brick chimneys, the satisfyingly proportioned sash windows and the small dormer windows above, an old man came out of the front door, adjusting his glasses. He threw his arms open wide in an unmistakable gesture of welcome before shaking Wyndham Lewis by the hand and bowing politely to Mary Anne. He was followed by Disraeli, looking mildly embarrassed.

'This is my father,' he said.

'Wyndham, isn't old Isaac the most lovable and perfect old gentleman you have ever met?' Wyndham Lewis looked steadily at his wife for a while.

'I would be happy for you to remember these people should you come on hard times.' Mary Anne did not consider the remark, becoming more aware that Disraeli's sister, Sarah, always known as Sa, neither smiled at her nor gave her a welcome.

When they sat down to dinner, Isaac looked around at them reassuringly.

'I assume that my son has told you that although we were born Jews we no longer practise the religion. Hence we are no longer Jews. Therefore there are no restrictions on what we may eat. *Bon appétit.*' It was a joyous meal, served with an excellent French wine.

'I found the whole family so natural and friendly,' Mary Anne later told Rosina. 'And their manservant Tita, Byron's former bodyguard.'

'Has Sa never had a lover?' Mary Anne asked Disraeli as they sat together after dinner.

'She was engaged for a long time to my friend, George Meredith. He died of malaria six years ago when he was on tour with my father and I in Egypt. Sa and I made a bargain. I would live for her and she would live for me.'

'Perhaps an unwise commitment,' said Mary Anne, looking into Disraeli's eyes. She observed the grey-frocked Sarah for a while. 'Certainly your sister lives for you, Dizzy,' she commented, feeling sorry for a woman living such an unnatural existence.

The visit lasted only a few days, during which she flirted discreetly with Disraeli. He wrote to her at Grosvenor Gate: *'After you went everybody and everything is most dull and triste.'*

Mary Anne wondered about Disraeli and took advantage of the situation when she found herself alone with a slightly drunken Edward Bulwer.

'Tell me, Edward, where did our Dizzy gain his experience?'

'Dizzy? I should not tell you.'

Mary Anne smiled at him encouragingly.

'Oh, the brothels of St James where he regularly picks up infections ... the Middle East ... and from Maurice of course, Byron's boatman.'

Mary Anne looked at Bulwer in horror. Did he mean what he said or was he just trying to shock her? She did not ask for further information for fear of the answer.

In November Disraeli entered Parliament. He expressed his excitement to Mary Anne.

'What fun, and how lucky I should esteem myself to be, I am now leaving a secure haven for an unknown sea. What will the next twelve months produce?'

Mary Anne felt a certain foreboding and spoke to Wyndham Lewis.

'I feel that Dizzy is naïve, Wyndham, overconfident. Look after my protégé, I beg you.'

It was on 7 December that Disraeli gave his maiden speech. Before they entered the Chamber, Wyndham Lewis suggested to him that a full stomach would be wise. They went into St Stephen's where they ate a Bellamy pork pie, washed down with porter. Disraeli looked at the waiter.

'We are being served by the man who had taken a Bellamy porker to Prime Minister Pitt at his home in Putney,' he said loudly.

'Wasn't he told that it was not required because the gentleman was dead,' replied Wyndham Lewis curtly.

'A good omen nevertheless,' responded Disraeli.

Disraeli took a seat behind Peel in the second row of three-tiered seating in the Court of Requests which served as temporary accommodation for the Commons while the Palace of Westminster was being re-built. O'Connell was addressing a bored House. Seeing the flamboyant Disraeli, he took the opportunity to continue their "duel" in a different manner.

'As you said, Disraeli, "I will see thee at Phillipi, then".'

The Chamber was restless. Members looked at the young Disraeli and then at the veteran campaigner.

'At that moment my heart sank,' Wyndham Lewis later told Mary Anne.

The Speaker, the Right Honourable Charles Manners-Sutton, nicknamed "the Laundress" by Disraeli, surveyed the House for a moment and then called out, 'the Right Honourable member for Maidstone'.

O'Connell stretched out his legs and waited. The House was in the mood for mischief. Disraeli began to speak, with unjustified confidence, about Parliamentary elections in Ireland, about which he knew precious little. His high-flown phrases '... the strains of borough mongering assumed a deeper and darker hue ... majestic mendicancy ...' without real substance, made the House restless and aroused the animosity of the Irish members. Voices called out.

'Old clothes, sit down.'

'Take a bite of pork.'

The Speaker sat back to enjoy the baiting. O'Connell crossed his arms and pretended to sleep. The Chamber was darkening. Soon more gas lamps hissed into life, but silver forks held high lit the Chamber. Pieces of pork dripped down onto hands pushing meat towards Disraeli.

'Shylock, take a bite.'

'Sit, sit, sit.'

Soon they were screaming at him hysterically, like a lynch mob. The Speaker rose to his feet, looking worried. Suddenly Disraeli raised his right arm high, the fist tightly clenched.

'Sit!'

' I will sit down now, but the time will come when you will hear me.'

The jeering stopped. Members sat back in their seats.

'What kind of a man is this?' whispered Wyndham Lewis to the Member next to him.

Disraeli left the Chamber in silence, looking neither right nor left. His report of the matter in a letter to Mary Anne shows that he had developed an innate resilience to such treatment.

'I made my maiden debut last night ... I can give you no idea of the unfairness with which the Rads and Repealers met me, but I fought my way with good humour and I hope not altogether without spirit thro' tremendous clamour and uproar ... I am not in the least dispirited by all this friction.'

'I will not enter the House until he becomes Prime Minister,' vowed Mary Anne.

After Christmas Mary Anne went by herself to Bradenham, feeling that Disraeli would need comfort and support before returning to the House. She found a man waiting for her whom she would hardly recognise. The mask which Disraeli would wear for the rest of his life was in place. When she returned to Grosvenor Gate she found a letter from Disraeli waiting for her.

New relations between these two people had begun.

7 New Relations

At breakfast on 14 March 1838 Wyndham Lewis signed a cheque, his knife clattered to the floor, his hand lolled forward, a gurgling sound came from his mauving cheeks and he lolled forward into Mary Anne's arms.

She looked up at Norah Rooke who took her master's right hand briskly, felt the pulse and then said quietly. 'Mr Lewis is no more.' Mary Anne looked at her maid incomprehensively. 'Ma'am, I think his heart has stopped beating.'

Norah Rooke bustled out of the room to fetch help. Mary Anne realized that she had joined the world of the lonely and perhaps impoverished widows.

Charles came into the room and silently removed Wyndham Lewis's body to lie in the drawing room for seven days. Lilies and candles were placed around the body. The undertaker replaced the salt on Wyndham Lewis's chest every few hours. Mrs Yate arrived to comfort her daughter and Mary Anne looked forward to Rosina's lively gossip to ease her loneliness and pain. She did not come, but much to Mary Anne's surprise Disraeli did.

'Where do I bury him, Dizzy?' Mary Anne asked. 'I cannot take him back to Wales.'

'Why, in the new cemetery, you know the one opened a few years ago, just after the cholera epidemic. Kensal Green.'

'So far away, so ungodly.'

'Better there than in a churchyard where his bones will be thrown away when the place becomes too crowded,' snapped Disraeli with unexpected force.

'I have relied so much on Wyndham, Dizzy. He was such a strong man. I had not realized how strong,' said Mary Anne quietly.

'You will not find such kindness again, my dear,' said Disraeli putting his arm around her. 'You cannot be seen in public before the funeral. You may not even receive. Society will be shocked you are not even yet in mourning. Leave things to me,' he said and as Norah Rooke returned to the room, he added, 'and Norah.'

She was clinging to him. He was stroking her hair.

So that's how things are going to be, said Norah Rooke grimly to herself.

Mary Anne felt Disraeli kiss her gently. She looked up at him with surprise. She had never sensed in him such real strength; cleverness yes; now she felt a man who could and would command … if the situation demanded it. Otherwise he would play the dandy, the gigolo and the fop. He looked at her kindly, tenderly and for the first time Mary Anne saw real friendship and understanding in his look.

As Disraeli and Mary Anne stepped back to talk about arrangements for the funeral, two mutes wearing sad expressions stepped from the mourning coach which had drawn up outside. They stationed themselves either side of the front door and were followed by two black clad, lady fitters, pattern books in hand who bustled their way past the footman, to inspect the body.

'Mr Wyndham Lewis makes a fine corpse, Madam.'

'Why should he not?' responded Mary Anne.

The women assessed the situation between themselves:

'One widow and one gigolo who would vanish into thin air the moment the will was read.'

As was customary, friends and relatives were invited to view the body, which was never left alone, in order to protect the soul of the dear departed from an attack by evil spirits.

On the day of the funeral just before the coffin was closed, Mary Anne placed a guinea piece in Wyndham Lewis's right hand, to pay the ferryman to take him over the river Styx to the underworld.

The mutes led the way through the West End, into North London to Kensal Green. The cortege was followed by a feather man carrying black ostrich plumes.

Few people followed Wyndham Lewis. The ones who mourned were in Glamorgan. As was customary passers-by bowed their heads, some prayed. Soon the cortege was out of the centre of London and into the suburbs of Maida Vale. Disraeli squeezed Mary Anne's hand.

Only the horses' clip-clop broke the silence.

'The horses are so beautiful,' observed Mary Anne. 'Wyndham loved black stallions so ...'

'These horses are brown. They are dyed.'

Mary Anne's depression vanished. She drew from her purse a notebook and wrote: *'Horses dyed. Discount 5%.'*

After the funeral Norah Rooke handed her mistress a letter written by the master on New Year's Day. 'He did not want to give it to you then ...'

Mary Anne read:

My own darling,

I was delighted to receive your letter last night it made the old year run out in happiness. I now wish you a happy New Year that we may live together many more years with equal solace to each other as heretofore ...'

Three days later Wyndham Lewis had written another note.

God bless you my affectionate kind dear, and believe me your own devoted and faithful husband.

W.L.

Make my regards to the D'Israelis and tell them how grateful I feel for their attention to you.'

From the time of the funeral Mary Anne ate little, grew thin and forgot to place geranium powder on her cheeks. Her mother felt concern for her naturally resilient daughter. Mrs Yate warned Johnny. *Write to me before you arrive at Grosvenor Gate because Mary Anne is in a sad state and cannot take any sudden surprises ...'*

And then to make Mary Anne even more miserable a letter arrived from Rosina later from Bath. It gave no consolation. It dealt with her own sufferings over her favourite companion, Fairy, a King Charles spaniel, who had just died.

'My heart, literally feels torn up by the roots - for everything is continually reminding me of that poor little darling faithful

creature, which seemed the only thing in wide world that never turned on me or against me, and that did not ill-use me for loving it ...'

Mary Anne told Mrs Yate, 'I cannot help feeling, Mama, that a loss of a husband is more serious than the loss of a dog.'

The letter made Mary Anne consider Wyndham Lewis's many virtues. She placed on Wyndham Lewis's tombstone.

"He was renowned for his charity, which in him did not cover a multitude of sins, but only heightened many virtues. This tablet was erected in his memory, by his widow Mary Anne Lewis, who was united to him for seventeen years of unbroken happiness."

Sir Philip Rose, the family solicitor, refused to read the will in public as it was of a surprising nature.

He told Mary Anne, accompanied by Norah Rooke, 'You and the Reverend Price-Williams are the executors of Mr Wyndham Lewis's estate. His holdings in the Dowlais ironworks have been bequeathed to his brother, Harry. You, along with the Reverend Price-Williams share in his properties, mainly in Gloucester. They include the lease of your Uncle James Viney's residence, Cathedral House. Perhaps you did not know he had mortgaged it to Mr Wyndham Lewis. You also have a share in his various investments, mostly in government stock, both home and abroad. In all your income will be somewhat between £4,000 and £5,000 a year: not as considerable as you hoped possibly, but quite comfortable nevertheless. Your jewellery and other like personal possessions are yours to keep or dispose of as you wish. Your home, at Grosvenor Gate, is yours for your lifetime. But, and this is why I refused to disclose the will in public, the house and your sources of income are entailed. On your death they pass to the Reverend Price-Williams or his heirs.'

'What if I should re-marry?' asked Mary Anne. 'Surely, my possessions shall become the property of my husband?'

'Ah, no Mrs Wyndham Lewis, remember that your late husband, ironmaster, landowner, Member of Parliament, businessman, was also a barrister. He knew the law. Your income, its sources and your house have been placed in trust and can never be placed in the possession of a new husband.'

'He bequeathed me independence,' murmured Mary Anne, overwhelmed by Wyndham Lewis's understanding and generosity.

Sir Philip leaned forward and paused.

'Mr Wyndham Lewis was an exceptional man in morals, in business and if I may say in his love and understanding of his wife.'

The next day Mary Anne and Norah Rooke set out for Dowlais to sort out affairs. This time she came to Greenmeadow not as a young expectant wife but as a sad, wan widow knowing she had lost a jewel of great price. It would be good to talk, perhaps, with the "Governor" again. But they could never be as they had been.

As she sat with Norah Rooke watching the reflection of the sun on the River Taff she observed, 'I think Norah I have been a selfish woman.'

'Youth must make its way, madam,' she replied and did not tell her mistress that coming up the valley in a most unsuitable London phaeton was Disraeli.

'There are papers, papers and more papers. Oh, how small-minded and claustrophobic I find it all.'

'Not for much longer, madam.'

Mary Anne did not notice her maid's comment as the bell rang, 'Who could it be? Nobody knew they were here.' Mary Anne rushed down two flights of stairs, excited at the prospect of an unannounced visitor swung open the door and Disraeli swept her into his arms.

'Dizzy, is it you?'

'I am staying nearby at the Cow and Snuffers.'

He assisted in putting Wyndham Lewis's affairs into excellent order. Perhaps not surprisingly, he and the "Governor" got on rather well together.

'I did not expect you to possess such an orderly mind,' said Mary Anne.

'You forget, I was trained in the law,' said Disraeli with a wry grin.

The couple returned to London and to the fiasco of the Bulwers.

The year before they had quarrelled bitterly and they decided to live apart. One day Rosina called unannounced upon her husband and saw a naked woman disappear into the next room.

'I don't do it with you, what do you expect?'

Disraeli suggested to Mary Anne that Rosina settled for a Deed of Separation and perhaps remembering Henrietta, said:

'There is in unhappy marriage a power of misery, which surpasses all the other sorrows of the world. The entire soul of a woman reposes upon conjugal attachment. To struggle alone against her lot, to advance towards the grave without a friend to regret you, is an isolation of which the deserts of Arabia give but a slight idea …'

Mourning did not suit Mary Anne. She was bored and entertained herself by telling visitors how Rosina had found Bulwer with a "stark naked lady".

Bulwer sent a sharp letter to Mary Anne. One, which few people would have ignored.

'My dear Madam,

You must permit me to place thoroughly before you what I venture to consider grounds for certain caution on your part … Paragraphs have appeared in more than one newspaper containing a very grave calumny upon me …'

Mary Anne read the letter and placed it in her inlaid rosewood correspondence box. It was too good to lose.

8 Coronation

Victoria washed Dash, her King Charles spaniel. The dog was unaware that his mistress had just been crowned and anointed Queen of Great Britain. He sat in sulky silence drying while his mistress wrote in her diary:

Thursday, June 28th 1838. I was awoke at 4 o'clock by the guns in the Park, and could not get much sleep afterwards on account of the noise of the people, bands, etc. Got up at 7. The Park presented a curious spectacle, with crowds of people up to Constitution Hill, soldiers, bands, etc.

Outside the crowds continued to chant: The lower orders calling for "Our Vicky" and the new young Queen could still hear the sound of horses returning to stables. Sergeant Majors shouted and carriages carrying the great and the good of the land lumbered home. London life was returning to normal.

Many years later the Queen and Mary Anne exchanged reminisces of the day. Mary Anne was far too excited and annoyed to think about dogs.

In her blue drawing room overlooking Hyde Park Mary Anne paced up and down. She wore mourning – plain black bombazine trimmed with crepe, which was already beginning to look tatty. 'Black,' she observed, 'has never suited me. And the cost of putting servants in black too depressing for words.' The only jewellery allowed to a widow was jet and the only attractive garment to be worn during mourning was the widow's cap which with a little theatrical rouge which made up for the ageing effects of such attire.

Mary Anne was wearied. She had had such a battle with Disraeli to make him go to the Queen's Coronation. He quibbled about the cost of hiring court dress, 'As if Dizzy you have ever bothered about money,' she admonished. She had refused to pay for it. 'I am now a widow with fewer means and no Wyndham to charm my way into his purse,' she told Disraeli sharply.

'Besides, Dizzy you have the legs for court dress.' Disraeli went immediately to Jermyn Street to hire his outfit.

Mary Anne could not believe it. At last the day of the Coronation had arrived and there was Disraeli sitting in Westminster Abbey along with dukes, duchesses, earls, countesses and mere lords and ladies. As dawn approached Mary Anne jumped out of bed. The hoi polloi were tramping into London. Most came on foot. The sound of their singing made the starlings chatter even more with excitement and circle in the blue skies above Hyde Park.

'Oh, how I hope Dizzy will come quickly to me the moment it is all over and tell me everything,' she told Norah Rooke eagerly. Sarah D'Israeli at Bradenham also hoped Disraeli would drive quickly out of London to recount to her the joys of the great day. Only, Isaac knew his son would never come.

And then just as Mary Anne and Norah Rooke stood on the balcony they heard the roars of the crowds greeting the State Coach leaving Buckingham Palace, surrounded by soldiers and dignitaries. The royal party came up Constitution Hill, down Piccadilly, through St James's Park across Trafalgar Square and into the Abbey. It was 11.30 am and all sounds were drowned by the booming of the Abbey bells.

'The noise of it all could be heard at Blackfriars Bridge,' the cook told Mary Anne. At half past four in the afternoon Mary Anne and Norah Rooke standing on Grosvenor Gate balconies heard a great cheer again. The Queen, now with her crown on her head and the orb in her hand was returning to Buckingham Palace.

Mary Anne could not wait any longer and poured champagne into two glasses. 'Will Dizzy never come?' she asked Norah Rooke, who muttering with a sniff replied, 'Mr Disraeli may be meeting people much more useful to him, madam.'

But Mary Anne did not hear the remark for Disraeli was stepping out of a barouche accompanied by eighty-year-old

Lord Rolle. Norah Rooke grimaced. She had been proved right.

'We have had such a fight to get through the throng,' Disraeli told Mary Anne.

Now, with a glass of champagne in his hand, Disraeli began in oratorical style, 'The Queen walked down the aisle, a lonely little figure, followed by the assembly of England. When the ceremony began I heard the Queen constantly ask, 'What are you doing?'

'She received no answer for nobody knew what they were doing,' interrupted Lord Rolle.

'The whole thing,' Disraeli continued was ill rehearsed except the part God played in it. He managed a ray of sunlight to fall upon her, just as the Archbishop placed the crown on her head. Otherwise I saw little for my attention was constantly caught by a gentleman, sitting in front of me, wearing a startling turquoise bespangled suit.'

'How disgraceful,' said Mary Anne.

'And, poor little Queen,' Lord Rolle said. 'She is at an age when many an old counsellor would find it hard to make the decisions she must make … But you know during the homage I tripped down the stairs and she came towards me with arms outstretched saying, "Lord Rolle, may I not get up and meet you?" Is that not a strange understanding in one so young?'

'She is not so young in mind,' observed Mary Anne. 'She can choose her own name,' and then paused, 'I wish I had been there.'

'This may be some compensation. When you are old give this to your grandchildren.' Disraeli placed in Mary Anne's hand the Commemorative Coronation medal.'

'Dizzy, I am now too old to have children.' Both men were surprised at the sadness in Mary Anne's tone. She had not meant to say it and said quickly, 'Dizzy, won't Sa be expecting this?'

Disraeli had forgotten Sa. Yes, she would be waiting for him and the medal. Nevertheless, he kissed Mary Anne's cheek and left the medal in her hand.

Lord Rolle observed, 'There was one revealing occurrence. I wonder if it augurs well for the future?' He smiled at Disraeli.

Disraeli continued, 'As the Queen walked towards the West Door all bowed low before her, except one individual, not expecting to see such a singularly beautiful young man, the Queen paused, half smiling and then remembering she was a Queen, moved on, leaving the young man bowing low murmuring 'Majesty, Majesty, Majesty ...'

'Who was that?' asked Mary Anne.

Neither man answered her question, but Disraeli gave an embarrassed smile.

As the noise of the day subsided Mary Anne, folding a black edged mourning handkerchief around her fingers asked, 'Gentleman will you join me?' She hesitated. The men waited. 'I understand on 9 July there is to be a Coronation Fair in Hyde Park, followed four days later by a review for 5,000 soldiers. Lord Rolle, Dizzy, will you watch the Review with me from the balconies here? Otherwise, I cannot stand alone on public view.'

'It is such a pity,' observed Disraeli, you should be holding one of your grand parties. We could have all been sipping champagne. Dancing all night – and I could have stood on your balcony beckoning to the Queen to come across and dance with us.'

As the Coronation festivities ended summer turned into autumn. Victoria settled into being Queen, and Mary Anne began planning her future.

9 Courtship

Mary Anne continued to dither over the date for her second wedding.

Already it was February 1839 Disraeli was becoming restless. Mary Anne was approaching her second year of mourning. It was now acceptable for her to consider another marriage. Disraeli angrily demanded of Mary Anne that she set a date.

'You are spoiling my reputation. Making me look a fool.'

Mary Anne overwrought cried out, 'You make yourself that.'

Disraeli went white with anger and she frightened exclaimed, 'Dizzy, stop bullying me. I will not have that from any man, especially my lover.'

He sneered, 'There have, of course, been so many.'

She could not bear his contempt. 'One of the reasons I dither is because Wyndham has been such a good husband.'

Rosina had asked, 'Do you expect Dizzy to be faithful for more that the first six months of your marriage?'

He stood looking at her. She knew he knew how attractive she found him and deep down inside her she wondered could such a man find me really desirable?

Exhausted, fearful, her control snapped. 'Dizzy, don't you dare ever come to me again!'

The moment she said it she regretted it. It was too late. He turned and walked silently out of the door, seemingly away from her forever.

She suspected he was standing on the landing wondering…

But after a few minutes she heard his footsteps going down the stairs. He thanked Charles for his hat. Charles murmured something. She just caught the words, 'And what of Madam? She … cares …'

The front door slammed shut. Mary Anne rushed to the window. Disraeli was tilting his top hat over his right eye, placing his thumbs in his waistcoat arms and despite the rain went whistling his way out of her life forever – or so she thought.

Charles placed Disraeli's umbrella in the waiting urn. Tapped it saying, 'He'll be back.' Meanwhile, Mary Anne picked up the pug sitting before the fire. It licked her face and snuggled up to her. Tears began falling down her cheeks making marks in her face powder. Charles opened her sitting room door discreetly and left a glass of brandy with a little water on a side-table.

Later in the evening Norah Rooke packed her mistress off to bed with a shrug. 'Good riddance Mr Disraeli,' she said under her breath.

The next day a note arrived from Disraeli to Mary Anne.
Am at Bradenham

By April 1838 Wyndham Lewis's affairs were settled. Mary Anne left London to journey to Bradenham and to Disraeli.

Mary Anne drove to Bradenham feeling a mixture of fear, expectation and excitement. Cottagers proudly showed Mary Anne their gardens and she remembered Disraeli's comments in Henrietta Temple on gardens. One day she would create him such a garden – and as the red roof and gables of the Disraeli's family home appeared through the still stark beech trees Mary Anne immediately dismissed the thought.

They were all there to welcome her, as Grandma and Grandpapa had been so many years ago. Disraeli opened the carriage door. 'The sun shines specially brightly for you when you come to Bradenham,' he said

Pepys, his younger brother James's dog, half-Alsatian, half-greyhound, bounded forward to lick her face, putting paw marks all over the tapestry silk of her dress and wagging his tail ran around and around. He evidently remembered a friend.

Sa looked worried. Disraeli annoyed.

'Pepy is all right. He's just thick, almost as thick as Jess the gamekeeper's daughter.'

'Enough James,' said Isaac. 'Jess gave you her precious dog.'

'Only after a poacher knocked Pepys on the head and he wasn't any good any more.'

'Be quiet James,' snapped Disraeli. 'Make sure you keep that dog locked up tonight. I don't want him prowling round the corridors in the early hours of the morning.'

'Don't you, my son?' asked Isaac, wryly.

'You seemed to like Jess enough. Are you planning a night's divertissement with her?' asked James mischievously.

'Be quiet James,' ordered Isaac.

By the knowing look the boy gave her Mary Anne wondered if he planned to eavesdrop outside her bedroom door.

Sa also looked across at Mary Anne and the agony in her face made Mary Anne remember Sa's letter written to her shortly after Wyndham Lewis's death.

'*No friends have thought more of your affliction than we have done, and none have prayed more devoutly for your happiness, dearer to all here than our own.*'

No, my dear. You did not expect me to take your Dizzy away from you, thought Mary Anne.

After a light supper of boiled beef, carrots and potatoes followed by ice cream straight from the ice house, they gathered round the new instrument, a pianoforte, to sing Tom Moore's Irish melodies, and lyrics by the recently deceased Sir Walter Scott.

'Why is your father looking at you so sharply, Dizzy?'

'Because in my youth I was involved with Sir Walter's son-in-law. We produced a political paper, lasted six months ...'

'With a loss of £20,000,' said Isaac.

'You never repaid it Dizzy?' Mary Anne asked.

'But it was John Murray, my own publisher, my good friend,' retorted Isaac.

'As I say Father something always turns up.'

Mary Anne joining in the singing of *The Ballad of Alice Brand* sang slightly out of tune. Was Dizzy completely irresponsible in all ways, she wondered.

Disraeli sensing Mary Anne's mood dug her in the ribs. 'How the devil did any woman find strength to break out of her two or three coffins so as to be found on her knees in the vault?' he asked above the ballad.

Mary Anne returned to sparkling but she had not forgotten Disraeli's carelessness. He would find she rarely did.

'Tell me, Dizzy, why is a pretty woman like a muffin?'

'Because she is toasted …'

In the early hours Mary Anne was soon woken by the sound of a light creak coming form the floorboards. She heard Isaac stirring and Sa sobbing into her pillow. Disraeli lay sleeping in her arms continually muttering, 'Sa poor Sa.'

The next morning Norah Rooke brought in her mistress's early morning tea. Disraeli had vanished to his room, leaving several trinkets behind him. Norah Rooke took them to Disraeli's room. Hearing no reply to her knock, she entered quietly and ignoring the apparently sleeping Disraeli, placed them on his dressing table.

This time Rooke left one trinket behind her, an enamelled snuffbox entwined with pearls and diamonds, and on its lid a picture of Lake Garda. Mary Anne, half asleep, snapped it open and looked into the face of a hazel-eyed, blond boy, whose mouth was slightly open. It bore one inscription. *Maurice*.

There was no snuff in the box but a carefully folded piece of paper.

My Darling Maurice,

The first time you rowed me about the Lake, our knees touched and a strange perilous intimacy grew between us. You told me as you rowed me forward and backwards across the Lake at all hours how you sat with my Lord Byron while he told you of his love for his wife, for boys, for girls, even his incest with his own sister and how eventually his wife left him wearied of his perversions, I knew Byron's shadow was over us, willing us … I saw in the swish of the oars, Caroline's face. 'Join us, join us … but a gull broke our reverie and I ignored the invitation in your eyes and returned like

*a coward to London ... Maurice, oh Maurice how I regret
... Remember your cowardly Englishman who so regrets but
remember I loved you then, I love you now, I will love you
for ever, my dearest boy.'*

Suddenly, the sun had gone in. A wind blew menacingly
through the yew trees where it was said the "Devil" hid. She
saw a figure coming up the drive, thumbs in waistcoat arms
whistling.

Not you, Dizzy, not you? Not one of the men mocked by
my brother and my uncles? Does Isaac know, your brother, or
Sa? As Mary Anne continued to be lost in thought, Disraeli's
footsteps approached. She was too late.

The snuffbox was in her hand as he entered the room and
without saying a word he took it away from her.

'I am not a Wyndham Lewis. Widows make good wives,
they do not expect much ... did you not tell me that?'

'But some love, Dizzy.'

'And that you will have.'

Disraeli locked the bedroom door.

Shortly after Wyndham Lewis's death Mary Anne had
received a letter. As she opened it the shadows of young men
appeared whistling invitingly to the little navy clad milliner
stepping her way through puddled cobblestones to the great
houses of Bellevue.

The letter was dated April 6 1838 and she knew even before
she began reading it – it was from him:

*'I hardly know how to address you. Time has done its
office, and what perhaps might formerly please may now
create disgust ... and thy name, Rose, flourishes still in the
only green spot of my memory, and there will exist ...'*

Thine Augustus'

Mary Anne screwed up the letter into a small ball, threw it
into the wastepaper basket, retrieved it, unfolded it, smoothed
it, studied the handwriting, and then filed it.

I remember, sir, the Waterloo Ball. Madame de Pompadour.
No, sir, I'll choose better than you or shall I?

In spite of Berkeley's letter Mary Anne continued to play with Disraeli, while he sought a 'suitable wife, such as dear Charlotte.'

'Unfortunately, Dizzy, while you romanced with Henrietta, Charlotte Bertie has married John Guest and is with her third child.'

While Disraeli played around Mary Anne heard whispering fans cry 'gigolo.'

In July Disraeli vanished on a Tory campaign to Rochester. In his absence Mary Anne received another letter from Berkeley dated 14 July: *'Three times did I advance to your door and three times did I as hastily retreat. Even now when I dwell in thought upon that brief and rapturous period when we were all in all to each other, my heart throbs with emotion.'*

But relations with Disraeli had suddenly deepened.

Disraeli was writing, after making a difficult after dinner speech. *'I was wearied, bilious and I lost my audience until I touched your miniature and then my voice became strong again. 'God bless you my own, sweet faithful Mary Anne, love me as I love you ...'*

Berkeley wrote to Mary Anne again on 27 July and in November Mary Anne was meeting her former lover. A note says: *'I shall be in town tomorrow, dear Rose. Send a line to meet me at the Albion in Cockspur Street.'*

There follows further notes of assignation.

'Any communication will be received privately and safely by directing it to this hotel. If my dear Rose, and dear she must be in every sense of the word, as she cost me £40,000 (well worth the money!) – if, I say, my dear Rose is at home and alone on Monday next let her leave word at the Albion Hotel for me to attend her at dinner.'

Mary Anne went to stay with Disraeli at Bradenham. Isaac beaten by Mary Anne at conjuring tricks wrote to her on her return to London in the October.

Thy Hand, fair Lewis, by the Graces taught,
Folds empty letters, but with meaning fraught;

I found my Match! my honour and my shame!
Oh skilled to snare me in they witty game!

Another letter arrived in the post. It was from Berkeley.

'Farewell Rose, then for ever. Tho' I confess your power un-diminished. Enjoy your triumph, it is your greatest and your last ... you are no more worthy of affection than I of Heaven. He who can best play the Fool to amuse the present hour becomes for that hour the God of your idolatry. Continue to play your fantastic tricks; 'till Angels seem to weep.

To a Nunnery, go ...'

Shortly after Wyndham Lewis's death Mary Anne had written to Disraeli.

'I do not know where to turn for love.'

He had told Sa, 'I will not marry for love.'

In December Disraeli was attacked by influenza, took to his bed and wrote pathetically to Mary Anne.

'I have been obliged to betake myself to bed again, and wish you were with me there.'

Ralph, Disraeil's brother, invited Mary Anne to spend Christmas at Bradenham.

Dear Lady! Leave the foggy town,
At Bradenham find a peaceful rest,
Now all thy tender cares are o'er,
Oh hasten here our loving guest.'

As the church bells rang out the old, welcoming in the New Year society learned Mrs Wyndham Lewis was engaged to Disraeli. The Montefiore girls asked their Mama, 'What does our dearest Dizzy, see in that old woman?'

However, it was Mary Anne who procrastinated over the wedding date.

'I don't know why I am dithering, Dizzy.'

And then one evening, while waiting for Disraeli to arrive, a messenger knocked on the door instead. It was a note from Disraeli's rooms in Duke Street. Mary Anne opened it expecting him to say he had been delayed and would be with her ...

'...*When I first made my advances to you, I was influenced by no romantic feelings. Why not let your Captain Neil have been the minion of your gamesome hours without humiliating and debasing me.*'

Poor woman. Few women could have received such a vicious letter – all Disraeli's genius was in it.

'Is there a reply, madam?'

'No reply.'

Mary Anne sat pushing her supper away watching the sunset creep through the trees in Hyde Park and the birds wheeling in the sky before settling into the branches.

Already, in a gentleman's club, a Mr Robert William Jackson, celebrating the New Year, made remarks about Mary Anne's morals. Mr William John O'Connell challenged Mr Jackson to a duel. They met at Battersea Fields at six o'clock the next morning. Mr Jackson and his friends were arrested and society twittered behind its fans.

The next morning Mary Anne wrote a "holding note" to Disraeli followed by a gentle letter.

'*For God's sake come to me. I am ill and almost distracted. I will answer all you wish. I never desired you to leave the house, or implied or thought a word about money. I received a most distressing letter, and you left me at the moment not knowing ...*'

The next day she wrote:

'*My darling, my love can be of no value to you dear Dizzy after all the harsh and unkind thoughts you have expressed and, of course, feel towards me ... I beg you to be explicit and answer this, also my letter of yesterday. In the meantime I will believe all that's kind and fond of you whatever your feelings may be towards your poor Mary Anne.*'

In the evening, when the candles were lit and Mary Anne was sitting alone. Norah Rooke announced grimly, 'Mr Disraeli, ma'am.' She showed Disraeli into the room and shut the door with a bang as Mary Anne fell into his arms, hugging him to her, almost as if he were her son.

The date of the marriage was fixed. An astrologer told Mary Anne 28 August augured well, except everybody had overlooked John Viney Evans who in June 1839 rose to become a Lieutenant Colonel.

'I feel my star rapidly rising as Napoleon used to say ... but the position has to be paid for ... I am like a horse with a large stone untied from his neck.'

Johnny came to stay at Grosvenor House. He was grumpy, miserable, out of sorts. He had been stationed in Mauritius and the climate had not suited his highly-strung nervous temperament. On 2 July he fell ill and subsequently died. Disraeli briskly despatched "the brother" to be buried besides Wyndham Lewis in Kensal Green Cemetery.

'Out of sight out of mind.'

A tearful Mrs Yate arrived. The sobbing was too much for Disraeli who suggested, 'Dear Mrs Yate, clear the house of trivia.'

He kept Mary Anne occupied by thoughts of her marriage but if he had known it she wrote in her daybook:

Time was is past – thou canst it not recall,
Time is thou hast – employ the portion small;
Time future is not – and may never be,
Time present is the only time for me.

The couple travelled to Bradenham to invite the family to the wedding.

The family replied, 'No thank you. We have made our own plans.'

Disraeli annoyed observed, 'I look forward to the day of our union in my life which will seal my career: for whatever occurs afterwards will I am sure, never shake my soul, as I shall always have the refuge of your sweet heart in sorrow or disappointment, and your quick and accurate sense to guide me in prosperity and triumph.'

'Quite so,' said Mary Anne.

'Lord,' said Ralph. 'Your speeches are why we ain't coming.'

The two joined the D'Israelis sulking around the pianoforte. Sa played Chopin, Ralph read a Shakespearean sonnet. The boys told riddles and giggled. Mary Anne's voice echoed out into the lanes, singing a music hall song.

On the last day of their stay, when the couple were just stepping into the barouche the head gardener arrived with an ephemeral flower.

'One flower alone has opened in every part completely double, bearing six leaves instead of three.'

'We accept it as a happy augury,' said Mary Anne and they waved goodbye for tomorrow they would be married.

Mary Anne had left lying on a bureau her character analysed from her dreadful handwriting by a Miss Richardson.

'Accustomed to every comfort and indulged in all her wishes, she has never learnt how to conceal her feelings or moderate their violence ... Naturally gifted with a warm heart and ardent disposition, she is capable of sincere affection and even of extraordinary devotion, but from the circumstance of having been constantly in the society of literary people, and adopting a strong language they sometimes employ, she gives to the expression of a sorrow a harshness ...Quick, clever – too fond of a jest – and too apt to ask a puzzling question, she makes society gay and her own house particularly agreeable ... She is conscious not vain of her attractions, and inclined to discover the merits of others rather than dwell on their faults.

'Dearest Dizzy, what a wife you have chosen,' sighed Sa.

Prior to their marriage, Disraeli introduced Mary Anne to the Jewish world of the Rothschilds, Montefiores, and Alberts.

'Mary Anne bore it like a philosopher,' he boasted to Sa , 'I sat at dinner next to Lionel de Rothschild, whom I admire above most men.' This was the man who would one day grant Disraeli the loan with which to purchase the Suez Canal.

It was to Mary Anne such a new world. These were international people who did not have cousins in the shires but in strange places like Lithuania and talked of pomegranates and of collecting gold. They lived in an enclosed world of their own, an exotic place, linked throughout the globe with relatives – who had often no language in common – except for their Jewishness.

Disraeli laughed in Yiddish and talked of his bar mitzvah to please his grandfather. These were sharp, quick, clever, bejewelled people with no roots; they even had their surroundings gold plated. They placed before Mary Anne strange tasting food: Gefilte fish, turtle soup and Pomerantzen.

One day Baron Solomon Mayer de Rothschild, second son of the founding father of the dynasty, Mayer Amschel Rothschild, decided to hold a ball. Mary Anne and Disraeli were invited.

The Gentiles, who attended came from the best society. It was uneasy for most of them were in debt to their hosts and so could not patronise them as they wished.

Mary Anne remained silent.

'What is wrong?' enquired Disraeli.

'I am agog for the place is more glorious than the Tuileries and pineapples are plentiful as blackberries,' replied Mary Anne.

'Disraeli, do you like the opera?' a voice asked. Shortly afterwards Mary Anne found herself in the best box in the Haymarket. It belonged to the Rothschilds. She prepared herself to be seen and to see. But the "quality" passed her by. She was now an honorary Jew – an outsider – a person to be ignored except when needed.

Grosvenor Gate stood not in the midst of society but cut off from it, in the centre of the Rothschilds' spider web: Rothschild Row, Natty lived at No 148, Piccadilly, next to Apsley House, Hannah Roseberry at 107 who Lord Roseberry married for love, even though she was plain, Ferdinand at 143 and Alice 142 and close to Mary Anne lived Louise, with eventually, baby Leo at 1 Hamilton Place and Alfred at 1 Seamore Place.

However, for Disraeli, the most important person was Mayer de Rothschild who had responsibility for the Vienna offices of the Rothschild financial empire and this connection led to invitations from Louis Phillipe and gave Disraeli an intelligence network throughout Europe.

And living in this world Mary Anne came to understand that for Disraeli to become Prime Minister was almost impossibility. Almost but not quite. I will cultivate Victoria and it is the Rothschild money, their international understanding, their family networks which will be a greater force than any Norman aristocratic background, she told herself

The Jews had been persecuted for nearly two thousand years. They were more complex, more intense than English people. Their servants knew their masters were richer than the Duke of Westminster. They had billiard rooms for their own amusement. When she had first known Disraeli she judged him lightly as an exotic Londoner, but Mary Anne began to realize that she had a more complex man than she could ever have imagined. He listened; his long fingers would tap on the table. He would ingratiate himself with the great and the good. 'Of course Lord So and So that is your view,' he would say bowing slightly. He would make others aware of how great the great man was. He would keep down upstarts who questioned him but he saw himself as a Messiah and one who touched the very depths of despair. A very Jewish male characteristic – and one unknown to a cheerful Devon woman.

It was a hard struggle for her to understand the nature of his illness and she learned to cope with it – eventually. She asked questions of physicians and priests. She learned Disraeli had been rejected by his mother and his father intellectually. Mary Anne recalled a brief meeting at the Llamas Fair. 'He suffers from the family illness of melancholia,' Mama had said.

Mary Anne, naturally warm and maternal, gave Disraeli the comfort, mothering, support and understanding he longed for as well as superb food for his stomach. In a world where his Jewishness was despised, as Mary Anne had already experienced at the time of Disraeli's maiden speech. She had already experienced the hatred of the Jew and the Rothschilds did not forget the woman who was reported to have called out from the Ladies' Gallery, 'I will not enter this place again until he is Prime Minister.'

Mary Anne with her cheerfulness, her lack of judging others and her obvious love for one of their own made her grow in favour with the Rothschilds. In her turn she felt one of them and not a ridiculous old woman who was an outsider. And Disraeli was obviously, at home amongst his own.

Mary Anne became so Jewish that in 1845 when Sir Anthony de Rothschild's nephew Leopold was born she cradled the baby in her arms, cooing like any Jewish woman with a newborn male. Leo looked up into Mary Anne's face and she exclaimed:

'Oh, my dear, what a beautiful baby boy, does he not look like the Messiah? Indeed he has the look of Dizzy about him?'

Thankfully for his parents young Leopold grew into a kindly man, "an angel, with a revenue" and is remembered, as the man who backed an outsider at the 1879 Derby and won £50,000.

But Disraeli's depressions were a threat to his life. At one of his many low points, he told Stanley, 'If I retire from politics in time enough, I shall resume literature, and write the Life of Christ ...' He spoke at this time with great earnestness about, 'Restoring the Jews to their own land.' Mary Anne felt that he was tempted to go to live in Jerusalem – alone.

Mary Anne's unselfishness was one of the reasons why when Disraeli was asked how he coped with that ridiculous old woman, thundered 'Gratitude.'

Lady Anthony de Rothschild was often alone in the evenings, as was Mary Anne and they would sit together, enjoying high tea and gossip. The housekeeper recounted, 'Mrs Disraeli used to turn up wearing an afternoon frock with the oddest headgear. She did not eat much for she just talked and talked incessantly about Mr Disraeli and his successes.'

10 Mrs Disraeli

The Times: August 28 1839

**The wedding of Mrs Wyndham Lewis
to Mr Benjamin Disraeli
At: 10.30 am
At: St George's Church, Hanover Square.**

At l0.30 am Mary Anne arrived at the church ablaze in a travelling costume of exotic brilliance accompanied by her relative, Mr William Scrope, solicitor.

At ll.00 Rosina bounced down the church steps.

'He hasn't come.'

'Dizzy was late for his own birth,' snapped Mary Anne.

She plonked herself down.

Five minutes later the vicar scuttled down the steps.

'Dear lady do come inside.'

Mary Anne sat in the furthest pew, facing the West door, her skirts lifted: 'So Dizzy will see my ankles and Rosina cannot see my face.'

As the clock struck the half hour, the West door was flung open. Disraeli entered arms outstretched.

'Dearest, I got lost.'

'Horse got the staggers, ma'am,' said a perspiring Lyndhurst.

The organist started up the Wedding March.

'No time for that,' snapped Mary Anne. 'Caterers being paid by the hour.'

'Dearly beloved we are gathered together in the sight of God began the Vicar … It was ordained for the procreation of children'

'Too late!' the couple said in chorus.

'With this ring I thee wed.'

Disraeli looked round to Lyndhurst.

'Over to you old man.'

'Are you sure?'

Both men began patting pockets.

Mary Anne produced the spare.

'I take thee Mary Anne to be my wedded wife.'

Mary Anne wriggled her fourth finger up and down as Disraeli pushed down hard on the middle finger.

'It won't go on,' whispered Disraeli.

'Wrong finger old boy,' said Lyndurst.

'And live together in Holy Matrimony,' concluded the vicar.

He said it to empty air for the two had rushed to the vestry, signed and fled to Grosvenor Gate.

On their arrival Disraeli was delighted to see the servants attired in his own colours of gold, silver and brown but as the couple did not consider their wedding a special occasion the best silver was not put out.

Disraeli rose to thank the guests for coming.

Rains began splashing against the windows.

'Tedious ain't it?' observed Lyndhurst to Mrs Yate, his American accent more pronounced than ever,

'They will be enjoying themselves at Bradenham.'

'The church bells will be ringing.'

'Isaac will be playing the fiddle.'

'Spectacles sliding down his nose.'

'Sun shining on his bald head.'

'Sa will be dancing a jig.'

'James kissing the kitchen maid.'

'Ralph jotting up the cost of it all.'

'Old Scrumpy will be coming up the drive with toffee apples for all the children.'

'And Tita will make sure they will be happy until midnight.'

Disraeli groaned on, 'Reform is the issue and I must add ...'

Lyndhurst raised his glass to Mrs Yate. They clicked glasses and together drank down second best champagne.

'Oh how we wish we were at Bradenham,' they said together.

Suddenly, Lyndhurst jumped up beaming, calling out, 'Mr and Mrs Disraeli. Your carriage is here.'

The couple were up and out, like two mice escaping from a cat, leaving the rest of the party calling for drinkable champagne.

'Magnificent carriage,' observed Disraeli, bouncing up and down on the seat. 'Whose is it?'

'Mine,' said Mary Anne.

'No, dearest, ours.'

'Mine. A wedding present from your dear Papa to me.'

Disraeli sat in miffed silence while they drove through the rain to Tunbridge Wells.

Occasionally, Disraeli muttered under his breath:

'The man is supposed to be in the driving seat.'

Rains continued to pour down as the carriage drew up outside 'The Kentish Hotel.'

The coachman yelled, 'Harry help me with this lot.'

The couple alighted with dignity, swished into the hotel. Disraeli announced:

'Mr Disraeli and Mrs Wyndham Lewis.'

Later Mary Anne wrote in her accounts book:

28th August 1839
In-hand £300

Incomings	*Outgoings*
Dear Dizzy Became My Husband	*Gloves 2/6d*

11 Honeymoon

The following morning Mary Anne woke. As she turned over she found a note pinned to her pillow – half asleep she sat up to read it.

'My Dearest Love,

After such traumas, gone to take the waters, back in time for luncheon.

As always Your Loving Dizzy'

Mary Anne sighed. She was not a young first time bride, nevertheless, it would have been nice to have woken up to find Dizzy snoring gently beside her. As she climbed out of the very old four-poster, she clung to its tapestries – they had been so tired they had not even pulled the curtains around themselves.

It seemed as if this second honeymoon was not going to be so different from her first. Wyndham had been pre-occupied with business and Dizzy seemed busy with life. Mary Anne looked out of the window on to small Georgian houses huddling together opposite. The roofs began to shine with rain. 'It is all very depressing,' she said to the red-nosed china dogs on the mantelpiece.

It was August and already there was a chill in the air. The damp seemed to seep into the room. For a brief second Mary Anne felt alone. She looked at the dress lying across a chair which she had worn for her wedding and pulled out from a tin trunk a sprigged gingham day gown. As she struggled into the dress she felt her spirits lifting and when she came downstairs her appearance met with approval from the assembled company. Nevertheless, when she arrived in the "eating room" Mary Anne asked for the logs to be lit in the inglenook.

As they blazed into life she called out to a passing waiter, 'When Mr Disraeli comes bring him sherry, a large glass of sherry quickly. He will be cold and wet.'

At which point Disraeli arrived – dripping with rain and about to sneeze.

'Only met Lord Monteagle,' he complained. 'He talks continually about everything and nothing in particular. Don't know why we came to Tunbridge Wells – not what it was. Waters taste vile and the Pantiles quite grubby.'

Food was placed on the oval table before them. Then with forks at the ready, Mr and Mrs Disraeli dug into game pie, steak and kidney pudding and took breath to survey the rib of beef being placed before them.

'Why did we come?' asked Disraeli between mouthfuls.

'So we could talk, eat, drink, sleep,' answered Mary Anne. A log slipped from the fire burning to a cinder in the grate. 'And to love and be loved,' his wife added.

The rain continued lashing against the windowpanes settling on the sill before splashing down making puddles for passers-by to try to avoid. The Disraelis watched the outside world getting wetter and wetter and then looked across the table at each other.

'Last night we had both been rather tired,' observed Disraeli. Mary Anne smiled and lowered her eyelashes. Disraeli smiled back and fingered his wife's wedding ring. They left a golden syrup pudding to its own devices and holding hands climbed the stairs, walking arm-in-arm to their bedroom. A few minutes later Boots wandering along the corridor read the first *Do Not Disturb* notice hanging from the Disraelis' bedroom doorknob. He pencilled in – *please*.

The rains continued to fall all that night. The next day continued grey and dull.

'What shall we do?' enquired Disraeli discontentedly, as the rain tumbled down.

'Visit,' said Mary Anne sharply, anxious to show off her new carriage.

On September 4 Disraeli wrote to Sa: '*Thankfully the hotel is comfortable but the weather remains so bad we have scarcely left it but have taken a drive amidst the squalls and rain.*

Lord and Lady Camden at Bayham were startled to see the Disraelis coming up the drive – the horses splashing through the rain.

'Are you not on honeymoon?' they enquired.

'Oh yes, but the weather is so dull is it not.'

The Campdens thought of their own honeymoon and smiled at each. 'We weren't bored were we dear? said Lady Campden.

'No,' said Disraeli, 'but you weren't stuck in Tunbridge Wells in terrible weather.'

Lord and Lady D'Lisle saw the couple approaching and resolved to be "out" and fled through the back entrance.

As the butler began announcing that His Lordship and Her Ladyship their three small children crept across the hall shyly and seeing moisture in Mary Anne's eyes became quite charming. Disraeli patted them on the head and rewarded each of them with a guinea. As the couple left they were startled to hear pandemonium breaking out as little voices cried, 'I'll have yours.'

The next morning the Disraelis' carriage could be seen trundling out of Tunbridge Wells along the road to Ashford. Here they stayed the night and then continued through Hythe to the Ship Inn, Dover, where they found two letters waiting for them.

One came from Sa saying: *'We had a wonderful party and in the morning we found on your wedding morning the ephemeral flower open in every part completely double, bearing six leaves instead of three and very large and splendid. Was it not a most curious circumstance? We accepted it as a happy augury.'*

And the other letter came from Isaac and finished. *'If you proceed to the Continent, I hope you will find some fragment of a lost summer.'*

The Disraelis hopeful of finding good weather and armed with Mary Anne's Baedeker boarded the new style continental steamship, paying four guineas for their carriage to accompany them, but Mary Anne refused to pay three guineas per horse preferring to hire fresh animals at Calais.

Once they were aboard and the cliffs of Dover began to disappear Mary Anne looked at the ship and seeing the steam coming out of the chimneys said to Disraeli. 'It is so unromantic. The wind is unimportant. It seems that only coal matters.'

'More reliable. It will be only coal which will matter from now on,' observed Disraeli. They stood together watching England vanishing and their old lives too. As the boat made its way across the Channel Mary Anne snuggled up to Disraeli. She had never felt so as one with Wyndham Lewis.

They could hear the sounds of the engines and men pushing coal into a raging furnace. The ship ploughed its own way, not dependent on the elements for support. As they came on deck for air before retiring to their cabin waves crashed over the side of the boat and the seas became increasingly turbulent. Mary Anne began to feel sick thankful that this journey would take only two hours and twenty minutes instead of several hours. In bad conditions it may have taken a day or more.

Disraeli lent over the side of the boat. The spray struck him in the face and when he turned around he was surprised to see Mary Anne turning green. He took his wife by the arm and rather smugly led her below deck. Wherever Disraeli went inside the boat he could hear the roar of the engines and men stoking coal into the furnace, which blazed away. They seemed impervious to the terrible heat or the waves crashing over the side. His fellow passengers lay moaning in their cabins. Disraeli, trying not to slip on the wet decks, rushed around looking after everybody, which much to his surprise he rather enjoyed. The boat continued struggling through the troubled seas until it docked at Calais.

'I was the only one who did not succumb,' Disraeli boasted once he was safely on shore. 'Mary Anne suffered dreadfully.'

'Nonsense Dizzy it was the oysters I ate,' snapped Mary Anne.

With relief they struggled wearily into their own carriage and hired horses at the equivalent of £2 15 6d each and began the tedious journey to Dunkirk and Ostend and finally reached Brussels on the evening of 8 September, tired and hungry. They had to search for several hours to find accommodation in the overcrowded town. Finally, they were forced to settle for an "entresol" at the Hotel Britannique.

From Brussels the Disraelis drove through Liege to Antwerp, and then travelling via Aix la Chapelle and Cologne to Baden Baden, arriving in the Spa on 19 September. Mary Anne had bravely agreed to travel the latter part of the journey on a river steamer but insisted on sleeping in her own carriage – comfortably.

'Such,' wrote Disraeli pompously to his sister, 'Are the revolutions of modern travel.'

Modern travel or not Mary Anne did not like Baden Baden. 'It is not much better than Cheltenham, the public dinners, balls, promenades, pumps, music and gambling are not up to snuff,' she complained.

They did not stay long in Baden Baden, but drove through the Black Forest to Munich and remained in that city during most of October sightseeing. They played the part of tourists in Rattisbon, Nuremberg and Frankfurt, but Disraeli quickly returned to being a politician when they arrived in Stuttgart.

Here, the Disraelis found fat little King William Frederick of Prussia sitting on a gilded throne granting largesse to pretty girl peasants and even more graceful boys who pranced around him.

'And this little oddity influences all the states of Germany,' Disraeli told Mary Anne.

'Does he now?' she replied.

The small gnome-like man took no notice of the odd Jew who kept talking at him, but laughed at his wife, who told him such risqué jokes and stories of life at Westminster. In return, perhaps, the King was a little indiscreet himself. His remarks, of course, were repeated by Mary Anne to Disraeli …

After Stuttgart the couple visited several other German cities and excitedly went down the Rhine from Bingen. They sailed through the dramatic Wagnerian scenery to Coblenz and it was here in the small wine-growing town that Disraeli recalled:

'The Rhine healed me when Father fearful for my mind brought me here. The doctors told him I would succumb for ever to the D'Israeli nervous disability and I was not even nineteen.'

Mary Anne, squeezed her husband's arm saying, 'Dizzy, you have me now, there will no more melancholia …'

But Mary Anne was approaching her late forties and becoming weary of constant travel and asked, 'Shall we go home now Dizzy?' She was taken aback by his answer.

'When I have met Nathaniel Rothschild.'

She had expected him to agree to their return immediately as Wyndham, as a gentleman, would no doubt have done. 'Is Nathaniel Rothschild not in Paris, dearest?' she enquired.

'Quite so,' said Disraeli sharply. 'We return to London when the network is in place, not before. It will mean a smile here, a bribe there and eventually I shall be at the centre of the spider's network – then we go home and only then.'

His great dark eyes were looking into hers without smiling, commanding her obedience.

She remembered writing to Johnny glibly. *'Mark what I say, mark what I foretell Mr Disraeli will be one of the greatest men of his age.'*

Mary Anne realized this man would bend to her, play the boy – when it suited him. Is this the price all women paid for such a great man, Mary Anne asked herself. She added sadly, it is his ambition, his will and that is what he is married to.

She whispered to Disraeli, 'And, therefore, you will be the only man suitable to become Foreign Secretary.'

'Quite so,' he replied.

And they travelled on to Paris even though Mary Anne was tired.

She realized as they entered the Hotel de' la Europe in the Rue de Rivoli that Disraeli had ordered the best suite in the place and laid on lavish entertainment, intending to entertain the best company in Paris – all without consulting her. By now it was early November and they had been away more than two months. Mary Anne was longing to be in London to buy presents and make Grosvenor Gate ready for their first Christmas together.

'Dizzy how are we paying for this?'

She did not know Disraeli had already written to his lawyer:

'Mrs D is aware I am about to raise a sum of money but is ignorant of the method.'

The Disraeli suite became one of the liveliest places in Paris. Here one could find a series of the richest people in Europe, politicians and artistic and literary cognoscenti. Actors came wandering in after the theatre and sat until the early hours recounting theatrical tales, as actors do, and from somewhere came a son of a friend of Isaac's introducing himself as Chidiock Tichborne Nangle.

Mary Anne asked, 'Dizzy, How could any parent give a child such a name?'

'Nangleis is a character in Father's *Curiosities of Literature* dearest,' he replied.

At the end of November Mary Anne would take no more. She said, 'Dizzy you have met Nathaniel Rothschild, now we do return home?' adding 'dearest' as an afterthought.

Disraeli nodded and to make sure her husband did not see her merely as a "doormat" Mary Anne asked, 'Have you noticed my clothes, Dizzy?'

Her husband looked up from *The Times*, which he read every day.

'They are out of date dearest compared with the French,' his wife told him.

'Really, I had not noticed.'

But, of course, he had.

An hour later the Disraelis were seen shopping in the heart of Paris.

'The shops of the Rue Etienne-Marcel rival those of Regent Street any day dearest,' observed Disraeli, but Mary Anne led him through a labyrinth of tiny streets: then down steps, clucking at the dirt and sweeping up her skirts calling out, 'Careful Dizzy.'

They went into a darkened place, where from below stairs could be heard the sounds of girls scuttling around. Mary Anne knew some twenty would be snipping and embroidering, by candlelight, even though it was midday outside.

A sharp-eyed black clothed Parisian woman looked across a cutting table at them. 'Your materials, madame,' demanded Mary Anne sharply and before her were laid out brocades, silks and embroidered linens. She fingered them, folded them, tucked at them, while watching Disraeli's expression and chose those which were brocaded, richly embroidered with flowers – in the manner of the eighteenth century. These she had noted Disraeli greeted with a smile.

'200 francs, madame.'

'No, madame, at that price I will make a loss.'

'No you won't you're dealing with a woman who still owns a milliner's shop.'

'And a man whose grandfather helped found the London Stock Exchange,' said Disraeli not to be outdone.

'200 francs my last offer.'

'200 guineas.'

'200 francs,' said Mary Anne. 'Dizzy would you go downstairs and give to each girl a guinea because they will all be blind by the time they are thirty ...'

The couple left the shop with the bell tinkling, and madame banging the materials back onto shelves.

Norah Rooke had joined them in Paris. She collected and packed Mrs Disraeli's new acquisitions immediately. The Disraelis decided to visit the opera.

Ahead of going to see Aubron's Fairyland, Mary Anne,

grubby, from the Parisian streets, decided to take a bath. Just as Disraeli entered the room she stepped out of the tub – naked.

'Dizzy, place my pearls around my neck.'

With shaking hands Disraeli did so. And then, not calling for Norah Rooke, Mary Anne put on her under things, her petticoats, her skirts and finally her bodice, drawing the square neckline down with her hands, straightening it to the waist so it emphasised her breasts.

Disraeli smiled, amused, 'You are a veritable Madame de Pompadour.'

She threw her head back. Her fists clenched.

'You think I am a tart, a whore?'

'No, no my dear,' said a startled Disraeli. 'Madame de Pompadour is a great courtesan …'

'You think I have sold my talents for money,' Mary Anne screamed.

'No, of course not I only meant you do look particularly well – it is only your beauty which is of a comparison.'

'Her face is painted an inch thick with powder and paste.'

'Mary Anne, Mary Anne. What is it? It is so unlike you?'

'I am a happily married woman and you imply …'

'Mary Anne I implied nothing,' he said walking to the door.

As he opened the door Disraeli turned.

'Mary Anne I only wanted to make love to you.'

'Oh, Dizzy, Dizzy why didn't you say so?' She put out her arms around him, as if to a hurt child. 'Come here.' She drew him close to her and kissed him with such passion they sank into the bed and as they fell Disraeli extinguished the gaslight.

After nearly three months of honeymoon, Mary Anne read a letter from the "Governor", which filled her with dread. *'On 4 November in Newport a thousand miners and ironworkers were fired upon at the Westgate Hotel by troops. Several were killed. They had congregated to ask for the release of the Chartist leader Henry Vincent from Monmouth jail.'*

'Now, is indeed the time to return to London,' said Disraeli.

Early in December the Disraelis found themselves driving through Hyde Park to Grosvenor Gate.

Mary Anne, disliking the swirling London fogs, snuggled up to Disraeli.

'Dizzy we cannot see. People come lurching up out of the mists.'

A voice called out, 'Careful you nearly ran me over.'

'Pity we didn't Lyndhurst,' said Disraeli opening the carriage door as Lyndhurst waved his umbrella at the coachman.

'Need a lift Lyndhurst?' asked Disraeli.

'No need to be impertinent now that you're married. I'm going to see a lady. Had a good honeymoon?'

'Excellent,' said Disraeli. 'I made several useful contacts.'

'I finished the daisy chain around the mats for the dining table,' added Mary Anne with a smile.

Lyndhurst raised his hat as the carriage moved away. The horses' hooves were the only sound to be heard in the enveloping gloom.

'Some people have a damned odd way of spending a honeymoon,' he said to the fog.

12 Christmas 1838

Mary Anne woke, toes tingling; from somewhere a clock struck four times. It was just four in the morning and already the house was coming alive.

'Dizzy, Dizzy, it's our first Christmas. I need to impress your family. They must accept me as your wife – a good wife to you at that.' But Disraeli merely turned over and continued snoring into his pillow.

'Oh, Dizzy, sometimes you are just like everybody else's husband.'

Norah Rooke swept into the room, ignoring Disraeli, as much as in the couple's pre-marriage days.

'I have laid out the pink changeable glace, madam, added a pelerine, extra ruffles to the cuffs and brooches at the collar. It has lost that severe look.'

Mary Anne jumped out of bed, waking Disraeli who sat up expectantly.

'No time for that,' said Mary Anne running out of the room, heel-less shoes tapping down uncarpeted back stairs and into the kitchen. The goose turning on the spit spluttered out a welcome, the beef and hams baked silently together in the range oven, maids sliced away at an enormous green sea turtle, others peeled potatoes, leeks, onions and carrots ready to go into the great boiling pot. The cook herself stirred sauces. Charles emerged red robin faced from the cellar.

'Will everything be ready in time?'

Mary Anne received no answer except a chorus of, 'A Merry Christmas, madam.' Even the cook joined in, forgiving Mary Anne trespassing unannounced into her kitchen.

Mary Anne chivvied the servants for several hours until finally Hortense, duster in hand, called out from the drawing room balcony, 'Madam, madam they are coming.'

Across the park, came the Bradenham carriage, horses' hooves crunching into gravel paths, harnesses jangling in time to the church bells. Tita, in best brigand attire, galloped them through the glistening Grosvenor Gates, across Park Lane, drawing alongside Mary Anne's mansion calling out, 'Whoa boys.'

Mary Anne pushed past a miffed Charles and called out, 'Merry Christmas, everyone.'

And then everybody fell out onto the pavement, giggling, hugging and kissing one another. 'We spent yesterday with Aunt and Uncle Basevi,' called out James.

'We must visit them, dearest,' said Disraeli quickly. 'They are our richest relations.'

'Indeed,' said Mary and returning to the business of day said, 'Come on in out of the cold.'

Disraeli called out, 'Mince pies and champagne.'

The door banged shut leaving one guest standing on the pavement. Then it opened again.

'Oh come on in, Mother, do.'

Once inside Mrs D'Israeli was immediately forgotten by her son, as she was by the rest of her family, who munched their way through mince pies, pulled noiseless crackers and gurgled with glee as they opened numerous parcels before the crackling great fire.

'Leave room for dinner,' instructed Mary Anne.

As the mantelpiece clock struck two they sat themselves down higgledy-piggledy around the walnut dining room table polished especially bright for Christmas dinner. Seven pairs of eyes watched expectantly as Disraeli poured champagne and then into the room entered Charles bearing the goose, followed by lesser beings carrying the beef, hams and game pies. The younger maids brought in dishes overflowing with vegetables: turnips, parsnips, onions, carrots, gravy and chutneys – the list seemed endless.

Isaac began to carve the goose but after a short time Disraeli asked, 'Allow me Father. The journey has tired you.'

'No, my boy, it is my eyes. I cannot see.'

Then came the sound of rattling plates, footmen, maids, rushing to and fro and silence as the party dug into the food only raising its head en block some twenty minutes later.

'We must pause for breath,' said Isaac.

Sa looked around her, 'Mary Anne, you haven't brought back any mementoes of your travels.'

'No, I have not. I do not like fussiness.'

'Do you not?' replied Sa glancing at the pink and blue glass objects encased in crystal and gilt scattered along the table.

When everyone had eaten as much as possible, the cloth was removed leaving the table clear for desert. Servants drew the deep green velvet curtains shutting out the winter mists that were beginning to creep across the park.

How they cheered as Tita entered carrying shoulder high on one large hand, a huge pudding.

Disraeli rose, 'Let us raise our glasses to Mary Anne's Spanish pudding.

As she began to serve it, 'Sa said, 'Mary Anne, you must give me the recipe.'

'Of course, I will, when I am dead and gone.'

'What an answer, Mary Anne,' exclaimed Isaac. 'I did not know you possessed such toughness.'

'I make sure nobody does dear Papa-in-law.'

Mary Anne glanced at Disraeli. He continued chatting, not noticing her careless remark, but she caught Sa's eye and in a second realized that the greatest intellect belonged not to her husband but to Sarah D'Israeli.

13 The Chartists 1840

The wedding, the honeymoon and Christmas were over and the business of living had to begin again.

Disraeli was writing to Sa from Westminster: *'Last night all the town was terrified with expected risings of the Chartists. The troops ordered to be ready, the police in all directions and the fire engines all full, as incendiarism was to break out in several quarters.'*

Disraeli's nerves were already strained during the day of the unrest as he had taken his new wife to meet his aristocratic relations – the powerful Basevis. The last words he had heard from his uncle's lips had been some twenty years before, when as a young man he had been articled clerk to his uncle's chambers. Uncle Basevi had told Isaac D'Israeli coldly, 'Young Benjamin has too much imagination for the law.'

As the butler announced: 'Mr and Mrs Disraeli,' it was obvious that his relations' view of him had not changed and that the oddly attired Mary Anne brought back memories to Uncle Basevi of Disraeli sitting in chambers, most wonderfully attired, reading Chaucer to clients who were put into such a good frame of mind they decided 'not to pursue the matter Basevi.'

The clock ticked away as the group made awkward conversation. Mary Anne grappling with an old fashioned hot cup of chocolate in a handle-less cup, desperately trying to have the little finger pointing outwards said, 'Dizzy, always says that only working in the law could he have gained such a knowledge of human nature which has stood him in such good stead ...'

'Indeed,' said Uncle Basevi grimly, rising from his chair, indicating the meeting was at an end. As the couple climbed into Mary Anne's carriage and snow began falling Disraeli observed, 'I feel we have lost the support of our only influential relatives.'

'Oh, no, dearest,' said Mary Anne, but Disraeli slunk

through Carriage Gate to the Commons 'looking uncommonly dejected' as one MP observed to another.

Mary Anne drove back to Grosvenor Gate and wrote a note inviting the Basevis to a soirée with the Duke of Wellington as guest of honour. Their refusal came by return.

While Disraeli was in the House Mary Anne sat in her sitting room listening to gossip saying, 'Our kind are threatened by the Chartists and their leader, Draper Frost, should hang.'

Mary Anne said quietly, 'I am not of this view. I know too much about industrial conditions in the Welsh Valleys.'

An old cat spat out, 'We all know Mrs Disraeli when there is a riot your windows are not broken by the mob.'

Mary Anne ignored the jibe but replied, 'We are two nations. One cause of discontent is that many of the new working people can read. Shoemakers, ale-house keepers, dissenting clergy, miners, factory workers. They gather together and discuss the wrongs our type inflict upon them. Even Mr Gladstone has expressed the view that he wonders how long the poor will be subject to the class system.'

One of her guests said with astonishment, 'But don't you know that on street corners, pamphleteers, non-newspaper sellers, even the broadsheets that are thrown into the gutters carry one message: 'Representation.'

'Is it so much to ask for responsible people to wish to vote to influence the great men who wield power.'

There was silence in her sitting room. From the street they could hear a beggar singing:

We will conclude our mournful ditty
Which fills our aching hearts with pain
Shed a tear for us of pity -
We never shall return again;
And when we've reached our destination
O'er the seas through storm and gales
O May you live in comfort
While we lament in New South Wales.

The women rose to go. These were Mary Anne's intimate circle and she said in desperation, 'All they ask for in their "People's Charter" is democracy.'

'Would you not if your sons had no future but to be mere cogs in the industrial machine?' Mary Anne added quickly. 'My dear, Wyndham Lewis always said these people are of a lesser sort and they should be kept in their place.' Her guests relaxed. She was one of them after all. 'Dizzy, however,' Mary Anne continued, 'being Jewish shows more understanding of working people and their ways.'

At that point Disraeli entered the room. 'Ah, yes,' he observed. 'It is a common thought that democracy has nothing to do with the lower orders.'

Mrs Disraeli's guests shuffled with embarrassment, 'Of course, the dear soul has a Jewish husband – what else could one expect?' They all sat down and returned to discussing the weather.

In the evening Mary Anne wrote in her account book. '*Mr Stebbbings given two weeks notice for impudence. We must never employ him again.*'

And during that evening Mary Anne, told Disraeli, 'I definitely agreed with cook's daughter that if a woman rules the country, should she not be able to vote?'

'Yes,' said Disraeli, 'but does cook realise the Queen would not be eligible. Some of the Chartists said privately that they would only give the vote to spinsters and widows, dearest.'

Mary Anne looked up from her embroidery with annoyance.

'Husbands and wives being as one, dearest, therefore only one vote,' Disraeli added with a smirk.

London as always had its own agenda but the newly prosperous merchants, bankers and factory owners, living in bright red suburban villas outside the Northern and Midland conurbations, needed to know Tory policy.

The great and the good of the party considered all options and decided: 'Self-made men like Disraeli, understand the new industrial men. They are not our sort of person.' Peel, an industrialist's son agreed with them but for different reasons. Nobody in that circle knew, except Peel, how well Mrs Disraeli, understood this new world.

'It is a great honour to be asked to represent the Party to a new class of person,' said Disraeli, as the two of them sat down in a first-class compartment in one of the new steam trains.

'Quite a comfortable way of travelling,' observed Disraeli. 'I do not know why the working-classes object so.'

'They have to travel without lids to cover them, Dizzy.'

Mary Anne, when rail travelling, wore as she always did an outfit of brightly printed wool, black, blue, green and orange, with a mantle of green and cream shot silk braided and fringed with matching bonnet with a curtain at the back of the crown to shade the neck. The outfit did not show the flecks from the engine, which even attacked those in first-class carriages and covered wagons.

The train steamed out of the newly built railway stations of Paddington and Euston. £5,000,000 had been spent annually to date on the construction of the railways.

'The network is almost complete,' said Disraeli.

'No,' said Mary Anne firmly. 'No shares, Dizzy. It is a bubble, Dizzy. No, not another word. We have your debts to consider.' Disraeli shrank back into his seat.

'You are a perfect wife, until we get to money,' he muttered with annoyance. To avoid conversation with his wife Disraeli looked out at the countryside speeding past at nearly thirty miles an hour. The steam engine raced through the old countryside into the new world of machines, muck and money, stopping at Manchester Piccadilly Station. Passengers tumbled out on to the platform and handed to the guard their copper disc with the destination engraved upon it.

Some years later when they were travelling back to Grosvenor Gate on Thursday October 16 1845 Disraeli read in his newspaper: '*The Bank of England has raised its discount. The effect is disastrous ... the price of stock is lowered. Panic has reached every heart and every home. Entire families are ruined. There is scarcely a town in England, what has not beheld some wretched suicide.'*

He did not show the article to Mary Anne.

It was Mary Anne who felt most comfortable in the worlds of Manchester, Birmingham or Sheffield. In these cities men were industrialists – dealing with realities – like Wyndham Lewis and his friends. They were not politicians and even a man like Peel had a way with words.

Sometimes, when her husband was trying to persuade this new breed of Tory to engage in Conservative policy, Mary Anne would walk beclogged, with only Norah Rooke for company, through back streets, head covered by a shawl, like any labourer's wife. She saw privies without doors, courtyards full of swine growing fat on the foulness swilling around them, She looked into windows and saw people sleeping in layers and the stench, the awful stench. These were the breeding grounds of typhus and cholera which in its turn destroyed the rich as well as the poor.

Mary Anne, leaving a Manchester slum, handkerchief over her mouth, was startled when a man stepped in her path. She shrank back, looking for a constable.

'I won't hurt you lady.'

'Where did you lose your eye?'

'Prison, ma'am. A steam bellows came down unexpected catching my mate under it. The owner was angry. It took me time to get my mate out. There was no guard on the machine – it took my eye out with it. The factory inspectorate told against me, ma'am. They said I was nothing but an agitator.'

Mary Anne told the story to Disraeli, omitting to mention how she walked around the slums almost alone. He remembered and dedicated his book entitled: *Sybil: Or Two Nations* to her.

When they returned from their tour the Disraelis looked forward to greeting Mrs Yate who would be waiting for them at Grosvenor Gate.

On one occasion she said, 'A meal of cold ham and cheese awaits you. The cook's daughter's baby has just arrived.'

'What is it?' asked Disraeli

'What is baby to be called?' corrected Mary Anne looking at her husband with annoyance.

'Feargus, madam, after Mr O'Connor, 'cos he's such a great leader of our movement.'

Lady Londonderry continued to snub Mary Anne.

Mary Anne had heard that Lord Melbourne came often to dine with the Royal couple. 'The Prince is bored,' she said. 'He wants the company of people like us …'

'Yes,' said Disraeli, 'he does.'

Sadly, for Disraeli the Prince did not consider him quite a gentleman and so Albert remained lonely, requesting a German secretary.

On one occasion Mary Anne said, 'Lawyer Edward Sugden and his wife send you their regards. They took us to church.'

Mrs Yate put her apron over her head exclaiming: 'I wish my own darling daughter would attend, you are in possession of so many amiable and endearing qualities …'

'But,' said Disraeli, 'sitting for a hour or so listening to the vicar is not one of Mary Anne's strong points.'

And Mrs Yate would always say, 'Dizzy dear. You are so pale. He has anaemia, Mary Anne.'

'Nonsense, Mama. Dizzy is in excellent health he has just a natural pallor.'

They would enter the Grosvenor Gate and sooner or late Mrs Yate would say her investments, which she depended on for a living, were giving her concern.

Disraeli who looked after the old lady's affairs would begin rustling papers and Mary Anne would say, 'Pass them to me dearest.'

Mary Anne's mother would journey on to Bradenham before going back home to Bristol.

She would say, 'Dizzy has put my affairs in order.'

But nobody believed her.

14 Debts

In February Disraeli invited sixty MPs to Grosvenor Gate with the Duke of Buckingham as guest of honour. Forty MPs came.

He wrote to Sa: '*There is scarcely anyone of any station in the House or society that I have not paid attention to, which was most politic, and would have created any sensation at any other time of year.*'

Mary Anne noted in her account book the vast quantities of alcohol imbibed. At a dinner party for only six – three bottles of claret, three bottles of sherry, one bottle of champagne and almost a bottle of port. Mary Anne made a mental note not to let the gentlemen continue until midnight again.

The next day she was surprised to receive a note which read.

'*Dearest, send watch.*'

The urchin delivering the message commented, 'He's forgotten it.'

'Again?' said Mary Anne. 'Yesterday he forgot his money.'

'Got something on his mind,' said the boy scampering back to the House of Commons, only to return some time later with another note.

'*Send black boots, wearing brown.*'

Disraeli's behaviour became increasingly odd, poking his nose out of the door at 7am looking up and down Park Lane only to return at midnight with his, coat collar muffled up to his ears.

'What is wrong Dizzy?' enquired Mary Anne.

'Nothing really except Melbourne's government is sliding into dissolution. There will be an election and if so …'

'And if you are not in the House …'

'Quite so …'

Mary Anne shuddered as she looked out of the window watching the sun dipping through the trees and the birds circling overhead before nesting. Some day soon all this would be but a memory and they would have to flee to Paris or be trapped in the prison for debtors, the terrible Fleet.

'People live and die Dizzy in that place, no light comes near to it. Human creatures crouch below ground in filthy bunkers, listening endlessly to the shouts of card players, whose game is followed by drunken brawls, while bony fingers claw at skylights begging for food, others behave like dogs in the streets, coupling with whatever passes by.' Her voice shook as she said, 'Oh, Dizzy, *no*.'

'Don't fuss, dearest, something always turns up.'

On 27 May 1841 Disraeli entered the House sat down with his hat over his eyes, looking occasionally up at the clock.

'The Honourable gentleman for Maidstone.'

Disraeli rose, shuffling about.

'Is that the great Disraeli?' enquired a young new MP.

Disraeli began to speak, softly at first and then his eyes twinkled, his lips moved into their customary sardonic smile and he looked around the Chamber. Every eye was upon him, watching a great actor at work, and he stood for a moment holding them all in utter silence.

'The career of Her Majesty's present servants has been a singular one: they began by remodelling the House of Commons, and insulted the House of Lords; they then assaulted the church – next the colonial constitutions: afterwards they assailed the municipalities of the kingdom, attacked the rich and the poor, and now, in their last moments, at one fell swoop, made war upon the colonial, commercial and agricultural interests.'

He did not acknowledge the cheers but sat down, placing his hat back over his eyes and seemed to go to sleep, but he was in fact watching Sir Robert, who seemed unimpressed by the performance.

But the young MP said, 'With a few words he has slashed the Government to ribbons.'

Disraeli, had he heard, would have agreed with the

verdict because he told Mary Anne, 'Peel must give me an appointment now.'

Shortly, afterwards, Melbourne was forced to ask the Queen to dissolve Parliament. Prince Albert disliked Melbourne and the Queen allowed her old mentor to fade out of her life with little regret. She wrote: *'the dream is past.'*

Now, Disraeli's creditors sensing blood began pressurising him.

He approached his father and Mary Anne and reported back to his new London solicitor G.S. Ford, 'There is no money from either source.'

'Even if they were willing,' said Ford. 'They couldn't meet £25,000 between them.'

The Maidstone Conservative Party informed Disraeli they did not want him to stand again. The constituents were bored with Disraeli's style.

Mary Anne observed that she was also bored with paying for their corruption, as it was one of the most corrupt constituencies in the country.

Disraeli's friend Lord Forester suggested Shrewsbury, where he had influence.

'But where,' said the Disraelis in chorus, 'is Shrewsbury?'

Disraeli arrived in the little Shropshire market town, so remote from London society, six miles by rail to Wolverhampton and a further six hours by carriage, drooping like some exotic house plant, to be followed briskly in the second week of June by Mary Anne, who immediately began to canvas on Disraeli's behalf. She knocked on doors from eight in the morning until sunset.

'You're such a gay lady, ma'am.'

Your wife never gives us a dull moment, sir.'

Mary Anne was particularly popular with the trades' people especially with a butcher known for his brawns, which Mary Anne bought in quantity and served to the quality of Shrewsbury, leaving his label on show.

But her husband was less favoured. A man drove his donkey cart up to the place where Disraeli was speaking, 'To take you back to Jerusalem, Mr Disraeli.'

Meanwhile, Mary Anne was promoting Disraeli as a man possessed of ample independence that rendered the attainment of state, except as a matter of public service, a matter of complete indifference.

While canvassing she found posters appearing around the town and as fast as she tore them down, they appeared again.

'Judgement for debts against Mr Disraeli. The sum of £22,000. Tailors, housekeepers, upholsterers – in short persons of any denomination foolish enough to trust Mr Disraeli. He only seeks election to avoid the debtors' prison.'

Disraeli placed his eyeglass in his right eye, watched by the crowd and his wife, removed the eyeglass and turned round.

'Ladies and Gentlemen the list is utterly false.' He took Mary Anne's arm and swept on.

'At least, I know who his creditors are.'

The crowds continued to heckle him. 'Honest electors of Shrewsbury, will you be represented by such a man? Can you be confident in his pledges: Take warning …This is an ambitious man.'

Disraeli replied, 'There is no doubt gentlemen, that all men offering themselves as candidates for public favour have motives of some sort. I candidly acknowledge that I have, and I will tell you what they are: I love fame, I love public reputation, I love to live in the eyes of the country; and it is a glorious thing to do for a man who had to contend with my difficulties.'

The crowds were silenced and then they cheered him and Disraeli was elected MP for Shrewsbury, but it was Mary Anne they called for. She threw out her arms and blew kisses to the crowd, especially to the brawn butcher, for she knew and they knew her canvas had been much more important than Disraeli's speeches. However, she watched as they chaired him, shoulder high to quaff the triumphal cup in forty Salopian public houses.

At the great public dinner which followed Disraeli told Mary Anne 'I found the pub-crawl gorgeous and fatiguing. A maltser named Taylor unexpectedly raised his glass and somewhat tipsily declared a toast, 'Being Mrs Disraeli's husband is good reason why Mr Disraeli should be Member of Parliament for Shrewsbury.'

The next day found the Disraelis relaxing with Sir Baldwin Leighton at Loton Park.

Over cigars, away from the ladies, the two men discussed their first meeting in an Eastern brothel. 'Those girls were a revelation to me. I'd never been East before.'

Mary Anne played with the children telling the beautiful Lady Leighton, 'Your children are lovelier than the dawn.' She thought so even when the baby decided to scream and scream and scream.

Sir Baldwin described Disraeli to his wife as 'a man devoid of any principle except that of getting himself on in the world.'

Much restored the Disraelis journeyed back to London to wait Peel's summons.

On 30 August 1841 Peel kissed hands with the Queen. It had been a great victory for the Tories.

For two years Disraeli had not baited Peel. Mary Anne had put up with snubs from Mrs Dawson, Peel's sister.

'I saw Mrs Dawson; she was most friendly and particularly disagreeable.'

By September the appointments had been made. Gladstone was Vice President of the Board of Trade.

Mary Anne offered to write to Sir Robert Peel saying, 'I am a particular favourite of his.'

'You know that no gentleman would accept such an offer, my dear.' As she left the room Disraeli wrote down a few notes for the next day and left them carelessly on a side table.

In the evening he retrieved them and casually picked up the blotting paper; then holding it up to a mirror he read:

Dear Sir Robert Peel,

I beg you not to be angry with me for my intrusion, but I am overwhelmed with anxiety. My husband's political career is for ever crushed, if you do not appreciate him.

Mr Disraeli's exertions are not unknown to you, but there is much he has done that you cannot be aware of, though they have had no other aim but to do you honour, no wish for recompense but your approbation. He has gone farther than most to make your opponents his personal enemies. He has stood four most expensive elections since 1834, and gained seats from Whigs in two, and I pledge myself as far as one seat, that it shall always be at your command.

Literature he has abandoned for politics. Do not destroy all his hopes and make him feel his life has been a mistake.

May I venture to name my own humble but enthusiastic exertions in times gone by for the party, or rather for your own splendid self? They will tell you at Maidstone that more than £40,000 was spent through my influence only.

Be pleased not to answer this, as I do not wish any human being to know I have written to you this humble petition.

I am now, as ever, dear Sir Robert

Your most faithful servant

Mary Anne Disraeli.

Disraeli put back the blotting paper, with a secretive smile.

In October 1841 Charles approached Mary Anne, 'Madam, there are two unsavoury men at the door. They have papers for Mr Disraeli.'

'What are these papers?' enquired Mary Anne.

'Writs for debt, lady, to be given into the hands of Mr Disraeli personally,' the two men said in chorus to the little woman half their size.

'Madam,' said Mary Anne snatching the writ out of their hands. The man with a red neck cloth and no teeth she merely nearly choked with his own necktie. Then turning to the other she pulled his top hat down about his ears and boxed him with it to Tyburn. Both men dived into the nearest public house saying, 'Gawd. Poor sod. I pity him when he gets home.'

Disraeli found his trunk discarded on the pavement outside Grosvenor Gate, for passers-by to see.

He knocked at the door. The writ was handed to him without a word. 'Shaving things dearest.'

The door flung open, a tirade of abuse greeted him. 'Thief, thief. You tricked me, running up such bills, such debts. You didn't tell me.' Great-aunt Mary Anne's second best china flew around Disraeli's ears.

Disraeli quite shocked, jumped into a passing hansom cab, the driver saying, 'Ladies do get excited sir, don't they sir?'

'Yes,' agreed Disraeli, 'especially when you don't want them to.'

As the cab disappeared Mary Anne sat down on the stairs and wept.

'Dizzy, Dizzy, you did only marry me for my money after all.'

From the Edwards' Hotel, George Street, close to St George's Church, Hanover Square, where they married, Disraeli wrote some notes:

'...the storm which has, more or less, been brewing in my sky for the last twelve months burst rather suddenly yesterday and I am present residing in a hotel, leaving Grosvenor Gate to its mistress.'

And to his solicitor: 'Please make sure in future my wife is not involved.'

Hortense was sent by her mistress to the back stairs of the hotel in order to enquire how Mr Disraeli was faring.

'Master's uncomfortable but well, ma'am.'

'Flowers arrived at Grosvenor Gate, then trinkets and finally Disraeli himself.'

'Who paid for that lot Dizzy?'

'I put them on your account, dearest.'

'Oh, Dizzy really!' But he could always charm her and he charmed her upstairs to bed.

Mary Anne departed to Bradenham. Shortly, afterwards she received a note from Disraeli. As the rains fell she signed papers securing a loan of £5,000 from Ford at 5%. Disraeli ended his request with *'My sweet, sweet love – do not despair, I will hope. I am very wearied – but I love you -with all my heart and soul, as you love me.'*

Mary Anne saw, in a mirror, an odd expression flash across Sa's face. Sa knew just at that moment an inventory of furniture and valuables of Grosvenor Gate was being taken: *'three foot feather bed bolster and pillow, Ormulu time piece etc.* Lists were made from attic to basement.

In a secret drawer in Sa's escritoire the note from the Carlton Club continued …

'My case is very clear tho' between ourselves it might be otherwise – there is only one point in which I felt a little embarrassment and used your name to carry me through. I said I was going out of town last Thursday to Bucks Assizes but I did not and Meyer Rothschild unintentionally let the cat out of the bag … So remember this – last Thursday.

I don't know how it will all end …'

When Sa opened the letter the perfume reminded her of somebody … and for a long time she could not remember who it was until one day at Grosvenor Gate, Smythe called. The perfume belonged to George Smythe.'

Sa's reply has been lost a long time ago, but a strange letter remains.

It is to Mary Anne from an admirer, perhaps a man, who saw her on honeymoon with Disraeli in Munich. It is written in French from a great rogue who had been overcome by a lady of noble appearance, so much so he had journeyed to England and had seen his lady strolling in Grosvenor Square arm-in-arm with a gentleman.

'Now they tell me it was you, Madame … is it possible to entertain the thought of your speaking with me? Of receiving

me for a moment? Alas! I think not. But I suffer so much that the cold proprieties and common laws of my life are useless to me ... tomorrow at noon I will come, Madame, to your door, if you deign to bend on me your gracious regard.

Your very humble servant G de La Grangechancel'

The gentleman wrote a dejected letter to Mary Anne:

You have not been kind, Madame. It is the common law, 'tis true. I accept it, for I don't know what dream of the mind ... I have said to a woman that I suffer – I am unhappy – help me! She has done – 'comme les hommes'. This will be a black page in the chapter of my life. You draw that page, Madame, you will see two portraits the features of which will reproach you.

Nearly fifty Mary Anne might be but it was not only Disraeli who received flattering invitations and she placed it in her handbag – just in case...

In December 1841 the Disraelis celebrated Christmas, wondering what the New Year would bring them.

15 Young Englanders

Mary Anne's visits to the mining folk of Dowlais had made her aware of the winds of change blowing through British society.

Most of London's decision makers shivered, knowing old French women sat muttering knit one, purl one and clicked their needles as yet another *aristo's* head fell into the basket.

London's upper classes did not understand the causes of the French Revolution. They knew nothing of the fear of the workhouse, which the new Poor Law engendered. The dirt and the crowded housing of the burgeoning industrial towns was an unknown phenomenon to them, but they knew it was a law of God that the poor should be poor. They pitied individual cases and Victoria wept for the little waif who slept outside her windows, but she knew nothing personally of the dirt and back-to-back housing of those who worked in the new industrial towns.

Out of all of this grew a new movement and a committee of the General Working Men's Association of London drew up the "People's Charter".

A few days later Disraeli commented, 'The Parliamentary campaign begins fiercely – war to the knife.'

Despite the Disraelis' concerns for the development of society, Mary Anne enjoyed herself travelling with Disraeli into the new conurbation and helping her husband to address the "new industrial classes." Mary Anne understood them better than Disraeli, for she had been involved in the ironworks of Dowlais.

The workplace might well be changing but high society was not.

Mrs Yate wrote to her daughter; '*You will find the house exactly what you could wish, the carpeting down, and everything else well cleaned. I am partial to Mary, she is such an excellent servant. I agree with you, the cook is a very good one – for her station in life.*'

The Disraelis when they needed a break took themselves to Brighton. Disraeli dined out on the tale of how Mary Anne taught him to eat shrimps: 'Under the pier, like a couple of cockneys.'

Mrs Yate was somewhat shocked at the story but was mollified when told her daughter, when a guest of the lawyer, Edward Sugden and his wife, was persuaded to attend church, Mrs Yate wrote:

'... *knowing how much it would enter into my feelings where I wish my own darling daughter would constantly attend, how happy it would make me, being in possession of so many amiable and endearing qualities as your dear self.'*

Mrs Yate would often make herself useful and stay at Grosvenor Gate in the Disraeli's absence. She would instruct the cook to prepare lamb shanks and onions for Mr and Mrs Disraeli's homecoming. Following her return to Bristol she received numerous missives from her daughter.

'*Mama,*' instructed Mary Anne. '*Pray take care that you dress yourself warm, very, and put your washing-stand by the fireplace as it used to be, and take care of your caudle-cup.*'

The family at Bradenham would invite Mrs Yate, to spend time with them. 'We will be delighted to see your dear face and affectionate smile soon.'

However, Mrs Yate did have one thing in common with her second son-in-law. She could not manage money either. Her interests in shares and property were in a complex mess and as for her pensions ...

Mrs Yate wrote on that subject to her daughter, '*I hope Darling will excuse my dwelling so long on one subject.*'

Disraeli, helped out, and made matters worse but he treated the "old scatty lady" with kindness and courtesy.

Mrs Yate wrote: '*Many thanks to Mr Disraeli for managing the business for me.*'

Disraeli was more successful when he went to the Middlesex Hospital and inspected the invalid carriages and chose one of a special kind, most suited to the needs of Mrs

Yate, and being expensive paid for it out of his own pocket. There were only two carriages in London and none in Bristol. Mrs Yate kept the catalogue tucked in the chair, showing the entry to friends.

The brochure of Marks & Co of Cavendish Square says, 'Invalids how severely afflicted may be conveyed any distance with perfect security.'

Disraeli looked after Mrs Yate and Mrs Yate looked after Disraeli.

'I am sure Mr Disraeli has an ailment,' Mrs Yate worried.

Mary Anne, replied gently, 'Dizzy, is strong-minded and well now, and ever so happy.'

Disraeli might be happy because he was quite certain he was heading towards some new and unknown disorder. Mary Anne, wearied by Disraeli's neuroses about his health, asked the eminent consultant, Dr William Chambers of St George's Hospital, to thoroughly examine her husband. Disraeli was most impressed. The eminent man could not see him for at least a week and when he did so he could only see Disraeli, by appointment, once a week.

Disraeli set out to St George's Hospital, in a buoyant mood. He returned in a mood of deep dejection.

'I ought not to be ever unwell again.' He immediately opened his pillbox.

On 10 February 1840, Mrs, Yate, Mary Anne, Disraeli and a few guests celebrated the marriage of the Queen to her Albert. They could hear the crowds cheering and the blare of trumpets and all wondered what the future held for the young couple.

On 17 February, with other Members of Parliament, Disraeli went to see the Queen at Buckingham Palace.

The MPs crowded into the great drawing room and they found waiting for them under the chandeliers, the Queen and HRH Prince Albert of Saxe-Coburg, dressed in high military fig.

The Queen rhapsodised on the Prince's delicate mustachios and slight, but very slight, whiskers, his beautiful figure, broad in the shoulders and fine waist.

The MPs hurriedly gave their congratulations and then departed into their St James's Clubs.

'The little German wants a German secretary, he would like to lose at chess, just occasionally, and even complains about poor old Melbourne coming to dinner two or three times a week.'

Only Disraeli noticed the Prince's firmness of mouth and suspected he might well, harness his plain, wilful little wife and become a force to be reckoned with.

In November Victoria looked down at her newborn daughter, Princess Victoria, and declared, 'She looks like a frog.'

In the November of the following year the Queen produced the future Prince of Wales. A man who was to be known for his continual bonhomie.

Mrs Yate's failing health gave her daughter and son-in-law ever-greater concern. In 1842 while staying at Bradenham she died in the early hours of a spring morning.

It was the magnificent summer of 1842, the scent of honeysuckle wafted in from her balcony, the vivid canary yellow curtains billowed around Mary Anne, sitting by the open windows, trying to write to "the Governor" in Glamorgan concerning his son.

'Tell, my dear nephew Ernest, take care, London is not Cardiff. It is rush and in that rush unseemly things happen. Messenger boys, for instance, dash hither and thither, from one gentleman's house to another, anxious to earn a half-crown piece, "by being kind to a toff." 'Do tell the dear boy, when he walks along The Strand, the men waggling fingers towards him – are not hansom cab drivers. Ernest, I fear is innocent. London is not for naïve youth. Stress, my dear former-brother-in-law, on no account, must Ernest wait for friends, near the County Fire Office, Piccadilly Circus, or

enter the inviting Windsor Castle Public House in the Strand. I know you are of the same view as Prince Albert who has asked, "What enjoyment, sir, can be had from chasing grooms and coachmen for a night's pleasure?" But I assure you, Lord Euston, Lord Arthur Somerset, Colonel Jervois – all gentlemen in good society have such reputations – or so Dizzy tells me.'

Mary Anne folded the letter in two, placing it in one of the new gum envelopes and stuck one of the new postage stamps in the corner. She hurried down the uncarpeted marbled staircase to post the letter looking into the park where shop girls in starched linen hurried along the paths, clutching at straw hats. A young soldier looked around him and vanished into a clump of trees.

Mary Anne walked briskly to the posting box along Park Lane but changed her mind and tucked the letter inside her shawl. She must maintain discretion about the gossip swirling around her. She remembered how during the night before Disraeli stirring uneasily in his sleep, and half-awake perched on his right elbow to tell her, 'I find myself, dearest, without effort, the leader of a new party, chiefly of youth and new members.'

Only a few hours before, dining at Lord Palmerston's Lyndhurst told Mary Anne, following the tenth course, 'The great game is being played out with Peel, O'Connell and Gladstone. Dizzy is but a bystander.'

Mary Anne pulled the familiar old paisley shawl around her tightly, a present from her mother long ago, so old now that the smell of rose petals, dogs, hyacinths, cabbage and homely things all mingled together.

She cried out beneath her breath, 'The crowd, I knew, I understood, D'Orsay, Bulmer, Melbourne, Caroline Norton, Lady Blessington … they are fluttering away. Butterflies, of course, they were but I felt at home with them … and gliding towards Dizzy comes now a group of aristocratic exquisites, fifteen years his junior and nearly thirty years younger than myself.' She shivered and pulled the shawl even tighter around her.

When she entered the crimson painted hall, perched on the stand Dizzy's battered hat dominated three tall shiny top hats of darkest navy blue.

High-pitched aristocratic voices floated down into the hall well.

'To speak, for two hours and twenty minutes on the amalgamation of the consular and diplomatic services is a remarkable feat, indeed, Dizzy.'

'What an achievement, Dizzy.'

They turned en block as she entered the blue drawing room, three tall thin young men, clean long manicured fingers tapped snuff boxes in rhythm and one fiddled with pearl enamelled cufflinks.

They stopped and stared. What is wrong, she thought. I am wearing my favourite morning dress. The one Dizzy said was quite remarkable. To give the outfit definition red flounced petticoats peeped from beneath the shot blue-pink of the satin skirt and red roses at the neck emphasised the bodice.

They gawped. Dizzy looks uncomfortable, thought Mary Anne, examining with a milliner's eye the quality of the cloth which made up the navy blue tight jackets and trousers.

'Do sit gentleman,' she said unkindly.

They did not move. How could they in those trousers. They would not give an inch.

Dizzy looked embarrassed and she could not think why. He was wearing the gold chains she bought him each anniversary. They wore no jewellery except pearl stud pins in their plain navy cravats.

One of them she recognised as the second son of the Duke of Rutland, John Manners. 'Don't you think to talk so well on such a subject was remarkable Mrs Disraeli?' He was but twenty-four. He was beautiful. The Master of Manners' college, Trinity, Cambridge, swore he would rather be Lord John Manners than any other young man.

'May I introduce George Smythe?' said Disraeli. Smythe was looking around the room in a state of wonder. His eye travelled over the golden flock of the curtains, the blue flock of the walls and the oriental carpet, orange, green, red, pink.'

'I bought the carpet in Brick Lane for 2/6d,' said Mary Anne proudly.

'I can tell Mrs Disraeli, quite *extraordinary*.' Smythe tossed back his golden hair and flicked imaginary dust off his pure white velvet waistcoat. Again Disraeli looked embarrassed.

Mary Anne said, 'Do you speak in the House, Mr Smythe?'

'No, I cannot allow him to speak. I speak for him,' replied Disraeli in a simpering tone. Mary Anne did not recognise her husband as he continued, 'Smythe's speeches are as elaborate and as unprincipled as his agreeable little self, showing ability but quite puerile.'

'Didn't you know, Dizzy was to speak?' asked Smythe. He was old Lord Strangeford's beautiful, golden, corrupt, promiscuous son, who should have had such a marvellous future. He would be the "son of Disraeli's existence" and one day would betray Disraeli viciously. In reality he is remembered solely as the last man to fight a duel on English soil, destined to die of consumption at only forty-one – a glorious, brilliant, failure.

I do not know how to compete with such men as these, Mary Anne cried inside herself.

Baillie- (Kok) Cochrane came to her aid. He would never marry, but be her friend for ever and when she was a dying old woman, proposed her health to a great assembly saying, 'I know what Mr Disraeli owes to his wife.'

'Mrs Disraeli, you must read Manners' treatise on National Holy Days for the populace ... and thoughts on how the upper classes should treat the lower classes,' said Kok.

Smythe shook with laughter, so much so that one of the buttons popped off his waistcoat and Manners cried out, 'Fatty, fatty.'

Smythe's lips curled unpleasantly and spite shone in his eyes.

Mary Anne crossed to the window, looked out into the park, longing for the fresh air of Bramford Speke. Then she turned to catch Disraeli, looking as he looked at her sometimes, into Manners' eyes who was fluttering his eyelids up at Disraeli like any girl. He caught her glance, her unease and suddenly snarled, as at a pack of curs.

'This young man urges dancing round a maypole on the village green and the restoration of the ancient order of the peasantry.'

Manners cringed back glaring at Mary Anne. He believed vengeance was a meal best served cold. One day he would write to Disraeli: '*I take this opportunity of communicating to you a piece of news, which I feel may not be always agreeable to you, I marry Miss Marlam.*'

Disraeli always thoroughly loathed both of the women Manners married.

Manners slamming the door behind him, walked out of the drawing room with Kok Cochrane. Unfortunately for Manners, he did not know any ex-milliners. Mary Anne slipped out of the drawing room and hid in the shadows on the landing in order to overhear Manners' leaving comments. 'Could I only satisfy myself that Disraeli believes all he says, I should be quite happy, his historical views are quite mine, but does he believe them?'

Motherless since he was eight, Smythe, stayed behind to sit at the feet of "Little Madam" as he would do on many evenings only to disappear as dusk approached, complaining to the other "boys" I hardly spoke to Dis. I was too busy conciliating his 'Prosperpine.'

One day Mary Anne ran into Meyer Rothschild.

'I thought, Dizzy was with you?'

Mary Anne hurried back to Grosvenor Gate, ordered a duster, rushed into Disraeli's study, pretending to dust it, a job she would allow no servant to undertake. On the floor, just by the wastepaper basket, she found a crumbled piece of paper.

'Remember, I love you. Meet you at the Naughty House … at 9. Thursday.

Dis

'Which one was it? Her instinct said Smythe.'

16 Paris Interlude

November 1842 approached. Soon Disraeli would be near forty and Mary Anne over fifty-two. The fogs of London added to their gloom. Despite, all their efforts they remained on the fringes of power. People splashed through muck-covered streets, the stench of London weakened constitutions and they weakened as enemies whispered, 'The puppets are moved by Disraeli ... he is unprincipled. He is a disappointed man.'

In a Piccadilly coffee house Mary Anne saw the Duke of Rutland and Lord Strangeford huddled together and she overheard them talking.

'It is sad that two young men such as John and Smythe should be led by Disraeli. The lack of experience of our sons makes them vulnerable to the arts of such a designing person.'

Ladies of fashion passed by ignoring No 1 Grosvenor Gate. The Disraelis looked out at the bare trees in the park and into drawing rooms devoid of company. The only human contact they seemed to have were the crowds passing beneath their windows going to a good hanging at Tyburn.

'It is no use, Dizzy we must go away. We can live in Paris for only £89 a month.' Mary Anne explained to the staff that they were being put on board wages. As the staff were of poor quality they were not offered other employment and as the Disraelis introduced themselves to the Duchess de Grammont society whispered, 'The Disraelis are finished.' But the Disraelis were meeting the best of Parisian society. Disraeli was smoking diamond-studded chibouques with the Turkish Ambassador. Mary Anne surprised her hosts by making diagrams of how orange trees appeared to grow out of tables. Back in their hotel room, while Mary Anne examined her diagrams, Disraeli complained about the food. 'Such sumptuous food utterly ruined, when will the French learn to warm plates?'

They were not however, completely ignore
Reception occasionally announced the arriv;
friends – Mr and Mrs Henry Hope, Anthony R(
his wife. Mary Anne took her guests to soirée
that the occasion would be reported back in London circles.
Disraeli wrote to Sa: '*I made it clear to the French, Hope and
Rothschild could buy up 100 men in France who had £10,000
per annum.*'

Mary Anne thought it was too tactful of her husband but
was startled one morning to see Disraeli in a new well fitting
black suit that she did not recognise. She had not been around
to remind the Parisian tailor, 'Remember Mr Disraeli's stoop.'

In the evening, Disraeli asked Mary Anne. 'Didn't I tell
you I had an appointment with the King?'

'Without me?' enquired Mary Anne. He ignored her
comment. If all goes well, will you forget me, Dizzy, she
asked herself.

'The King,' continued Disraeli, smugly oblivious of her
unease, 'escorted me around the Tuileries acting as a guide.
It was a successful visit, dearest.' Disraeli handed his wife a
copy of a confidential memorandum. It was meant only for
the King's eyes:

'*The Government of Sir Robert Peel is at the moment upheld
by an apparent majority in the Commons of 90 members.*'

'I told the king that I am now in a position to influence the
affairs of state,' he added with a smile.

Paris danced its way through the Christmas Festivities and
in mid-January 1843 the Disraelis packed to return to London
for the new Parliamentary session.

Train and steamboat tickets were booked, hotel rooms
cancelled and within a few hours they would be in Dover, but
just as they were taking a last look at Paris, Mary Anne, saw
in the distance coming along the Rue de Rivoli two figures
walking with canes in unison. She said to Disraeli, trying to
avert his attention, 'Look is that not?' She was too late, he saw
them and held out his arms.

Smythe cried out, 'Dizzy, are you coming to the Masked Ball?'

'It's at the Opera House this evening,' said Baillrie-Cochrane.

Soon they were in front of them, kissing each other, hugging each other – as if they were all friends. Disraeli's eyes were fixed on Smythe. Mary Anne drew slightly away from the group. He was slimmer, blonder and more beautiful than ever.

Smythe looked back at Disraeli, who began to simper like any silly girl. They were so absorbed in each they forgot her.

Kok smiled kindly. 'How I hate the coldness of Paris. Only here could you have had Madame Guillotine. Things are different in London.'

Mary Anne looked into the mocking eyes of the Parisian women passing by. 'No French woman would have allowed such a situation to develop,' she said to Kok who pretended not to understand. In that moment Mary Anne drew herself up, clenched her fists. I will fight to end this battle, she said to herself easily, but knew it would be the shortest and hardest fight she had ever fought. She continued watching. Smythe kept smiling at Disraeli. The two continued to ignore the little woman standing by the hansom cab.

It was the coachman who broke the reverie. 'Monsieur. Do you want it or don't you?'

'He wants it,' said Smythe mockingly, 'don't you, Dizzy? You want it.'

Kok handed Mary Anne into the cab, squeezing her hand sympathetically. Disraeli followed. The two journeyed together in utter silence. Mary Anne prepared her mind for the forthcoming battle against an enemy younger, brilliant – ruthless.

The Disraelis chose not to wear fancy dress costume to the ball thus ensuring that they stood out from everybody else. Disraeli sneezed as the scent of opium hung in the stifling air. Mary Anne's eyes grew round as perfumed young men in sequined covered suits clamoured around them. A young naked man entered on a golden horse, making the animal rear on its hind legs in time to the music, a half-naked girl rode around on a young elephant. 4,000 masked devils "beyond fancy" whirled in and out dancing as if they were already in hell and then as if by magic Smythe appeared, dressed all in white as the angel Gabriel. It was such a surprise to Mary Anne that she allowed him to whisk Disraeli away from her. The noise, sense of despair and loneliness made her almost lose consciousness.

Kok came to her side and escorted her to a box.

From the centre of the floor, Smythe looked up. He bowed low to her, kissed Disraeli upon the cheek and again looked up at her – mockingly. Disraeli remained quite still gazing into the eyes of the young man. Mary Anne watched spellbound.

Suddenly, a polka was being played. Boys danced with boys, girls on trapezes flung flowers down to the crowds below and in the boxes old men and old women watched youth having its way.

The music seemed to say to Mary Anne: *youth has gone; life is going.*

'Dizzy,' she cried out, but he did not hear her. She saw Smythe taking her husband into his arms. In that second Mary Anne stood up, her chair banged to the floor. 'No' she called out. 'No.' People in neighbouring boxes looked up amazed. She ran down the stairs, flinging off her shoes, picking up skirts. She pushed open the doors to the stage, knocking two turban wearing black minders off balance. 'Madam, not suitable Madam.'

'No,' she called back. 'It is not.' She pushed her way through the crowds. People began standing back to observe the progress of the ridiculous old woman. At last she arrived. Smythe looked down at her, hair fallen down, grey showing, powder smudged, eyes cheapened by black lines, every wrinkle in view.

'Tell me Dizzy, how do you tolerate such a silly old woman?' Smythe drawled.

Disraeli swung round. His eyes bore into Smythe who shrank back. At that moment the music stopped playing. The crowds held their breath. Disraeli said quietly, 'I have a word in my vocabulary which is not in yours.' He then thundered out – 'Gratitude.' The music began again. A faint cheer emanated from the crowd.

Mary Anne took Disraeli's arm and together they progressed through the assembly. She kissed him lightly, 'Remember, dearest, Madame de Pompadour.'

He smiled and his eyes looked at her teasingly. She had her Dizzy back. Mary Anne looked over her shoulder, so that Dizzy did not see her looking back, and saw Kok comforting Smythe and the crowd around them laughing and jeering.

'Silly old woman. She outmanoeuvred you, sir.'

Shortly afterwards the Disraelis returned to London to find no commission from the French King. He was not willing to pay Disraeli to spy for the French court.

On the surface Mary Anne had coped with the strains well, but she was a middle-aged woman and occasionally she behaved oddly.

However, Baroness Lionel de Rothschild, sitting listening to her children's prayers was startled to have Mary Anne rush unannounced into the room, bonnet in hand, knocking against the rocking horse.

'Charlotte send the children away. I am quite out of breath, my dear. I have been running so fast, we have no horses, no carriage, no servants, we are going abroad, I have been so busy correcting proof-sheets, the publishers are so tiresome, we ought to have been gone a month ago. I should have called upon you long ago ere now, I have been so nervous, so excited, so agitated, poor Dis has been sitting up the whole night writing … This is my farewell my dear. Life is so uncertain, poor Mrs Fitzroy has been so very ill. Dizzy and I may be blown up on the rail-road or the steamer.'

Mary Anne thrust into Lady Rothschild's hand a document.

'*In the event of my beloved husband preceding me to the grave I leave you and bequeath to Evilna de Rothschild (Baroness Rothschild's daughter aged six) all my personal property.*'

'I love the Jews, I have attached myself to your children and it is she who is my favourite, I will not be deterred Lady Rothschild.' Lady Rothschild gave the note to Disraeli.

Some years later Lord Clarendon mentioned the incident to Queen Victoria whose only comment was, 'Mr Disraeli was a very good husband.'

Eventually the boys drifted away and Disraeli told Mary Anne, 'We have carried to a happy conclusion a highly successful campaign, unquestionably raised our names in the country, ascertaining the feeling of the nation is with us and having supplied the world with sufficient suggestions the wisest thing we can do is to leave them to chew the cud.' ...'

17 Peel: Potatoes and Corn

May 1845 was the wettest anybody could remember. This was followed by a fine June. Farmers looked forward to a prosperous harvest, but in August the rains fell again and continued to do so throughout September and the harvest was disappointingly poor.

Disraeli was still MP for Shrewsbury. Many of his constituents were farmers and Corn Law repeal was an important issue for them. He told Mary Anne, 'I suspect Peel will give way to demands to repeal the Corn Laws.'

Mary Anne paused, 'Surely, that would be a good thing, dearest.'

'Good thing? Have the country flooded with foreign corn? What will happen to our farmers? They will get next to nothing for their wheat and barley. What then?'

Disraeli removed his eyeglass and looked questioningly at Mary Anne. 'I'll tell you what then. They will not be able to pay their rents. Then … the landlords' income will drop and who is at the heart and core of the Tory party – they are.'

Mary Anne remembering her Dowlais days enquired, 'But what of the labouring classes? Fewer and fewer of them are cottagers able to grow food for themselves. They rely on bread for their very existence.'

'Oh, yes,' said Disraeli. 'And how will it be for them to change their circumstances? When we have good harvests – the price of corn is lowered by market forces then the industrialists and such people lower their wages.'

'Dizzy, when I spoke to Mr Cobden he assured me wages do vary, it is true, but it is not related to the price of bread. He also told me that reducing duties on corn imports should be carried out along with reducing duties on many, many more things.' Then Mary Anne paused for breath. Disraeli waited, half-smiling and amused. 'Then they will also be able to buy other things and if they buy from our neighbours, then they in their turn will be better able to buy the goods which our industries produce.'

'Is there more?' enquired Disraeli.

'It occurs to me that Sir Robert is dithering on reform of the Corn Laws. If you oppose him with good argument, could it be people will see you as a more suitable leader of the party – even Prime Minister.'

Disraeli took the advice. Aided and encouraged by Lord George Bentinck he led the attack on the Sir Robert Peel.

His constituents were angry at his attacks. 'It is only because he did not give you office.'

Disraeli tossing back his ringlets replied angrily. 'Sir Robert Peel knows me too well to think for a moment that any pecuniary circumstances influence my conduct. Sirs, I was his supporter when in adversity – in prosperity I will not be his slave.'

If the market town was becoming wearied of Disraeli it continued its love affair with his wife. Mary Anne came to Shrewsbury as much as possible with her husband. He would write: *'The more we are apart the more I cling to you.'* She attended the Bachelors' Ball, over fifty, wearing white with dark velvet flowers entwined with diamonds in her hair or attended the races. As much as she could she supported her husband.

On 28 August 1845 Disraeli wrote to Mary Anne.

We are alas, parted on our wedding day. We do not celebrate birthdays but our marriage, which we feel has been a gift of the Gods. The women shed tears which I can hardly myself restrain... Our wedding feast must be on Thursday, but if I die for it, I will write you some verses tomorrow,' which he did.

The seasons change, sweet wife, but not our love,
And the revolving year, that all its moons
Hath counted since thy bridal hand I pressed
Brings us yet moons of honey. Blessed day!
That gave me one so faithful, and so fair,
To glad and guard my life! A graceful sprite
Hovering o'er all my fortunes; ever prompt

With sweet suggestions; and with dulcet tones
To cheer and counsel. O! Most perfect wife!

On the Disraeli's 1845 anniversary Sa wrote to Mary Anne to thank her for a bonnet and ending the letter with: '*We will not be emerging into the light of the world until spring.*'

Mary Anne and Disraeli had no intention of entering into a "grub like state". In addition they found an increasing debt burden draining and he needed peace and quiet to finish the third part of his political trilogy, *Trancred.*

One late September evening in 1845 Mary Anne packed Disraeli's things and a few of her own, leaving jewellery, fashionable crinolines and low-necked gowns, staff on half pay, friends, relations, society and even Norah Rooke behind. The Disraelis could be seen during the early hours of the morning slipping out by the side door of Grosvenor Gate and into a carriage to journey to hide away in the little Flemish town of Cassel. Society greeted their disappearance with glee. 'The Disraelis,' they said to each other, 'have gone to live in Paris – for good.' And waited for the "To Let" signs to appear outside Grosvenor Gate.

The couple seemed to the inhabitants of Cassel to be a "solicitor and his good lady" enjoying a rest, living in a small house, reading only English newspapers, going to bed early and rising late. The town's people sensitively ignored them.

The Disraelis asked each other, 'Do we stay in this paradise – for ever?' They were tempted to do so.

Mary Anne wrote to Sa:

'*We do not know and have not interchanged a word with a single person of even average intelligence on any subject. The names of the Duke of Wellington and Sir Robert Peel and all those sort of people are quite unknown here …We have walked 300 miles.*'

Disraeli added a postscript: '*She is as plump as one of the partridges which we can't purchase here.*'

Disraeli wrote to Bradenham.

'*As we walk out in the late afternoon, about 5 o'clock … we sometimes hear the bells of half a dozen surrounding valleys sounding at the same time. There are oratories and little chapels certainly every half-mile, and a carv'd image or two in almost every field ... the autumn here of the most mellow nature: continuing fine and mild tho' we live on the top of a mountain. And we never have a fire except in the evenings. We have a pretty little garden, which grows us mignonette, and Alpine strawberries, which Mary Anne picks for me, and often wishes she could do the same for my father ... Mary Anne cannot leave her young pigeons, who live in the house and breakfast with us.'*

They had almost decided to sell up, retire and become nobodies but as their energies returned and the sun shone less, a brisk wind touched their bones and they decided to return to a more interesting life. At the end of November, Disraeli and Mary Anne found themselves wrapping travelling rugs around their knees against the winter winds. They said to each other "Paris" vowing to return next year to Cassel; of course, they never did.

Parisians saw an old hired coach banging its way along Mon Marché through the noise of French clamour and the stink of garlic. As the coach trundled into the courtyard of the hotel the Disraelis were grateful to be back amongst their sort of people again.

Immediately, hostesses invited the glamorous Londoners to take part in Le Ronde but just as the Disraelis became the toast of Paris a political crisis arose in London. On 27th November, *The Times* published a letter from Lord John Russell to his City of London Constituents, condemning the government for prevarication in face of the Irish potato famine and advocating the repeal of the Corn Laws.

On 2 December, Peel, having met with no success with persuading his cabinet to accept even temporary suspension to the laws, announced he would bring in a bill 'involving the ultimate repeal' of the duties. Frustrated by his cabinet's obstinacy, he resigned office on 5 December. Russell was unable to form a government of his own liking and Peel returned as Prime Minister after a fortnight of wrangling.

Disraeli wrote to Sa from Paris:

'Politics seem more wild and confused than ever. It appears to me that Peel's difficulties are insurmountable: but what is to follow I cannot divine.'

Such was Peel's determination to repeal the Corn Laws that he had the open support of the Queen and Prince Albert, so much so that MPs were again shaken to see the Queen's husband entering the Strangers' Gallery to listen to the Corn Law debates.

Throughout the proceedings Disraeli, aided and abetted and encouraged by Lord George Bentinck, led the attack on Peel. These two who had previously shown disinclination to one another, were now drawn together by other circumstances. Over time, this created a firm friendship, which lasted until death.

There was a relaxed interlude amongst all this in-fighting. In the early summer the musical deaf Disraelis sat on little gilt chairs, in full evening dress, in the shuttered ballroom of Buckingham Palace, fidgeting their way through a celebration of music performed on the pianoforte by Herr Mendelsohn. The thin oriental bird-like creature cocked his head on one side, bowed to the audience, sat at the piano and began to play. The Queen and Prince Albert nodded in time to the music, obviously tempted to join in. Perhaps the three remembered the delightful occasion in July 1842 when they had sung together *How lovely are the Messengers*. During the interval the Disraelis rushed to mingle, avoiding commenting on the performance.

He had finished with the enchanting *Es ist ein Schnitter* during which Mary Anne was seen to nudge Disraeli and whisper, 'The piano needs dusting.'

The Queen was now standing in front of it, discussing the performance with the Archbishop. 'Indeed, Archbishop, Sir Robert is undeniably musical. He is one of the few people to appreciate Prince Albert's great qualities.'

'I thought his dancing master ways got on her nerves,' murmured Disraeli anxiously.

Soon, it was 22 January 1846 and time for the Queen to open Parliament again.

Peel addressed the House, 'I have thought it consistent with true Conservative policy, to promote so much happiness and contentment among the people that the voice of disaffection should no longer be heard.' Disraeli watched and did not forget the Queen's comments.

The battle between Disraeli and Peel continued. Another poor harvest threatened famine and this time it would affect the whole of Europe.

During the autumn, it was not only famine which exercised Disraeli's mind. Peel offered Smythe a job as under-secretary for foreign affairs. Unknown to Disraeli, Smythe had written to Manners, several years before, '... *to be of power, or fame, or even office, we cannot trust ... too much lies with Disraeli.*'

Mary Anne had read the letter. It had been given to her in a fit of jealousy, by Manners and Smythe. They had seen Disraeli kiss his wife with a tenderness never shown to them.

They stood together, one fair, one dark.

They passed her the letter, smiling at the silly little woman standing before them. She placed it, smiling into her handbag, 'For further use gentlemen, if required.'

She left them standing – together – not daring to look at each other – feeling somehow they had lost the day.

Since that time, and perhaps always, she had been frightened that the 'son of Disraeli's existence' who had every gift he had not would one day betray him. Disraeli took Smythe's letter, newly delivered, from Mary Anne, recognised the writing and went into his study to read the letter alone. It was from the man he saw as his son and who had perhaps been his lover.

'... *I am sorry to pain you – as I know I shall by thus becoming a Peelite ... whatever your feelings towards me, I shall ever feel to you as to a man of genius who succoured and solaced and strengthened me when I was deserted even by myself.*'

He emerged from his study and as his feelings had been really touched Disraeli did not discuss Smythe's desertion with Mary Anne or anyone else.

Except he clung to Mary Anne more than ever, saying things like, 'You are the only one I can trust.' She saw his face become more sphinx-like, the hooded eyelids covering the eyes more deeply and when he spoke of Peel or to Peel, he did so with a special viciousness.

And soon the battle between the two men would come to a head.

Late in the evening of 15 May 1846 a carriage stopped outside Dean's Yard close to the Abbey. A middle-aged woman stepped out and made her way through the mellowing brick gateway into the courtyard. She sat down on a seat away from the lamplight.

A breeze danced around the old Abbey walls and she pulled her shawl closely around her. The woman sat bolt upright, hands clasped – waiting. A few moments later, a tall blond young man hurried through the archway, looking round him as if frightened of being seen.

'How goes it, Kok?' Mary Anne called out.

'The Prime Minister is defeated. Peel is no more.' Kok continued, 'I saw Disraeli come to the Members' Staircase, march across the lobby, speaking to nobody as he passed by. Suddenly, as he entered the Chamber the gaslights were alight, flinging strange shadows around him as he walked on. They seemed to hiss Disraeli, Disraeli, Disraeli.

We all knew it was his hour.

He sat down, folded his arms and remained quite still … waiting. The eyes of the Chamber watched him. Eventually, Disraeli rose, staring straight ahead of him; he placed his hands on the table. He took his hands off the table, looked around him, smiled and thrust his hands into his waistcoat pockets. The Chamber shuffled uneasily and when Disraeli began to speak, not a soul stirred. He held the House like a great actor. For three hours Disraeli attacked the Prime Minister. Few remembered exactly what he said but some recalled Disraeli's opening fire several years before.

"Ours was a fine child. Who can forget how its nurse dangled it, fondled it? What a charming babe … then the nurse, in a fit of patriotic frenzy, dashed its brains out and came down to her master and mistress to give an account of the terrible murder. The nurse, too, a person of very orderly demeanour not given to drink and never showing any emotion, except of late, when kicking against protection …"

And so for three hours Disraeli baited Peel.

Disraeli sat down to such cheers that Peel, who loved the place, found it difficult to make himself heard and tears rolled down his face. In his left hand be held his little daughter's watch. Before entering into the Chamber, I met him on the stairs and he told me he had just collected it from the jewellers.

But then the great presence of Gladstone rose, dominating the Chamber. "If Mr Disraeli, has so much contempt for Sir Robert Peel, why did he ask for a post in his Government?"

The chamber gasped.

Disraeli turned corpse-like ashen white.

"I assure the House nothing of the kind ever occurred."

Sir Robert restored, lifted up his carpetbag and began to open it.

Now it was Disraeli who seemed hypnotised.

"I have not approached, Sir Robert – ever."

From the bag Peel took out an envelope.

Disraeli watched.

Peel slit open the envelope drawing out a letter.

'What happened then?' cried Mary Anne. 'Tell me, quickly.'

'It was odd. Sir Robert paused. I think he muttered, "I do not wish any human being to know that I have written to you …"

Kok paused before he said, 'Disraeli seemed in a trance.'

'And then?' cried Mary Anne, 'tell me.'

'Disraeli sprang forward. In a second it was all over, Sir Robert was no more. Disraeli left the House in utter silence, leaving his colleagues sitting in utter disbelief.

Lord Ashley exclaimed, "Disraeli, must have taken a vow of hatred to Sir Robert Peel, no ordinary condition of mind would lead to such ferocity."

Baillerie-Cochrane walked through the archway and away into the night. Mary Anne returned to the coach, 'Coachman quickly, get me home before Mr Disraeli arrives …'

He came through the front door smiling. Mary Anne was waiting for him. ' I've won, dearest, I can see being Prime Minister ahead of me.'

They walked hand in hand into the small drawing room where before a spring fire, on a neat little table, sat an expectant bottle of champagne, together with a Fortnum and Mason special game pie and a fine bird.

Disraeli whirled Mary Anne around the room laughingly exclaiming, 'You really are more like a mistress than a wife.'

Once more he was the young man who had fallen in love with Henrietta Sykes and as she danced in his arms, Mary Anne's heart cried out, 'You do not know what you have done, Dizzy.'

And he would not do so, until he was a very old man but as they went up to bed Mary Anne told him, 'Henrietta died yesterday, at Missenden.

Disraeli stopped at the top of the stairs. 'Oh the terrible catastrophe of Henrietta, she nearly ruined by career.'

Hortense coming along the passage carrying their night-time drink was warned by her mistress, 'Be careful Hortense, men ruin women's lives.'

Mary Anne went into the bedroom – to Disraeli.

18 Hughenden

For some time Disraeli had sought a country house and just outside Beaconsfield he found it. The innkeeper of the Red Lion in High Wycombe told him Hughenden Manor was available. Immediately Disraeli went to see it and then he took Mary Anne.

At a clearing in the trees Disraeli stopped the carriage.

'Can you see Hughenden Manor,' he enquired.

Mary Anne peered through the dusk and saw, just below the top of the hill, a square, attractive old house, whose mullioned windows looked out unseeing into the darkness while the beech trees surrounding it stood like white sentries on guard. The cloud obscuring the moon cleared and the house stood bathed in white light, friendly, now, inviting. She noticed for the first time the japonica flower growing up the walls. They had japonica in the garden of Sowden and Moors.

'Obviously, it has deep foundations,' said Mary Anne.

'And you will provide us with the anchor.'

The house looked back at her and seemed to agree. Against her will – Mary Anne loved it.

Disraeli was no longer in the carriage. Mary Anne looked around her and saw him standing with arms uplifted before the house, as if a supplicant before an altar. Mary Anne shivered, pulling her shawl closer to her and then suddenly Disraeli called out, 'Eloi, Eloi, Eloi.'

A startled sparrow flew out of a tree and the poacher by the stream, looked up and seeing a figure 'like no living creature' crept away. Then Disraeli turned and came running back to Mary Anne, no longer reminding her of 'the potent wizard of the Llamas fair' but he was once more, her enchanting young man, who tickled her feet and whose kisses left her moaning through the night for more.

As Mary Anne opened the carriage door for him, Disraeli fell into her arms, saying, 'We have a home at last, my dearest.'

She did not have the heart to tell him, 'We cannot afford it, Dizzy.'

On 19th January 1848 Mary Anne and Disraeli suffered a terrible blow. Isaac died suddenly at Bradenham. He was eighty-one years of age, infirm and blind. He had been lonely since the shadowy presence of his wife left his side nine months before. They all were. She was one of those people you only notice when they are not there. Disraeli was in difficulties. He had made an offer for Hughenden and his father, with his mother's advice, made a provisional contract of purchase on his behalf.

Isaac left Disraeli one third of his estate, £11,000. The residue being divided amongst his other children. History for Mary Anne repeated itself. Bradenham was only a rented property.

'*To my beloved daughter-in-law I leave my collection of prints. To my son Benjamin my books.*' Disraeli did not take his father's library to Hughenden but instructed Sotheby's, 'These were my father's books, some 25,000 – theology, history, and philosophy. Sell them en block if you can.'

Sotheby's complained, 'The politician, Disraeli, is filling our hallways and passages with books.'

The rest of the library, including Isaac's study of the life of Charles 1 was placed in the loft-like library of Hughenden.

'The place looks like a circulating library, Dizzy,' snapped Mary Anne. But slowly over the years, the almost empty dark wooden shelves became filled with rare books on the Renaissance, philosophy and history, all purchased by Disraeli.

Isaac's will had ended: '*To the care of my family Tita.*' Shortly afterwards Disraeli met by chance Byron's old friend, Sir John Hobhouse, who placed Tita as a messenger to the Board of Control.

Following Tita's departure they had all gone. Sa left the Buckinghamshire countryside to live alone in the suburbs at Ailsa Avenue, Twickenham. Ralph stayed in London where he had chambers as clerk in Chancery. James remained a gentleman farmer living in the house opposite to the Manor which had been his family home.

Sometime before, while so many dramas were being played out, my Lord Bentinck had been seen shuffling up the drive towards the Manor House at Bradenham and asked to see Disraeli. Through the open windows the D'Israelis heard the conversation between "Big Ben" and Disraeli. 'It would be no object to them and no pleasure to me unless I played the high game in public life; and that I could not do without being on a rock.'

'Oh, no Dizzy, no. We cannot afford Hughenden,' Mary Anne whispered. 'You know my income is limited. It comes from investments, rentals and legacies. There is no really large amount.'

Overhearing her sister-in-law asked, 'When has a mere lack of money ever stopped Dizzy pursuing an objective?'

Lord George was seen to nod at Disraeli and began to walk towards the wrought iron gates. Mary Anne alarmed ran after him. To the watchers at the windows Lord George seemed to assure Mary Anne. A few days later a letter was delivered at Grosvenor Gate to be placed in her hands only. It was from Lord George and gave a brief summary of his negotiations with his brothers.

'I went to my place at Welbeck. I had invited my brothers to dinner. What is it that is distressing you?' they asked me over the meal.

I replied, 'It is this, I have found the most wonderful man the world has ever seen and I cannot get these fools to take him as leader because he is not a country gentleman.'

'The remedy dear brother is perfectly simple make him one.'

I said, 'If you are willing to help me. You are perfectly right. The matter is perfectly simple.'

And so, shortly afterwards, Disraeli, cravat askew, waved a piece of paper in Mary Anne's face. 'Lord Titchfield, Lord

George and Lord Henry will advance us the necessary £25,000 to purchase Hughenden, dearest.'

'No,' corrected Mary Anne. 'Advanced £25,000 to you.'

On 6 September 1848 Disraeli wrote triumphantly to Mary Anne

'*It is all done and you are the Lady of Hughenden.*'

However, it was not so for just as the papers were to be signed, Lord George died on 21 September at his home Welbeck Abbey.

Disraeli had lost an honourable friend and support for the purchase of Hughenden. He told Mary Anne, 'Lord George's death is the greatest sorrow I have ever experienced.'

Disraeli began desperately trying to find money to purchase Hughenden. He approached his many contacts including, Lord George's father who was the fabulously wealthy 4th Duke of Portland. The Duke considered granting the mortgage in return for rents but did not. Negotiations with solicitors and bankers resulted in Mary Anne and Disraeli moving into Hughenden.

It took six weeks to do so. Disraeli complained that he felt he was living out of wagons like a "Tartar Chief". In the middle of all this Tita announced his marriage to Harvey, Maria D'Israeli's maid who had become housekeeper at Bradenham.

Mary Anne observed sourly, 'An event which I suspect took place some years previously.' But she was grateful for Harvey's assistance with the re-organization of their lives.

It took six weeks for Mary Anne to move furniture from Bradenham into Hughenden, supervise Disraeli with the books and to supplement the furnishing and fittings with new ones – Aubusson crimson and yellow carpets from Maples, shields to place in the hall from Mr Lacey of High Wycombe and a marquee for garden parties from Edgington's of the Old Kent Road.

Ralph and James exclaimed, 'Such clever arrangements and magic touches.'

The servants at Grosvenor Gate had no wish to come to live in the middle of the country and the ways of country servants did not please Mrs Disraeli.

A Charles Newbury received a reference from the Chief Justice's housekeeper but at Hughenden he did not behave himself. He wrote to the butler, Evans:

'Sir, I am truly sorry of my past crime more partickular of telling you such falsehood by saying that girl was a fellowservant of mine, as it may be the means of bringing you into trouble about what I know you are quite innocent but I hope their won't be any Blame attached to you and that you will forgive me and except of my umble repentance as I can't find words to express it but it will be a lesson for me for my life and for others I hope I think of coming to see if Mr Disraelia will forgive me tomorrow as I don't know what I shall do if he don't give me a caracter

Yours respectfully
Charles Newberry'

There was also trouble at Grosvenor Gate without Mary Anne being present. Mrs Rogers, the cook wrote to Mary Anne at Hughenden:

'...But waited to be able to name the day that I should leave Grosvenor Gate, which I intend doing this day (Monday). I can assure you Madam On Oath I made use of no abusive language to Susan, I only tould her that she did not give the cats the milk that you allow them, wich is the truth. She instantly exclaimed 'You are a lying Bald Old Devvel', and threw a glass of beer over me, and also acted as I have before described to you Madam – but I have no doubt it was a premeditated quarrel on her part as she had two persons ready to supply my place one of them your late kitchenmaid, the other a person the name of Ryan, a cook out of place.

Mrs Rogers was informed that Mrs Disraeli was very upset by such behaviour in her house.

Mary Anne struggled with the house move, fought with neurotic servants, and tried to clear "too thick" beech wood saying, 'This is where the German forest will be.'

Disraeli wrote to his wife in January 1849 from Grosvenor Gate. '*My dearest Wife, I was very much disappointed by your letter of this morning, as I took it for granted that it wd only be the herald of yr immediate appearance ... may I soon embrace you.*'

Unfortunately, we do not have Mary Anne's reply.

At the end of the 1849 parliamentary session Disraeli returned to Hughenden to assess the current political situation, he was leader of the House. His relations with the Earl of Derby, who much preferred racing to politics but felt the latter was his duty, were described as a "Jew and his Jockey."

Disraeli's, financial situation again became precarious because of the purchase of Hughenden and his more prominent position brought creditors out of the woodwork.

His marriage also came under threat from Lady Londonderry, an attractive, rich, society hostess, who had adored Disraeli in his Henrietta days and dropped him when he married "that odd common little woman." Mary Anne heard rumours of a liaison and in a temper she changed the locks on Grosvenor Gate, forcing Disraeli to spend a night at the George Hotel. In a letter to Sa 'Disraeli says: '*It might have been otherwise,*' but the brief affair, if there was one, remains a mystery and the two returned to loving each other.

Mary Anne had written to Disraeli before their marriage '*Dizzy, I deserve your love so give me all you possess. Me and only me in mind.*'

Now, in the comfort of Hughenden she reread his reply: '*I think if a woman be faithful and amiable she will never lose the heart she has once gained, at least judging from my own feelings and my own life.*'

And so, as Mary Anne always did, when her position was threatened, she planned a social event. This time it was a housewarming at Hughenden. A marquee was erected in the grounds. Gilt chairs and tables were placed inside it. Musicians were hired as well as extra servants. Mrs Cripps, the washerwoman and general handy person helped organize the refreshments. Norah Rooke curled madam's hair into ringlets, and placed her into a dress of pink and blue taffeta, flounced and full skirted over six flounced cream coloured buckram petticoats and at her neck great-aunt Mary Anne's pearls.

At 3 pm in the afternoon, along the driveway came carriages, four-in-hands, phaetons, barouches all carrying the great and the good of the land. They were all there except Lady Londonderry, who unfortunately Mary Anne had forgotten to invite.

The establishment drank champagne, ate lobster mousse, salmon soufflés, ginger ices, strawberry ices and numerous cheeses.

'The cost, dearest,' said Mary Anne, as the last carriage vanished from view.

'But dearest, they will now have to ask us to their country houses and I shall be able to feel the pulse of the ablest on all questions of the day over dinner.'

They stood together on the terraces, watching the sun dip behind the hills, rooks circling around the beeches and then an owl hooted announcing the approach of dusk.

And while Disraeli settled into Hughenden, Lord Stanley discussed him with the Queen.

'You well know, my Lord, we do not approve of Mr Disraeli. We remember if others forget, Mr Disraeli's treatment of dear Sir Robert Peel.' The Queen stared at Lord Stanley who replied evenly, 'Mr Disraeli, ma'am, has to make his position and men who make their positions will say and do things which are not necessary to those for whom positions are provided.'

The Queen considered this remark. 'Lord Stanley, it is with reluctance I agree to this appointment but you will ensure that Mr Disraeli is temperate.'

Disraeli was now Leader of the Opposition, sitting on the front benches. He sat close to his main competitor, William Ewart Gladstone, an establishment figure, a Saviour to prostitutes, deeply religious and a friend of his wife's. When he returned to Grosvenor Gate Disraeli sometimes found Gladstone taking tea with Mary Anne, smiling into her eyes saying, 'Sweet for the Sweet' as he ate Hughenden strawberries.

'Thank goodness,' Disraeli told Mary Anne. 'You are the only woman he seems really comfortable with. If he ever develops charm ... the Queen ...'

Being leader of the opposition was a boring and frustrating pastime. On 4 November 1849 Disraeli wrote to Sa: *I am myself not physically ill – but hipped and dispirited beyond expression. Indeed I find this life quite intolerable – and wish some earthquake would happen, or something else of a decided nature occur, that would produce a great change.*

No great change did occur but Hughenden provided an escape from the pressures and disappointments of Westminster and Disraeli remained unconcerned that not one shilling of the purchase price of Hughenden was being repaid to the Bentinck brothers.

So while Disraeli continued to climb the "greasy pole" Mary Anne went planting *Mrs Dizzy's Pleasance* as Disraeli called the gardens and named the walks, *Lover's Walk, My Lady's Walk, Italy* and teased his wife about her garden dress of a short skirt and gaiters. He did not know his wife had read *Henrietta Temple* and that the plans for their retreat were based on the gardens her husband described in that book.

She told Baroness Lionel Rothschild, 'I take a little luncheon and some bottles of beer for the workmen and sit there all day while paths are cut through the thick woods surrounding our house. I also planted pines and yew trees and laurels myself and these plantations I call my German forest and sometimes I help with the digging and planting.'

Disraeli on the other hand saw nothing strange in his costume. He wore a squire's outfit of brigand hat with a very long feather in it, leather leggings, and velveteen coat of a startling colour.

Disraeli who delighted in showing off his house and gardens told visitors. 'This is all due to the cleverness of Mary Anne, she devised this walk and she made it with the help of only two old men of the soil.'

People who were innocent of Disraeli's lack of direction agreed to stay as country houseguests. On a Sunday they were given a hearty meal of sausages and cold meats. Mary Anne and Disraeli ate together, away from their guests who could hear sotto voices and Mary Anne exclaiming, 'Don't do it Dizzy, don't.'

But he would go ahead.

'Do you care to see the countryside and nearby farms?' he asked the visitors.

Innocently, they replied in chorus, 'Oh, yes please, how nice.'

Mary Anne sighed, waved them off and settled down with Disraeli's secretarial work, correcting articles, preparing speeches and drafting letters.

At about 3 o'clock Mary Anne would call out, 'Go and find the master, William.'

Sadly, Disraeli's brilliance did not extend to a sense of direction. The footman would lead the party back to Hughenden. Manor. Weary and mud-stained they collapsed into the hall begging for hot baths and whiskey leaving Disraeli to face Mary Anne, 'I thought if I turned right, dearest …'

Even with such annoyance, Mary Anne continued to love Hughenden and its gardens.

'Green fingers,' Mary Anne told Disraeli is a sign we are getting old. On 28 June 1850 he arrived at Grosvenor Gate in the early hours, following an all night session of the House and slept late.

Mary Anne was missing the flowers of Hughenden. 'The rose garden in Regent's Park, is marvellous just now, Dizzy,' she said as he came downstairs at midday. The sun was shining through the roof's glass section down the four flights of stairs.

They decided to drive around the Nash terraces and through Cumberland Gate, when two horsemen stopped them.

'You might be interested to know, Mr Disraeli. Sir Robert Peel is dying, thrown from his horse. It pleases you sir?'

'It pleases me not. His passing is a great misfortune for this country,' came Disraeli's sharp reply.

On the third day following the accident Peel's agony became uncontrollable. The Disraelis were attending a morning fete at the riverside cottage of Lady Londonderry. The fate of Peel overshadowed everything. Lady Londonderry bustled about in the conservatory, serving tea from golden utensils wearing a deep blue satin apron embroidered in crimson, blue, green and white silks together with tassels. Lord Londonderry slipped away to gain reports of Peel. The next day Sir Robert Peel died.

But everybody's attention was distracted. The Prince Consort was considering a Great Exhibition of the Works of Industry of All Nations.

The purchase of Hughenden, finally, gave the Disraelis status. They were landowners, with a house in the country and the urgent departure of the Duke of Buckingham to Europe 1848 pursued by his creditors for some £1,000,000 of debts gave room for Disraeli to become the MP for the county.

But in 1845 the Disraelis had already visited the Duke's country house at Stowe where the Queen and Prince Albert were guests of honour. Mary Anne wrote to Sa:

'... We were for the first hour in the vestibule, like a flock of sheep, half lit up, and no seats or fire, only a little hot air and a great deal of cold wind; and a marble floor. Fancy dear, shivering Dizzy and cross-looking Mary Anne ... After a time we passed Her Majesty and the Prince, the Duke and Duchess and the rest standing behind, the Duke giving our names exactly the same as an ordinary groom, and we making our curtseys and bows. About eleven, or soon after, Her Majesty retired, and then all became joy and triumph to us ... The Duke almost embraced Dizzy, saying he was one *of his oldest friends; and then he offered me his arm, taking me all through the gorgeous splendid scene, through the supper room and back again ... all making way for us the Queen and your delighted Mary Anne being the only ladies so distinguished. After this I retired to a sofa with the Duchess, who told me that Her Majesty had pointed Dizzy out, saying "'There's Mr Disraeli." Do you call all this nothing? The kind Duchess asked me to luncheon the next day and to see the Queen's private apartment..'*

When her Majesty pass'd us to go from one room to another, she almost paus'd to look at mine own, who was in his best looks, ... My heart, dear Sa, was full of gratified ambition – oh no, of the most devoted love.

Mary Anne was less impressed the next day when she saw the Queen's private apartment. She describes the sleeping arrangements of the Queen and Prince Albert.

'But how do you think they sleep? Without pillows or bolster. Lady Anna assur'd me of this over and over again ... The head woman ask'd me if I would like to see the room which had been prepared for Her Majesty. On my asking her what a large red curtain was for, "Oh," she said, "to hang across the staircase when Her Majesty went to the cabinet." On her return the Queen ask'd the woman where the Prince could go – but there was no second convenience.'

Mary Anne had entered with gusto "the glittering bustle" of the country house visit – dressing as one of the greatest ladies in the land, wearing pale velvets, flowers entwined, with diamonds in her hair, with no airs and graces added.

As their carriage drove from the railway station, Disraeli told Mary Anne, 'I am able to feel the pulse of the ablest on all the questions of the day ... over dinner ... when they scarce know I am listening.'

Mary Anne, who confessed to disliking political talk found amusement in the country house visit. She wrote to Sa:

'One of our greatest amusements were two honey bears, tolerably tame, who I often went to play with; fancy my fright

when these horrific-looking pets came howling after me the first time! I went to take a composing draught. Sometimes they are chained, but oftener have their liberty, and use it by frightening the maids and running round the fine galleries – you never heard such a noise. I never kept company with them without witnesses, fearing they might in their fondness hug me to death.'

But it was the purchase of Hughenden which gave the Disraelis an entry into high society.

'As the strains of the Eton Boating Song closed the year for the young pupils, society went to visit its friends and relatives in the country – for the season was now over.

The Queen and Prince Albert went first, then the nobility, and trotting after them all – came the Disraelis.

The Royal couple called first on young Manners' parents, the Duke and Duchess of Rutland, who lived in a castle called Belvoir, perched on a spur, overlooking the Leicestershire countryside.

The great coaches trundled into the courtyard where Mr Taps, head coachman of great abdominal dignity, organized the massive domed shaped trunks. On the arrival of the political couple, Mr Taps, barked, 'Boy, put 'em trunks by the door, them Disraelis won't be staying.'

It was at Belvoir Queen Victoria was to recall as a widow, 'Dear Albert, enjoyed Belvoir's regular fox hunt.' The Queen had forgotten she had been much surprised by this and exclaimed over dinner, 'How well Albert's hunting answered.'

Mary Anne could not boast of Dizzy's brilliance in the killing of things. Once, on a horse, he could not get off.

Gamekeepers unkindly said, 'The guns, Your Grace, cause the gentleman to become agitated, then we must give 'im a draft of brandy, and then he don't hold steady at all ...'

On the first evening of the visit, the gentlemen would don the hunting colours of the Belvoir hunt, except Disraeli. He arrived in black, his perfumed quilted waistcoat a perfect foil for his gold chains.

The Duchess picking at her food explained later, 'No, I was not ill. I spent much time studying Mr Disraeli's gold buttons, wondering, what breed of duck his tailor had in mind?

The talk, over dinner, was of foxes, hounds and horses. Disraeli, much to the butler's surprise, had placed himself centre stage, but each time he opened his mouth to say, 'A Protestant, if he wants aid or advice on any matter, can only go to his solicitor,' his voice was drowned under the strains of the Duke's brass band launching into *The Roast Beef of Old England*.

In desperation, Mary Anne drew Disraeli's attention to the magnificence of the plate, 'Look dearest, each day, we will be served on a different display.'

Disraeli's look would have withered a lesser a woman.

In vain did Mary Anne read to her husband: *The Habits of Good Society. The main point in a country house visit is to give as little trouble as possible, to conform to the habits of your entertainers, and never to be in the way.*

The following morning, Mary Anne took toast in her bedroom. Disraeli entered the breakfast room, promptly at 10 am to sample kidneys, bacon, ham and eggs.

The gentlemen, when suitably nourished, picked up guns and fishing rods in order to go out and kill something.

Usually, Disraeli made his way to the library, (occasionally he fished) to finish a brilliant speech or add to a novel. He would take down from the Duke's shelves his own reference books. Disraeli's man had placed his host's vellum covered volumes, by the fireplace.

This practice embarrassed Mary Anne, but as Disraeli said, 'Dearest, you heard His Grace say most graciously, make yourselves at home …'

A cold luncheon was prepared but after such a repast as breakfast few guests took advantage of the meal. Disraeli entered the dining room promptly at midday.

Half an hour before dinner the guests assembled in the drawing room. The gentlemen in black tie and tails discreetly made eye contact with the married ladies. These were in *grande toilette* bosoms and diamonds on display. Aperitifs were not served and in the drawing room no drinks of any kind were offered, neither was smoking allowed. However, towards the far end of the room, half-hidden behind a walnut whatnot, Disraeli sipped sherry.

The host would suggest which gentleman should escort which lady into the dining room in order of precedence. Mary Anne muttered to her shaken escort – 'We are like animals going two by two into the ark,' as they progressed with solemn dignity and sat down as directed. Wines were served, but it was usual for a guest to sip one glass only – for attention was drawn to you by the footman washing your glass before serving you again. Disraeli continued to drink several glasses of sherry while sampling a variety of soups, game, fish and meats.

Disraeli would then eye the display of desserts soaked in cream and despite Mary Anne's entreaties of, 'No, dearest,' tucked into as many as possible.

Early the next morning would find Mary Anne asking her hostess for something to settle "Dizzy's stomach." The hostess would summon the overworked housekeeper, who marched along endless passages to the key room and then, gimlet-eyed, escorted Disraeli to the medicine cupboard. Disraeli, terrified, obeyed the instruction to, 'Sit, sir, open wide.' The most dreadful tasting mixtures that the housekeeper could prepare were poured down Disraeli's throat.

Disraeli, staggered off to his bedroom, leaving the housekeeper, wondering if wages of £70 per year, her own parlour, uniform and maid, were adequate recompense for the annoyance of Mr Disraeli.

On the fourth day of their stay Mr Taps would call out, 'Disraelis' trunks round to the 'ouse.'

Disraeli would say to Mary Anne as they waved their hosts goodbye, 'I detest society really, for I never enter into it without my feelings being hurt …'

19 The Great Exhibition

It was August 1850 and Mary Anne was furious. 'Leicester Square, sir, that's what Dizzy promised me. Your monstrosity would be built in the square. He promised me,' Mary Anne added desperately.

Joseph Paxton was startled by this odd little woman. He muttered to himself, 'Visitors are not allowed on to the site. How did she get in?'

She heard his questioning but did not give an answer. The sight of a small woman whose little gold shoes were sinking into the mud and whose petticoats frothed above it was almost too much for Paxton. Mary Anne caught his suppressed laughter and Paxton began to cough almost choking in his attempt to suppress it. A large contraption squelched past turning Mary Anne's tartan frock into a mud-spattered article. Her lips pursed. A sign which, if Paxton had known, was one that made Mary Anne's family shake with fright.

Instead he smiled superciliously, but the broadside Mary Anne now threw at him shook him to his very soul.

She said very softly, almost purring, 'If you build your monstrosity in the park you will ruin my husband's career. How can we entertain? How can we be fine folk with a builder's yard opposite sir?' She paused for effect. 'I tell you I will fight you to the very death. You ruin me and I shall ruin you …' And she meant it.

Mary Anne looked into Paxton's brown eyes and she saw his face turn white. He was no longer amused but evaluating the danger from the terrible wife of the Leader of the Opposition, but he did not respond to her attack. In fact he seemed inarticulate. Mary Anne asked herself, was this the man who coped with Colonel Charles Sibthorp of "Hyde Park is to be desecrated" fame? Had he not discussed delicate issues of the Great Exhibition with the Prince Consort himself and manipulated endless committees?

He did not reply but stood back, lent against an elm and

said, 'Madam. Who have I the honour of addressing?'

Mary Anne knew that Joseph Paxton was obsessed with his Crystal Palace as much as she was with Disraeli. But despite herself Mary Anne thought him a "fine figure of a man" and unable to think of an answer poked him in the ribs with her umbrella and burst out, 'You, sir, will ruin my husband's career, my life, my neighbours' lives – for what? Hyde Park will never return to its beauty – houses, houses, houses, rows of them I can see filled with wretches like those over there.'

Paxton swivelled round to look at a dozen whistling red kerchiefed workmen who were entering the park.

'They will get our maids pregnant and steal the silver. We shall never keep a decent servant.' Mary Anne stopped in the midst of her diatribe. 'Don't you dare cut them down,' she said boxing the ears of a young man holding a tree tape preparing to measure the three magnificent elms.

Paxton hoping she had now finished with him began to retreat towards the Grosvenor Gates. 'Sir,' Mary Anne called out after him. 'Stand still 'till I have finished with you.'

Even his Duke did not dare to thunder at him like that. He swung round angrily. 'Madam!'

Mary Anne checked herself. 'I am sorry Mr Paxton but I am so angry with you.' Her hands returned to her hips, 'Build your damn glass house somewhere else because I will not have my life ruined for a greenhouse nor lose my Dizzy through the whim of a mere gardener's boy.'

It began to rain again, a fine August rain. The ground became muddier.

Suddenly, Paxton and Mary Anne were aware of a great presence. Plodding through Grosvenor Gates, head bowed low with weariness, came a workhorse some eighteen hands high, his tail plaited with red and orange grubby ribbons. He was Dobin from her childhood.

The noise, the workmen, the clip clop of city traffic and the foul stench of London vanished. Mary Anne was once again in the farmyard of Bramford Speke.

She called out to the horse, 'Why are you here Dobin, not grazing in the water meadows?'

It was at that moment, Mary Anne saw in Paxton's face, that he realized nestling amongst the London finery, hid a farmer's child.

The horse hearing a kindly voice moved quickly towards the two of them. The overloaded chain-filled cart, bearing in faded red lettering the legend MESSRS. FOX, HENDERSON CO rocked from side to side. The driver called out, 'Steady boy, steady.'

In order to divert Paxton's gaze from herself Mary Anne bent to clean the horse's right hoof with her scarf just as she had done for Dobin when grandfather was taking him to the Llamas Fair.

'Mr Paxton, sir, these are the chains for measuring out. Smethwick's boys will be round with the iron frameworks.'

Mary Anne was about to ask about the property prices but just as she was about to do so the Secretary to the Government, to the Royal Commission and to the Great Exhibition regional, national and London Committees, Stafford Northcote, frock-coated, suitably galloshed and carrying a number of crested papers walked towards the party. He observed the mud, the deepening puddles and sidestepped his way around them all until he found a plank, which he crossed primly, balancing himself uneasily. The others took their attention away from the horse to watch him with fascination. He landed before them quite in control of himself and events that even the rain stopped falling. He bowed to Mary Anne and Paxton and began to address Mary Anne as if she also was a "public monument".

'You will see Mrs Disraeli from the minutes of … it was the Chancellor who voted the necessary money for the Great Exhibition to be built. When discussing the matter Mr Disraeli refers to the project as *enchanting*.'

Paxton smiled. Mr Northcote continued, 'Of course, Mr Disraeli had the backing of the Regional, National and London

Committees headed by the Prince Consort himself and, of course it has the blessing of the Queen.' He paused for breath. 'It is also in memory of dear Sir Robert Peel. It was a project dear to his heart, ma'am.'

But Mary Anne had disappeared – only a whiff of lavender remained to remind the men of her presence.

In fact she was crossing the park, running through the Grosvenor Gates, pushing past Charles in an undignified manner and calling up the front stairs, 'Dizzy, Dizzy.'

Disraeli emerged from his study. 'Dearest,' he said. 'Oh, the Great Exhibition, dearest. You mean the one in Hyde Park?'

Mary Anne stamped her foot, 'Where else Dizzy?'

There are little exhibitions all over the place – even Brussels, I believe.'

When Disraeli spoke like a gentle clergyman and his kiss curl fell over his right eye Mary Anne was grateful she did not have a knife in her hand.

'Dizzy, we are ruined because of you.'

'Are we dearest? I don't think so. You know my speech on the subject was one of my best … I have asked Hansard to forward it to you. Allow me to quote.' Disraeli put his hands in his waistcoat arms and began to speak as if he spoke to the whole of the House of Commons. 'Prescience philosophy of an accomplished and enlightened Prince was raised for the glory, the instruction of two hemispheres …'

Mary Anne looked up at the landing and even she could not think of a suitable put down.

Disraeli took stage direction left and looked out of the landing window.

'If you stand here, dearest, you have a magnificent view of the building of the Great Exhibition. It will consist of 3,000 columns, 1,245 roof girders, 1,073 square feet of glass with 293,655 panels of glass …'

'And Dizzy what do we do about the noise and confusion, 5000 workmen at least. We cannot escape to Bradenham and as for France …'

Disraeli continued to gaze out of the window. 'Do I see, dearest, the dear old Duke coming along the street? I believe he is coming in here.'

As the Duke of Wellington banged the lion knocker of the front door so that the whole house heard it, Mary Anne fled up to her bedroom calling out, 'Norah, Norah, my best pink day gown, quick.'

Fifteen minutes later Mrs Disraeli curtsied low to the Duke of Wellington, as if she had been prepared for his visit all her life.

'What a wonderful thought of yours my dearest Mrs Dizzy. Only you would invite us all to breakfast to witness ...'

To witness what? Mary Anne froze. She had done no such thing, but coming along Park Lane, were the Gladstones, Lady Londonderry, Rosina Bulwer, Caroline Norton, in fact, many of the best of London society.

Disraeli smiled charmingly at her. He offered his bewildered wife his arm, ignoring her whisperings of, 'What is going on Dizzy? I swear Dizzy I will hang for you one day.'

Disraeli escorted his wife with great charm, into her own dining room which was set for breakfast, using every item of the 400 piece Royal Doulton breakfast service, a wedding gift from Uncle and Aunt Basavi. Never used before.

It was too much for Mary Anne she needed air and walked out on to the balconies and found they were draped in purple velvet for entertaining.

When she returned to the dining room Charles asked her, 'Shall I serve now, ma'am?'

'Serve what?' she wanted to ask. Instead Mary Anne nodded and crossed her fingers.

First came devilled kidneys on a silver tray, followed by sausages, chops, eggs done every way, pots of porridge, fruit, bacon, coffee, tea.

People mingled. People ate. They gossiped. They laughed and just as they thought they had finished in came bowls of sweet strawberries from Hughenden.

Mary Anne vowed to herself to have words with Dizzy later.

During 1850 and the spring of 1851 Mrs Disraeli's breakfasts became legendary. She was the only hostess in London to have Joe Paxton cross the road to put into her hands personally his scheme of work. He never knew whether his master, the Duke of Devonshire, would be present at one of Mrs Dizzy's "do's" but every guest saw how the three great elms remained in their places. Seventy foot iron girders rose about them fading into the grey Victorian clouds of London as if they were part of some gigantic cathedral dedicated solely to a new god called "commerce". Nearly a million square feet of floor space was utilised and then the whole was encased not in stone or brick but in glass, crystal glass, nine hundred square feet in all.

The medieval mason had been replaced by mass produced standard units. Mary Anne's guests sat marvelling at it all as much as the feudal peasants had done as the cathedral grew up on the hillside.

By the end of April the Crystal Palace was almost completed and articles of wonderment were placed inside to be shown to people of all nationalities and religions. Mary Anne's guests drank champagne and spoke of the marvels of the age which was theirs.

At midnight on April 30 Mary Anne's Great Exhibition entertainment came to an end. Passers-by saw excited guests climbing out of carriages, shawls around their shoulders because they were to stand in the night chill on the balconies of No 1 Grosvenor Gate. The house was in darkness. The park was deserted. The workmen had gone away, the noise was still, rows of exhibits stood like children's toys waiting to be played with in the morning and someone said Joe Paxton had gone alone into the shadows of Hyde Park. Just before midnight the few loiterers wandering along Hyde Park Lane saw flares light up the palace so it shone like a gigantic Taj Mahal in the moonlight. It was not a place dedicated to a man's love for a woman, but man's love of power and money.

'This Great Exhibition will change the world for ever,' Disraeli told his guests. Marry Anne continued to wave towards the Crystal Palace. She did not know that the Exhibition would change their lives for ever.

The old Duke, coming to the end of his days said to Mary Anne, 'My dear you have truly taken us into fairy land again.'

Even Paxton muttered, 'You have made my palace look like the entrance to paradise.' Of course Disraeli started a speech but for once nobody listened to him. His guests drank champagne until nearly dawn and as people left, coming from behind No 1 Grosvenor Gate, the stirring of London waking up and the little girl who was Paxton's daughter, the child who stood on the leaf in the middle of the lake – suddenly turned back to Mary Anne and hugged her.

Disraeli ignored the opening ceremony, pretending the stream of carriages, the endless pedestrians making their way up Constitution Hill and Piccadilly, the red-faced policemen and sweating horses of the Horse Guards did not exist.

Mary Anne called out, '40,000 are coming, dearest,' and departed to witness the historical event with chattering Mrs Gollop, a friend of one of her Scrope cousins.

They agreed with the Queen. 'The park presents a wonderful spectacle … I never saw Hyde Park look like it does.'

It took half an hour of queuing before they could sit down in the gallery and observe 15,000 stalls from all over the world, draped in red or pink calicoes, and be thankful for the bleached white awning stopping the sun blazing down on them.

The large crowd and the multi-lingual clacking of tongues quite disconcerted Mary Anne unused to hearing other than English dialects in the capital. The air became stifling with the smell of oriental spices, sickly lilies, sweet beer and people and their heads began to split with the everlasting throb of machinery.

Then came a fanfare of trumpets and the little Queen entered wearing a coronet of diamonds with Prince Albert handsome in full dress uniform, the ten year old Princess Royal and little Prince Edward, dressed in a tartan kilt.

The crowds roared their welcome. The vast organ began to play; six hundred voices and two hundred instruments welcomed the Queen and her party who advanced to the middle of the palace. The Queen hesitated, tears filling her eyes, lips trembling and she began her speech. The Prince stepped forward. The National Anthem boomed around the dome. There was a hushed silence and the Prince began speaking.

'Oh dear, to pay so much and not to hear a word the man is saying especially in that thick accent,' snapped Mary Anne.

This was followed by a prayer by the Archbishop of Canterbury and then the choir of six hundred launched into the *Halleluiah* chorus.

'Magnificent!' drooled Mrs Gollop.

'Terrible noise with all that glass,' observed Mary Anne.

They visited George Jennings' public lavatories. Disraeli was much impressed when he was told about them and even more so when he learned at the close of the Exhibition 827,000 had visited them, without mishap.

They ooh'd and aah'd before a gas-lit gilded cage containing the Koh-i-noor diamond sitting on a red velvet cushion, and as for the British stand, this left them speechless. Wedgwood pottery, carriages, an electroplate system, much church furniture but few specimens of ordinary furniture for general use.'

Little Prince Edward wrote to Baron Stockmar, his father's tutor: *'I am much excited by some waxwork models of the murderous Indians.'*

The Baron replied: *'Sir, you are born in a Christian and enlightened age in which such atrocious acts are not even dreamt of ...'*

'Let's come when it's quieter,' said Mary Anne, 'and choose modern things for Hughenden, there is certainly no place for visitors to dine plainly and well.'

On May 21 Mary Anne woke Disraeli, 'Dearest, it is the crack of dawn. It is ten o'clock Dizzy. 'Get up. We need ideas for Hughenden.'

As if it was all his idea, Disraeli wrote to Sa: '*You must contrive to go, if only once.*'

On Wednesdays and Thursdays ordinary people could enter the Great Exhibition for a shilling. Thomas Cook brought trainloads of people to London. On the last shilling day, Wednesday, October 3 just before the Exhibition closed, Disraeli escorted Mary Anne to say goodbye to their exuberant neighbour. Some of the stalls had been dismantled and the Sousaphone, which played, to the hoi polloi on these cheap days was now silent, much to Mary Ann's disappointment.

'It might have had a humanising effect on the dog-stealers, cabmen and coal heavers – not to one of any sensitivity,' observed Disraeli while they pushed their way through smelly crowds guzzling from paper bags, throwing beer bottles to the left and right of them and endless crying, snotty-nosed children.

'But dearest,' said Disraeli, through the smoke filled haze. 'Did you not stress we must live according to our means. We have saved at least 2/6d each.'

'Actually,' observed Mary Anne. 'I have found Mr Jeremiah Smith's new invention, gummed envelopes a most useful item, but sadly he would not sell them to me cheaply even today.'

Disraeli enjoyed telling everybody, 'The £213 profit from the Exhibition is to purchase sites for museums in Kensington and a great concert hall. Mrs Disraeli and I look forward to availing ourselves of such cultural delights.'

'Do, we?' said Mary Anne. 'You are forever telling me, Dizzy, I never recall who came first the Greeks or the Romans.'

The Disraelis watched the dismantling of the Crystal Palace. 'And how sad,' they agreed. 'It is going into South London. Sydenham isn't it?'

The Exhibition masked Disraeli's dejection. In August he learned of the death abroad of one of the companions of his youth, D'Orsay. Lady Blessington had fled from her debtors and he was no longer close to Bulwer and "his beautiful young men" saw him as an ageing sphinx.

It seemed, at the end of that year that the Whigs would be in power – for ever. Stanley and Disraeli had failed to form a Tory Government and he was feeling unwell. Mary Anne squabbled with Sa and with James, who was making a nuisance of himself. He constantly requested Disraeli to get him an appointment as Justice of the Peace. Disraeli gave the same reply over and over again. 'It is impossible, under the current rules, for anyone in trade to hold this office.'

'I am not in trade,' insisted James. 'You are a farmer and therefore in trade.'

'I am a gentleman farmer …'

Wearied, of the constant exchanges Disraeli urgently requested a County Court Treasureship worth £900 a year for James.

In August when the Parliamentary session ended Disraeli wrote to Sa: '*As so many things have really turned up and always turned up when they were most wanted, the end will be as right as we all wish.*'

And it did in a most strange form. It was during the August recess Mary Anne became aware of Mrs Sarah Brydges Willyams of Torquay. She was one of the women who wrote regularly to Disraeli admiring his speeches and writings. In fact, Mrs Brydges Willyams, was one of his greatest fans.

'Dizzy, you should not ignore elderly ladies, you never know who they know … or how much money they have,' said Mary Anne. But Disraeli continued to ignore the widow from Torquay until he received the following letter:

'*I have, often before, addressed you in reference to your political speeches and your published works: but now write to you upon a private subject. I am about to make out my Will, and I have to ask, as a great favour, that you will oblige me by being one of the executors. I think it is right to add that whoever are my executors will also be my residuary legatees*

and that the interest they will take under my will, although not
a considerable one will, at all events, be substantial.'

While staying with Monckton Milnes, the MP for Pontefract, at Fryston, Devon, Disraeli asked, 'Do you know a mad woman living in Torquay called Mrs Brydges Willyams?'

Mary Anne delved to find out that Mrs Brydges Willyams was a widow of a former colonel in the Cornish Militia. She was of Spanish origin, whose Sephardic maiden name had been Mendez da Costa. She had no children and regularly attended the little church close to her home in Mount Braddon.

Disraeli asked advice of their solicitor, Sir Sir Philip Rose, who advised, 'Wait six weeks.' Mrs Brydges Willyams complained that her bookseller had sold out of *Tancred*. Disraeli sent her a copy, '*As a vindication, a complete one, of the race from which we all spring,*' together with a recent edition of his father's *The Curiosities of Literature*. '*You will find the name of your father, incidentally mentioned.*'

Mrs Brydges Willyams asked Disraeli to meet her by the fountain at Crystal Palace at 11 o'clock. Disraeli found the wide circular seat surrounding the pool. Mrs Brydges Willyams was on a visit to a married niece, and did not wish the niece to know of her wish to ask Disraeli to be the executor of her will, on the understanding that if he did agree to act in that capacity he would be her residuary legatee.

Disraeli was shortsighted. The old lady dodged out of sight of her niece – sitting at a slight distance away and neither saw the other. Mrs Brydges Willyams returned to Devon the next day and sent bulbs for Mrs Disraeli's garden and lobsters for Mr Disraeli together with a note.

Disraeli said, 'However, I must take Sir Philip Rose's advice before I act. Mrs Brydges Willyams is willing to wait and has invited us to visit her in Torquay this autumn.'

'*I should be delighted to meet you, and to pay my lawful debts; as to other debts, I must not soar to impossibilities.*'

Disraeli wrote back: '*Where did you get the lobster which arrived for my dejeuner this morning? From the caves of*

Amphitrite? It was so fresh! Tasted of the sweetness – not the salt- of the ocean, and almost as creamy as your picturesque cheeses ...'

In the autumn Disraeli travelled to Torquay and said to Mary Anne, 'I was handed a thousand pound note, "For election expenses" as if it were a paper handkerchief. Our lady has piercing black eyes, wears a jet-black wig, with an enormous top knot, but no crinoline. She is quite a miser, starves herself into a skeleton ... keeps neither horses nor carriages, nor men servants – only an enormous watchdog to protect her and her gold and her only exercise is to walk on sturdy leashes, two large and very ugly bulldogs. She is over eighty but expects to live to be 100.'

Disraeli returned to London clutching a memorandum concerning Mrs Brydges Willyams's will. Sir Philip Rose, on reading it, suggested Mrs Brydges Williams employed a local solicitor. Disraeli was still appointed an executor and she made him her residuary legatee.

A fortnight in Torquay became part of the tenor of the Disraelis' lives. They stayed in the Royal Hotel, breakfasted in their rooms, walked along the beach and in the afternoon called on Mrs Brydges Willyams, and later wandered through the dusk, hand in hand, along the palm tree lined promenade back to the "Royal."

Mary Anne wrote her a thank you note.

'I appreciate your constant kind thoughts of Mr Disraeli. I have never heard him appreciated so highly as by yourself, or by anyone, man or woman.'

From then on they exchanged letters, flowers, plants but the bric-a-brac Mary Anne hid away in cupboards.

'I dislike clutter.'

The New Year was to bring the Disraelis an even greater surprise.

20 Chancellor of the Exchequer/ Plus Secretaries

The morning news on 3rd December 1851 was dramatic. Lord Russell could not believe it, the Queen was utterly dismayed, the Prince Consort horrified, Disraeli amused. Old Palmerston, had secretly supported the coup d'état of Louis Napoleon Bonaparte, 'making a strong, clever man, – dictator of France.'

The Second Republic had been overthrown by a coup led by its own President. He was now proclaimed Napoleon III.

Lord John Russell 'exhausted by him beyond belief,' sacked Palmerston. They all agreed, 'The mischievous old man must now rest upon his laurels,' but after only two months, "Lord Pumicestone" announced. 'I've had my tit-for-tat with John Russell and on Friday last I turned him out.'

At last Disraeli's long wait was coming to an end as Lord Derby became Prime Minister and formed a new government.

Mary Anne, peeping from behind a lace-net curtain watched his Lordship stride purposefully across the park towards Grosvenor Gate. He whistled slightly under his breath.

'A good sign in a man,' observed Mary Anne and worked out which costume she would wear to open the door to the press, wishing to photograph and interview the new Foreign Secretary. Mary Anne shivered slightly on hearing Lord Derby's knock.

'Oh dear, Dizzy is opening the door himself. Lord D will think him either over keen or we have no decent servants.'

Murmurs.

'How softly men can speak.'

As you know Disraeli I am forming the next Government.' Murmurs again as the door shut sharply behind Disraeli.

Mary Anne remained behind the potted palm, ready for action.

'Should I take in tea, perhaps not. I hope he doesn't notice the cushions need plumping up.' Grandma Evans training remained even in a London society hostess. 'No, he won't, Dizzy says Knowsley is a slum compared to ...'

Charles emerged from below stairs, looked around him and placed his ear against the keyhole. Mary Anne dashed down, pushed him out of the way and put her own ear there instead.

'I can't hear a word, Charles.'

'No, madam, I could not either.'

On the sound of chairs being pushed away, the door began opening slowly. 'Thank you for the great honour, my Lord, I am most unsuited ...'

The two eavesdroppers looked at each other and grimaced. Mary Anne disappeared into the breakfast room and Charles into the servants' parlour.

Downstairs Charles said, 'Don't know what he's got.'

'I do,' sniffed the cook. On a Sunday afternoon, I take tea with Lord Derby's cook.'

On the first step of the backstairs, Hortense clutching a large brandy on a small tray, appeared to be waiting for a word of command.

As Mary Anne's shriek echoed to below stairs, the cook called out, 'Up those stairs girl quick,' and sat down with aplomb, pouring herself whisky with a little tea out of the brown teapot.

'It's too much for any poor soul to bear 'im Chancellor of the Exchequer.'

Upstairs Mary Anne sipped the brandy, stared up at Disraeli, unbelievingly. 'Dizzy, whatever is Lord D thinking of the country will be broke in a week. Dizzy, I see before me, you in handcuffs, a bankrupt country, the Crown jewels being sold to the French, starving hordes cursing "that Disraeli" and tearing down Grosvenor Gate, its curtains strewn around a deserted Park Lane.'

Disraeli slightly miffed at his wife's reaction, observed icily, 'His Lordship obviously realises creditors make the best negotiators, dearest.'

Perhaps he was right. One day, his secretary young Monty Corry would call in on Lord Lionel Rothschild who ignored the stuttering young man standing before him, concentrating instead on the grape he was peeling.

'Well?'

'Please, my Lord,' the Prime Minister wishes a loan.'

'For what purpose?'

'To purchase a canal, my Lord.'

This remark made even Rothschild look up.

'How much?'

'Four million, my Lord.'

'Security?'

'The British Government.'

'Tell the Prime Minister, the loan is his.'

Lord Rothschild threw the grape into the fire; it sizzled into nothing. Corry was dismissed.

But this all happened when Disraeli had become a great statesman and Mary Anne was long dead.

A few days, after Lord Derby's visit. Mary Anne, with sinking heart, wrote:

'Bless you my darling, your own devoted wife wishes you joy. I hope you will make as good a Chancellor of the Exchequer as you have been a husband to your affectionate Mary Anne.'

'Loyal to the last,' muttered Mary Anne as she went into the Chancellor's office where Disraeli was putting on the black and gold robes of the Chancellor of the Exchequer.

'Do you know dearest, these are the very garments worn by Pitt the Younger. They are a good augury, dearest,' Disraeli informed Mary Anne.

'That gentleman understood, Dizzy, two plus two makes four not three.'

The younger MPs enjoyed themselves, taking bets on how long Disraeli would last and sneering, 'finding the robes heavy, Dizzy?'

'On the contrary,' retorted Disraeli. 'I find them uncommonly light.'

'Really?' said the Whigs. 'The situation is gentlemen of England with a player thrown in.'

Meanwhile, the Duke of Wellington, placed his ear trumpet to his ear bellowing, 'Who? Who is Chancellor?'

However, luckily nobody knew before Disraeli took up his appointment that he had written to Sir Philip Rose, '*For a loan of £1,500 just to see me through.*'

And how Disraeli enjoyed being high powered. Mary Anne complained to friends, 'I have lost Dizzy, now that he is in office.'

Meanwhile in Torquay, Disraeli's position enabled Mrs Brydges Willyams, to gain friendship, 'My friend the Chancellor tells me.' She displayed the envelope marked House of Commons on her mantelpiece and Disraeli's letter left open casually lying about.

'*It has been a very gay and brilliant season, at least Mrs Disraeli tells me so, for I never go anywhere except Wednesdays off or Saturdays. I went, however, to two fetes on Thursday and Friday last, which amused me...*'

Disraeli told Sa, 'I go to Lord Derby's reception and nowhere else but Mary Anne is for ever gay and ubiquitous.'

And so she seemed. Every time Mary Anne walked through a drawing room door, alone she was reminded of the Clifton Assembly Rooms, of how the women stared at her unsuitable little frock and wrong jewels. How the women's eyes narrowed with jealousy and the men's with desire.

Now men smiled kindly at her. Women sneered behind their fans at the sight of an old woman in pale pink satin, 'suitable only for a young girl' or as Mary Anne had decided 'to be worn by a woman with a terribly attractive but much younger husband ...'

So, Mrs Chancellor of the Exchequer walked towards her hostess, hand outstretched, *A spirit I am, and I don't give a damn.*'

But she did.

Henry Lennox

One evening on her arrival at Grosvenor Gate Mary Anne found a note waiting for her. It was in Lennox's hand: *'D. is waiting – has done his work, and will be very glad if you will come down and fetch him home now.'*

Disraeli was waiting for Mary Anne in the House of Commons lobby. He fidgeted about with impatience. By his side stood Lennox, right hand on his hip. He looked like Disraeli's greyhound puppy. The silken suit showed off the thinness of the body it covered, the luminous skin shone, unnaturally for a man of thirty. His eyes glittered. The pupils distended and teeth so neat that they seemed to belong into a doll's mouth.

'The Chancellor of the Exchequer has been kept waiting.'

Mary Anne flushed with annoyance, wanting to box the young man's ears and waited for Disraeli to snap hard at the boy.

Disraeli laughed.

'Dizzy, says I have the sweetest disposition, don't you Dizzy?'

'I say you are incorrigible little flirt.'

Once he had called her a flirt and a "rattle" and had ended up loving her.

She watched Disraeli taking his books, his pens and his files into the Chancellor's rooms. He had never emptied his study before. She was furious to be told by Mrs Dawson, 'How do you feel Mrs Disraeli about young Henry Lennox sitting in your husband's office, administering what one wonders.'

Mary Anne wondered for she had heard Disraeli say to Lennox, 'Write to me very often, and tell me how you are. I am amused about *Coningsby* and am rather surprised that you never read it before. If you ever have the inclination or power to read another book …'

Mary Anne, overhearing Lennox describing one of his circle, "as a great bellowing booby," suddenly realised

Disraeli had a hidden agenda with the young man. Will you use anybody, Dizzy, she thought.

Although impoverished, Lennox was the 3rd son of the 5th Duke of Richmond and he possessed the insider's view of aristocratic circles. He crawled where Disraeli could not walk, listening to spiteful gossip and pillow talk providing Disraeli with information for his articles and endless intrigues.

Smythe, Manners and Kok danced less around Disraeli. Manners was married, Smythe a promiscuous drunk and Kok went on quietly and steadily. But Lennox was different for although stupid he had a cleverness. He inveigled himself into being invited to Hughenden, delighting staff and guests alike, making himself useful to Disraeli and one and all, smiling at Mary Anne and saying loudly, 'Mrs Disraeli, there is cheese over. Shall I take it back to the grocer in the morning?'

Society gossiped behind its fans. Smythe reported to Manners on a visit to Hughenden, 'I was puzzled ... to see how Dis was governed by Henry Lennox.'

Lennox's brother, Alexander was intensely disgusted at Henry's fawning over Disraeli.

Endless little notes passed between Disraeli and Lennox.

'Needless to say that I am quite effete without good news, without the Chancellor and without champagne cup! – I go on Saturday to Hatfield ... How I wish you had accepted to do the same.'

Lennox wrote from Hatfield:

' Thanks, a thousand thanks for your charming letter ... I dine at Hatfield tonight, but shall be down here tomorrow at 11.30. Till then Farewell! My dearest D! How could you suppose I should not be dull without you.

Disraeli's answered: *'I am glad you are dull in my absence, I also feel lonely.'*

Then the note: *'I can only say I love you, Dizzy,'* which Mary Anne found.

Had he sent the note, had Lennox planted it? She continued to polish the desk over and over again.

She was so disturbed she went to the Chateau of Waddesdon and amongst the glories of Sèvres and chandeliers, Mary Anne told Lady Rothschild, 'Few women know how much to give but I know exactly how much to give to a man or little. I was brought up in the west, but a young man my dear Lady Rothschild is a different matter.'

Lady Rothschild looked at the little woman in her afternoon dress, funny hat, who called in so often unexpectedly and now sat with the tears falling down rouged cheeks.

'I am nearly sixty and Dizzy is only forty-eight. Is that what is wrong? Does he need an adventure, men sometimes do, but that side of our marriage has always been so warm, so good but now he does not come to me ...'

'I can offer no comfort it is outside my experience,' replied Lady Rothschild leading her to the door.

One evening on a wet dreary night, a group of young men called out to Disraeli, 'Let us go to the Carlton Club for supper, coming Dizzy?'

Lennox stood invitingly close, but just as Disraeli stepped towards him a messenger arrived, 'A note for you, sir, from Mrs Disraeli.'

'Dearest Dizzy, a Fortnum's special game pie awaits you, together with a chicken, champagne with extras ...'

Disraeli patted Lennox's cheek and vanished into the London fog. He would gradually leave Disraeli's life to seek a rich wife. He died in 1886 unmarried and still poor.

Mary Anne learned that Lord Derby commented on the relationship, 'In two things D's character is more amiable than most persons suppose, the one his willingness, and often with considerable trouble to himself, to encourage and help rising men of talents for which several instances occur to me; the other, which would be well understood by those who knew his domestic position, but which I mention only by allusion, the gratitude which during many years he has never ceased to evince towards a person to whom he owes much of his success, but whose claims upon him in return are neither slight, nor easy to satisfy.'

How Mary Anne agreed with those sentiments.

Ralph Earle

It is obvious from Disraeli's letters he enjoyed power. He intrigued Mary Anne and Henry Lennox supplying him with political gossip. Now a more dangerous young man replaced Lennox, Ralph Earle. Earle assumed, as did Disraeli and Mary Anne, that his employer's next position would be Foreign Secretary and on March 4 he offered his services to Disraeli and skilfully eased Mary Anne away from the Circle of Power.

The young man undertook secret errands for Disraeli to foreign leaders. Mary Anne did not know who they were or what game was being played. Never before had she been so cut out from Disraeli's beloved intrigues.

At this time Disraeli's intelligence network abroad was stronger than ever. He relied heavily on Earle, who had links with the Ambassador to France, Lord Cowley. Earle told Disraeli much of what should have remained confidential.

In the winter of 1856-7 Disraeli and Mary Anne visited Paris, trying to persuade Napoleon that the Conservative government would serve his purposes better than Palmerston's. The French Government continued to support the leaders in power.

In 1866 Earle received a junior ministerial post and once removed from Disraeli's immediate life soon fell out with his former employer. Disraeli began to understand Mary Anne's warnings that Earle was unscrupulous and disloyal.

Montague Lowry Corry, Secretary

During the emotional vacuum caused by Earle's departure, Mary Anne and Disraeli visited the Duke of Cleveland's country house, Raby Castle. Their attention was caught by

Montague Corry, the son of Henry Corry, a First Lord of the Admiralty and Tory MP.

On a wet afternoon, the Disraelis were bored and sat in the library waiting for dinner. The rest of the party was out hunting. Mary Anne was reading unfashionable, unladylike *Tom Jones* and Disraeli was writing letters.

'How I miss gaslight when I am in the country,' said Mary Anne.

'Perhaps, we could look at the pictures in the long gallery,' suggested Disraeli. 'They always make us laugh.'

Suddenly from an adjoining room came the sounds of a very improper song, sung very loudly and out of tune.

They rose as one and went along the corridor to where the noise was coming from, opened the door, to find a young man, performing an explicit, vigorous solo dance, clicking his heels and making eyes to a circle of unchaperoned young ladies, who giggled at the song.

'Surely, properly brought up gals could not possibly understand,' whispered Disraeli with a smirk to Mary Anne.

'Oh you think not, dearest,' said Mary Anne. 'In fact, we do, from our earliest years.'

The girls, sensing a new presence looked up and saw, Mama and Papa's dear friends, looking directly at them. They froze in their crinolines, mouths open, wide-eyed with fright. Montague Corry spun round, stood stock still, not believing what he saw, removed the red scarf quickly from around his waist, threw it to a mousy girl who began crying, 'I shall never get a husband now.'

It was all too much for the Disraelis, who fled, collapsing with laughter to the library.

After dinner, a crestfallen Montague Corry, who believed his career was over, felt a pat on his shoulder. 'I think you must be my impresario,' said Disraeli smiling down at him.

At that moment Mary Anne saw the ghosts of Lennox, Manners, Smythe, Earle leave the room and she knew she would never again have to fight a beautiful young man for her Dizzy.

Monty was twenty-eight years of age. He was educated at Harrow and Trinity College, Cambridge. Sympathetic, intelligent, without being clever, well connected enough for Mary Anne and Disraeli. His grandfather was the 2nd Earl of Belmore, his mother, the daughter of the sixth Earl of Shaftesbury.

Within the year Montague Corry became Disraeli's friend, confidant and general factotum. He remained with Disraeli until he died and then became Lord Rowton and established the charity: Rowton House.

During the Reform Riots when the mob tore down iron railings and threw bricks through windows, except No 1 Grosvenor Gate, Monty sent a note to Disraeli who was waiting anxiously in the House for news of his wife.

'Mrs Disraeli wishes me to add that the people in general seem to be thoroughly enjoying themselves, and I really believe she sympathises with them. At any rate I am glad to say she is not in the least alarmed.'

Neighbours suspected Mary Anne' sympathies lay with the rioters.

In *Endymion* Disraeli described the relationship between a chief and his private secretary.

'The relations between a Minister and his secretary are, or at least should be, among the finest that can subsist between two individuals. Except the married state, there is none in which so great a confidence is involved, in which more forbearance ought to be exercised or more sympathy ought to exist.'

21 Out of Office

'Mr Gladstone is not a man of the world,' Disraeli told Mary Anne.

'Dearest, you cannot keep the Chancellor's robes. They belong now to Mr Gladstone.'

'They belonged to Pitt, the Younger.'

'Yes, dear but he gave them back.'

Gladstone, exasperated, wrote to Disraeli: *'It is highly unpleasant for Mr Gladstone to address Mr Disraeli without the usual terms of courtesy but he wants the robes back.'*

'No,' said Disraeli hanging the robes in the hall of Hughenden. 'Pitt the Younger's Chancellor's robes as worn by The Rt.Hon. Benjamin Disraeli MP when Chancellor of the Exchequer. Unfortunately the robes are not just a constant reminder of success they are my success. I need an official salary, we can no longer pack our bags and go to Bradenham every time money gets tight.'

If Disraeli's debts continued to be a drain upon resources Mary Anne said they could go and look at Disraeli in the new Madame Tussaud's waxworks. 'At least, Dizzy, you are well known, even the British Museum has asked you to be a trustee,' Mary Anne would say.

'Her Majesty, herself congratulated me on the appointment,' said Disraeli smugly.

'What a pity, dearest, they have not got your little Imperial beard quite right.'

'Indeed, they have not got me quite right, but has anybody, except you of course, dearest,' agreed Disraeli standing so that admiring mothers and fathers could say sotto voice, 'There is the gentleman himself children.'

Disraeli smiling benignly, patted little children's heads, giving the little creatures a penny, in return Ma and Pa told grandmamma and grandpapa, aunts, uncles, friends, cousins, in fact the whole of Bethnal Green that "old Dizzy" was a very decent sort.

Disraeli greatly encouraged by Madame Tussaud's, wrote long letters of application to editors signing himself "a gentleman of the press" together with the enclosed photograph. When a photographer asked Disraeli to lean on a pedestal Mary Anne pushed it away, 'Dizzy, has never had anyone but me to lean on, and he shall not be shown with a prop now.'

Mary Anne refused all blandishments to have her photograph taken with her husband. She was sixty. He was but forty-eight.

Disraeli's efforts seemed to generate little work. Mary Anne sighed, counted candles, ordered leftover pieces of soap to go in the boiler and continued upsetting the grocer by returning uneaten cheeses. 'Mr Disraeli did not require them after all.'

The baker could not believe it. He received, wrapped neatly in a napkin, six uneaten rolls, from a breakfast for the Royal Tecks. A year later, the Duchess, a formidable young woman, invited the Disraelis to dine with them. The main topic of conversation was the Crimea.

'Mr Disraeli, you have such influence, the Queen is for greater action, the House is for it, the people are for it, what are you waiting for, Mr Disraeli?'

'At this moment, madam, for the potatoes.'

Life continued on but as always, suddenly, the beech trees around Hughenden turned a deep glorious brown and orange. This was the season Disraeli felt most at home with, but Mary Anne hated autumn, the winds of winter approaching, the growing damp and frosts. Her time was spring. She fell ill and did not shake off her influenza until the following April. Hidden away in her bedroom Mary Anne could hear saucepans dropping, tealeaves left on carpets and when she picked up rugs, 'There is enough dust underneath to bury twelve mice.'

She called the cook, the housekeeper, Charles, even Norah Rooke but Mary Anne was too frail to use her tongue sharply enough and her tight control of her household slipped away from her.

Disraeli who never had anything to do with the servants, never noticing them, or remembering their names, imagining the house cleaned itself and food was prepared out of the air wrote to Lady Londonderry: *'As she is the soul of my house, managing all my domestic affairs, it is irrespective of all other considerations, a complete revolution in my life. Everything seems to be in anarchy.'*

While Mary Anne was sick, Disraeli stayed at Derby's country house, Knowsley Hall, near Liverpool from 9th to 12th December. Derby was suffering from the gout and Disraeli compared this household to his usual well-run homes and complained to Mary Anne, 'Nothing comes out except haunches of venison. It is a wretched house.'

It was suggested Derby never returned to the place. Perhaps he had not forgotten Disraeli had introduced his brother Henry to the Hell Club in St James's Street. And the boy had vanished for a time.

While Disraeli was visiting Knowsley, Mary Anne tucked up in bed, worried that without her he would show his dislike of country house society. He said of Crichel about one thousand and two hundred birds were shot and the sky was darkened with their up-rushing and the whirl of their wings was like the roar of the sea and then they fell to the ground – dead with the dogs nuzzling them.

Mary Anne explained, 'Whenever we go to a country house the same thing happens: Dizzy is bored, and has constant ennui. He takes to eating as a resource, he eats breakfast, luncheon and dinner; the result is, by the end of the third day he becomes dreadfully bilious, and we have to come away.'

But Mary Anne was a welcome guest. Sir Stafford Northcote wrote to his wife saying:

'She is great fun and we made capital friends in the train, though I could not help occasionally pitying her husband for the startling effect her natural speeches must have upon the ears of his great friends. Still, there is something very warm and good in her manner which makes one forgive her few

oddities. She informed me she was born in Bramford Speke, and I told her they must come and see her birthplace some time when they are in Devonshire. What do you say to the idea of asking them to Pynes? It would complete the astonishment of our neighbours.'

The neighbours would indeed be surprised. Mary Anne enjoyed shocking people by telling them, 'My parents eloped. I was once forced to be a milliner. I had to marry you know.' Fortunately, nobody believed her.

'Mrs Disraeli is so amusing with her stories.'

As Christmas approached, Mary Anne received a strange letter from James, who she so often quarrelled with and was annoyed to find Sa had won acclaim again acting as "peacemaker."

'I am so unhappy that you think I intended to behave rudely to you in London when you called on Sa. The truth is, on the chance of a visit from you I had prepared a grand dinner in the hope that you would do me the honour to partake of it, and really was much disappointed that you did not stay. I hope in this season of general Love you will forget this unlucky day...'

A year later Mary Anne was the first to be told by James: *'I am engaged to Miss Cave, of Brentry, Gloucestershire, who is reckoned "very clever, agreeable and accomplished" – of course I think that and a great deal more. I hope very sincerely that she will gain your good opinion. I am a far luckier fellow than I deserve to find a fortune of £7,000 with further expectations...'*

Mary Anne thought to herself: James, on no account must you tell your brother that Miss Cave has money. No never James ... If you do, I guarantee, you will be broke within the year.

Crimea War

In February the newspapers were full of how Lord Aberdeen was trying to preserve the peace, but nevertheless, England and France decided to declare war on Russia.

Uncle Leopold wrote to his niece: *'How the Emperor could get himself and everybody else into this infernal scrape is quite incomprehensible.'*

This was the Queen's view that she let her intimate circle know which, of course, filtered down to Mary Anne, who was of the same view as Uncle Leopold. The thought of such a waste of money upset her, 'I can see rationing ahead.' The cook found herself storing provision against the inevitable starvation day.

Mary Anne read in *The Morning Post* how bravely the Queen waved goodbye to her troops from a boat heading out to the Channel from Spithead. The reporter did not foresee that the name Crimea would be forever associated with death, disease and disaster.

From the beginning things went badly. In fact so badly that only two months after the outbreak of war, Disraeli was shaken to learn that the Queen was rather startled to be asked for a day of national humiliation.

Disraeli wrote to Mrs Brydges Willyams: *'We seem to have fallen into another Walcheren Expedition, and in my opinion the Ministers ought to be impeached.'*

The Prince Consort spoke against the lack of organisation, the lack of munitions, insisting men shot each other with rifles instead of the traditional musket.'

The war dragged on and on. The Queen presented medals, 'From the highest Prince of the Blood to the lowest private, all must receive the same distinction,' she said firmly. 'The Queen's heart bleeds for them as if for our nearest and dearest.'

Eventually in 1856 the Peace Treaty was signed.

Letters from Grosvenor Gate to Mrs Brydges Willyams spoke of: *'London gone mad with fetes and festivities every night, and an invitation to the palace where we shall have the honour of dining.'*

As the Disraelis drove through the great iron gates of Buckingham Palace and walked along endless corridors until they entered the Banqueting Chamber and feeling like two outsiders they sat down, the outsiders at the feast. Another guest reported that the Queen sat at the head of her table in the Great Banqueting Hall under a richly carved and gilded ceiling, the walls hung with crimson brocade and life-sized portraits of Kings, Queens and Emperors quick and dead, she too sat, the descendant of many, the equal in Majesty of all. She was still plain, still little, her plump and homely figure lost of its youth in frequent childbearing, yet in that brilliant galaxy of uniforms and diamond be-sparkled gowns she shone among them in her splendour like a star. Those light blue eyes darted from one to another and then rested adoringly on Albert and sometimes she threw back her head and laughed showing "not very pretty gums".

Disraeli watching the scene and remembered a young girl who smiled up at him invitingly, who then remembering she was a Queen moved on ...

22 Hatfield and Paris

Mary Anne had continued to feel unwell throughout most of the war. She stayed with Mrs Brydges Willyams, alone. Disraeli remained at Grosvenor Gate preparing a major speech.

Mary Anne said, 'I know good gossip, good food and Devonshire air will soon improve my health.' But walking on the promenade she was so busy noting the way other women clung to their straws, 'So silly, wearing such large hats, quite unsuited to seaside breezes,' that she tripped, falling badly, blacking her eyes and scratching her face. The large hats bent over her and raised her to her feet. 'Oh the indignity of it all,' Mary Anne said to a concerned Mrs Brydges Willyams, whose dogs, bored with the proceedings, tugged at their leads. The next day she travelled to the Salisburys at Hatfield, the train jolting every nerve in her shaken and badly bruised body.

As Mary Anne drove along the drive seeing the mullioned windows and great porch of Hatfield House dogs came bounding out. 'I will miss Mrs Brydges Willyams and her dogs,' she said to the coachman.

On her arrival Lady Salisbury welcomed Mary Anne, standing at the bottom of the staircase, clinging hold of the devil carved on the balustrade. At first she did not see her guest, for the light was so dim in the great panelled hall but as Mary Anne moved into the light Lady Salisbury exclaimed, 'Mrs Disraeli, whatever has happened?'

'Lady Salisbury, please allow me to go straight to my room, so that Dizzy cannot see me and sit me far away from him at dinner for he has lost his eyeglass. If you put me a long way from him he will never see what condition I am in.'

While Mary Anne stayed in the "Great Houses" she relied on Mrs Blagden to keep her informed of how life went at Hughenden.

'There are a number of glow worms in the *Ladies' Walk*.'

As a thank you the vicar's wife received a large piece of venison, 'A present from Hatfield, my dear.'

At the end of 1856 Mary Anne felt quite well but Disraeli suffered from his nervous debility again. He and Mary Anne departed to Spa in Belgium without telling any of their friends. They returned to Hughenden and fell once again into local affairs. Disraeli advised a startled farmer how to cross his sheep.

'I have studied these things,' he said.

On Sunday mornings, parishioners' lives could be enlivened by watching Mrs Disraeli driving her demure little pony and trap along the pathway leading to the church accompanied by the "Squire" walking beside her. Disraeli nodded to the left and right of him, Mary Anne waved graciously from the trap, rather like royalty. He patted the cleaner children on the head and shook the hands of the very elderly.

As the sound of the pony's hooves ceased, choirboys nudged each other. The congregation settled down for a long wait, the vicar remained seated. The churchwarden opened the door wide and sat down with a sigh.

Disraeli could be heard exclaiming, 'It is indeed a delightful little foot not to be met outside paradise.' Then sweeping off his hat and bowing low, he held forth on the beauty of such a delicate little foot, 'so exquisite a foot, worthy of the angels,' laying it on with a trowel the beauty of his wife's foot placed on the church step.

After some five minutes or so they would enter the church, graciously acknowledging the vicar.

Mary Anne would say to a tearful Mrs Blagden, 'Don't take on my dear. Relations between the vicars of Hughenden and Mr Disraeli are often strained. Mr Disraeli only comes down to Buckinghamshire at weekends and has to rush to catch the Sunday midday Paddington train.

The Reverend John R Piggott, for instance was high church, given to preaching on, 'The great and inevitable change we must all face.' He was a godly man, but against his wife's advice and mine he wrote to Mr Disraeli about: *The breach of that commandment to keep the Sabbath sacred, which not, so rigidly enforced as on the people from whom with natural pride you record your descent, is still not less binding now that you are a Christian.'*

Disraeli travelled on Sundays.

Dear Reverend Blagden replaced Mr Piggott. Mary Anne commented to his wife, 'Your husband does not distress Mr Disraeli so much, my dear. Dizzy only looks at his watch during Mr Blagden's sermons.'

However, relations did become strained when Mrs Blagden, near her time with her tenth child, insisted on playing the organ with such vigour that the organ trailed off, the choir stood aghast, the vicar went white and Mary Anne threw off her cape and rolled up her sleeves.

'Mr Blagden, boiling water if you please. Boys, blankets. Gentlemen out. Dizzy fetch the doctor from Wycombe.'

He came into the church just as the baby gave her first cry. The Reverend Blagden stood looking down at his newborn daughter.

'What shall I do now? '

'Nothing. You did too much, nine months ago,' snapped Mary Anne.

Mary Anne visited the baby often while Disraeli played the Squire.

On November 19th 1856 Disraeli announced to the local newspaper, 'I have become chairman of a committee set up to establish the new Rural Police.'

The Disraelis then left immediately for Paris. Usually it was Mary Anne who suggested visits to France because funds were becoming low. This time Disraeli proposed an overseas visit. He needed to keep out of the way of his colleagues, especially Derby and the French Emperor who wished to make contact with the Leader of the Opposition.

Disraeli and Mary Anne dined out eleven nights in a row and on the twelfth night they were invited to dine at the Tuileries with the Emperor Napoleon and his beautiful Empress Eugénie. Mary Anne wore a dress of crushed strawberry satin and diamonds were woven through her hair and hung from her ears and around her neck. She moved her hands so the rings caught the light, flashing so everybody could see them.

They timed their entrance well. Heads nodded as they walked towards the Imperial couple. 'In English society, how difficult I would find this, even with Dizzy by my side, besides the French are not so unkind, so reserved as the English upper classes.'

Mary Anne saw the Emperor note Disraeli's little Imperial beard and smile. She saw him turn to his wife.

'How remarkably young and pretty Mrs Disraeli looks,' and seeing the look of jealousy in her eyes added, 'in the candlelight.'

These were old friends, who went back to the Emperor's long English exile, and in recognition of this friendship Mary Anne sat next to Napoleon and Disraeli on the right hand side of Empress Eugénie.

In the seeming intimacy, Mary Anne, ignoring the coughs and sneezes of Disraeli, told the story of how during her engagement to Disraeli the Emperor had almost drowned them both in the Thames.

'Do you remember, your Majesty, Bulwer had invited us all to breakfast at Craven cottage?'

Disraeli froze. Mary Anne gabbled on. 'You sir, rowed us on to a mud bank in mid-river. I told you to be careful and you ignored me. We were in constant danger of tipping out because of the swell from the steamboats.'

'Much to the amusement of their passengers,' added Disraeli desperately.

'And I cried out, 'Sir, you are a clumsy creature. You should not have tried to row, you are far too adventurous and should not undertake things you cannot accomplish.'

At that point Disraeli smiled into the eyes of the Empress.

'Your diamonds are like something out of Aladdin's cave.'

Mary Anne annoyed by Disraeli's interest in the Empress began to speak again, but the Emperor said quickly, 'But I managed not to drown you.'

'Did you have to admire her diamonds so, Dizzy?' asked Mary Anne as she removed her jewellery that night.

'Dearest,' replied Disraeli, 'the Emperor had just made two unsuccessful attempts on the throne of Louis Philippe.

They returned to the "little fog bound island" to try and cope with Disraeli's £60,000 debts, the shock of the Indian Mutiny and the death of Smythe.

23 Deaths in The Family

On June 13th 1857 Dr Cummings foretold, 'A mighty comet would devastate the earth.'

The Disraelis, like most of the population of London waited. 'The comet did nothing,' said Mary Anne disappointedly to Disraeli, but from then on she found her own immediate troubles easing, while Disraeli's world was gravely shaken.

In 1854 the Duke of Portland died. The Peelite, Marquess of Titchfield succeeded his father and as the 5th Duke, three years later, called in the Bentinck mortgage on Hughenden.

Mary Anne, when she heard the news, could not believe it. She left the terraces, not noticing the peacock fanning out his tail, walked along *Lovers' Walk* in a dream, through the German forest, to the lake where Disraeli was talking to Hero and Leander.

Mary asked, 'How could he do this to us, Dizzy? I thought all the Bentinck brothers were our friends.' The birds drifted downstream.

'Remember, Sir Baldwin, dearest, we are political animals. We have no friends, only each other.'

'Dizzy, Hughenden is a beautiful place and we are at home here. We are together against the world and the evil that lies beyond its gates. Without Hughenden you cannot hold office.'

'Do you think I don't know that and without Hughenden the debtors' prison beckons?'

Mary Anne clung to her husband realising it was not only his home which was being threatened but also the reason for his existence. As always Disraeli seemed so slight, so highly strung to her. She was the strong one and yet in a crisis it was Dizzy who proved to be the rock.

'Dizzy, how can we trust a recluse so odd he won't speak to his servants and puts his carriage on the train with drawn blinds.'

Disraeli arranged to talk to Lord Henry. On 30 April 1857. Lord Henry wrote to Disraeli: *'I am very jealous of the course that my brother may take with us re: Hughenden and as the blow may be sudden it may be as well that arrangements should be ready for the worst.'*

Lord Henry told Disraeli, 'I posted up to London the moment I became aware of it, went to the Jews and borrowed enough money to pay off sufficient of the debt to prevent the possibility of you being disturbed in the possession of Hughenden.

In November 1857, Disraeli was reading *The Morning Post* contemplating getting out of bed. He judged by the sound of the traffic in Park Lane it was midday. His eye caught an announcement, *'Lord Strangford, (Smythe) is postponing his marriage to Miss KinCaird Lennox in consequence of his illness.'*

'Do get up, Dizzy. It is midday and even George is up by eleven,' Mary Anne said poking her head round the door.

Disraeli snuggled back under the sheets saying with a smirk, 'I apprehend our George does not want to marry her unless he is sure of dying. He means the coronet for a legacy. God grant he may be spared to us, and not mar a future with any sentimental "tomfoolery."

Shortly afterwards Disraeli met Lyndhurst.

'Smythe is dead.'

'Dead,' repeated Disraeli.

Lyndhurst, old, wrinkled, disappointed repeated, 'Smythe is dead,' and with glee added, 'Just forty-one. He died a glorious failure …' He stumped off, oblivious to the distraught look on Disraeli's face.

Crowds passed by Disraeli, a girl picked his pocket, another offered him 'a good time, dearie.' He walked in a daze back to Grosvenor Gate. He did not continue on down Whitehall to Shepherd's Market. Here he took his chaise. The horse broke into a trot and then galloped off through streets of suburban villas. Disraeli quite forgot the MPs in the House, waiting for "old Dizzy" to speak. Suddenly, he realised they were in Buckinghamshire. Slowly the horse picked its way through winter stark beech trees, Disraeli rode on, crying out against the gloriousness of the setting sun.

'You there God, why does the old Pantaloon go on and on. George,' he called out. 'George,' he called out again but received no answer.

At Hughenden the horse took himself and the chaise into the stable yard, stopping and turned round for his piece of sugar but Disraeli was throwing his reins to the groom ...

Mary Anne heard the commotion, coming to the door with arms outstretched, saw Disraeli coatless, rushing in the gathering dusk to his father's obelisk.

'What's wrong with the master?' asked the groom.

'Let him be.'

Mary Anne waited a while and then put on her "planting clothes" picked up a trowel, pretending she was making her way back to the house.

He was standing ashen white before the obelisk. She touched his shoulder gently.

A peacock's shriek rent the air.

'Smythe is dead,' he cried out.

Mary Anne held him like a mother does her hurt child.

Again, the peacock cry rent the air.

Deep, deep down inside her she was glad, not that Smythe was dead but that he was gone out of their lives – for ever.

'The voice of the peacock is heard in the land,' said Disraeli. His will be like me a mere footnote to history ...'

'No, not, you my dear, not you.' And then briskly, 'Come along now. I need your advice. This morning we had the first severe frost. The garden is dead – help me so it comes alive in spring.'

Mary Anne also wanted James's wife to live. She was frightened of her brother-in-law's "irresponsibility." Shortly, before they left Hughenden to go to Torquay, a note was delivered by hand.

'My dear little wife died this morning. Our baby was not even properly formed and we had spent less than eight months together.'

Mary Anne thought of a night long ago, when she had seen a baby, not properly formed and her heart went out to James, alone in the farmhouse.

On their return from Torquay the couple went to Hughenden via the farm, with little gifts hoping, 'To give comfort to dear James.'

On their arrival, a longhaired mongrel leapt forward and a huge woman stood in the doorway, hands on hips, black and grey greasy hair falling down.

'Who might you be?'

'Please announce Mr and Mrs Disraeli have come to call on their grieving relation.'

The door shut.

'He's out.'

'Oh no he's not,' said Mary Anne firmly. 'He's in and I am going to see your kitchens.'

Disraeli muttered something about clarets.

'Drawing room, Dizzy. You, kitchens.'

'The name is Mrs Betty Bassett, widow.'

'I sincerely hope so,' said Mary Anne looking at the woman's enlarged stomach.

'You have taken against the woman rather unkindly, dearest,' observed Disraeli as they drove into Hughenden.

'Experience has taught me such women are dangerous, Dizzy.'

She was remembering the letter which arrived while James was courting Miss Cave, addressed to Disraeli.

'Mr James D'Israeli is fond of the aristocrace a scandal in High Life I would wonder how it would affect Mrs Disraeli to hear of it a delicate high minded woman...Sir will you not induce him to keep his promise as a gentleman ...'

Augusta Leigh (Mrs)

Mary Anne never showed the letter to Disraeli. He would have been shocked and done something about it. Now, she said, 'We must remember we are not quite respectable or really rich. We cannot afford to have our name besmirched by a scandal involving a servant.' Every time there was an odd caller at the door, Mary Anne expected to meet Mrs Leigh with a request for money.

Shortly after the visit, Mrs Bassett produced a daughter, followed a year later by another.

During this time, early May, the country rocked under the atrocities of the Indian Mutiny. Disraeli had seen it coming, so had the Prince Consort. Palmerston took it all lightly but the Queen wrote to the King of the Belgium: *'the horrors committed on the poor ladies, women and children – are inhuman in these ages, and make one's blood run cold ...'*

Disraeli told Mary Anne, 'The stories of atrocities are greatly exaggerated.'

However, Mary Anne recalled the tales told her by Sam and his friend on the Exeter Dockside by sailors about the carnage of the French Revolution.

The newspapers were full of meeting atrocity with atrocity. Many people, shaken by Darwin and a rapidly changing world, crept into a depression. Could there be a loving God, who could allow such evil as the tales told of the Crimea and the Mutiny?

Disraeli and Mary Anne did not. They felt that education would ease religion out of the human need for such superstition.

Shortly before Christmas 1857 the Queen wrote to Lord Canning in India.

'The Indian people should know that there is no hatred to a brown skin, none; but the greatest wish on part of the Queen is to see them happy, contented, and flourishing.'

Mary Anne brought up directly in the country on a farm had no doubt of the bestiality of nature but, 'I owe my happy disposition to my childhood, never having been thwarted, never made unhappy … I am fortunate, therefore, to be able to withstand the horrors of this world.'

It was fortunate for Disraeli too for Mary Anne's "happy disposition" counterbalanced his Jewish melancholia.

The following year saw Disraeli briefly, Chancellor of the Exchequer, for the second time,

However, during 1858 Disraeli was again out of office but with a government pension of £2,000 a year. He fretted here, he fretted there and so got under Mary Anne's skin that she complained to her sister-in-law. Sa replied in a letter:

'Remember what great things you have seen, and that we have never known dear Dis experience a disappointment, or more than a disappointment, but that it has proved the very step to greater eminence – nor can we one moment doubt but this will prove so – the pear is not yet ripe.'

The 'pear' thought Mary Anne is fifty-four.

That summer became unbearably hot. In September Sa paid her annual visit to Hughenden and Mary Anne noticed and remarked, 'Dear Sa, how thin you have become.'

'It is the heat which has weakened me.'

After a month at Hughenden Sa returned to Twickenham and shortly afterwards Mary Anne received a summons to go to Sa. On her arrival she sent immediately for Disraeli.

On the particularly cold night of 19 December Sa passed away. That evening Disraeli wrote to Ralph:

'I have had a sleepless night and so have you. Language cannot describe what the sudden and by me never contemplated catastrophe has produced on me. She was the harbour of refuge of all the storms of my life, and I hoped she would close my eyes.'

At Christmas, Disraeli, James and Ralph buried the first of their siblings to die, in the new cemetery at Willesden away from the fear of grave robbers.

Disraeli looking down at the grave heard Sa saying as she did so often, *your career, is the only thing in my life which has never disappointed me.* 'It is a good thing she cannot see me now,' Disraeli told Mary Anne who herself was mourning the loss of an illusion – his sister was closer to Dizzy than she would ever be.

Life continued on. "The Old Pantaloon" formed yet another Government.

In 1860 the American Civil War caused a diversion.

In January 1861 the Leader of Her Majesty's Opposition and his wife received an invitation from Windsor Castle to spend two nights with the Royal couple.

'*It is Mrs Disraeli's first visit to Windsor*,' Disraeli wrote proudly to Mrs Brydges Willyams, *'and it is considered very marked on the part of Her Majesty to invite the wife of the Leader of the Opposition when many Cabinet Ministers have been asked there without their wives.'*

The ladies, after dinner, gathered around the Queen, waiting for the gentlemen. The Queen made small talk to each lady, 'And you Mrs Disraeli, how long have you been married?'

'I have been happily married to Mr Disraeli for twenty-two years, ma'am.'

'A happy marriage is a great gift from God, as I, of course, have reason to know.'

'And I too, ma'am. I thank God at the end of the day Mr Disraeli and I sleep with our arms around each other every night.'

Conversation stopped. The Queen glanced at her ladies.

'As so do we,' she said gently.

At dinner parties Mary Anne was surprised to hear, Disraeli telling friends, with something like relief, 'Her Majesty is a most gracious hostess and the Prince Consort possesses the most richly cultivated mind we have ever met.'

The November of 1861 saw a tragedy for Victoria which would enable Disraeli to climb to the top of his greasy pole. Gossip travelled fast from Windsor to Buckinghamshire, and remarkably fast to Mary Anne. She learned the Prince Consort, feeling unwell, travelled by train to Cambridge, to rescue The Prince of Wales from some scrape with an actress Albert returned worn out and wearied but still continued with his duties.

Mary Anne heard from a lady-in-waiting that the Queen did not know where his illness could come from. 'She went to her room feeling as if her heart must break.'

It became common knowledge the Prince Consort was dying in Windsor Castle.

24 Death and Restoration

Throughout November 1861 heavy rains swept through Buckinghamshire announcing the beginning of winter. Mary Anne watched the rains slash against the mullioned windows of Hughenden.

Midday, 15 December, a horseman galloped into the Manor grounds. 'Message for Mr Disraeli. Prince Albert is dead.'

Disraeli handed a letter to the messenger. 'Deliver immediately into the hands of the Queen's own Private Secretary – No other.'

'Dizzy, the man is not yet cold.'

'Quite so, and my condolences will be among the first the Queen will receive.'

'It is a good job, Dizzy, you are married.'

'Is it not, dearest?'

They smiled at each other and neither spoke a word.

'Sometimes, you are not quite a gentleman, Dizzy.'

'Not quite,' he agreed as he kissed her hand.

Disraeli was not a cynic, later he told Count Vitzum, the Saxon Minister, 'This German Prince has governed England for twenty-one years with a wisdom and energy such as none of our "old stagers" would have given us, while retaining our constitutional guarantees, the blessings of absolute government.'

Disraeli's letter caused the Queen to sob and call for Mary Anne and Disraeli and to say to her, 'You cannot tell how forlorn, I feel.'

'I did not know where to turn for love, ma'am, when my first husband died.' They both looked up at Disraeli. 'Dizzy, married me for my money and now he would do so for love.'

Disraeli smiled and bowed.

The Queen's mind for once was taken off her great loss to wonder about the nature of the Disraelis' relationship.

Disraeli gained the Queen's approval by advocating a memorial to Albert's blessed memory. 'It should, as it were, represent the character of the Prince himself in the harmony of proportions, in the beauty of its ornaments, and its enduring nature.'

Listening Members of Parliament were most impressed.

Immediately Disraeli had finished the speech he delivered a copy, already prepared in his own hand, into the hands of the Queen's astonished private secretary.

Mary Anne, who had no idea that Disraeli had delivered his speech, was surprised to find a messenger from the Royal household standing on her doorstep, 'Urgent parcel, ma'am.'

'To the Right Honourable Benjamin Disraeli. In recollection of the greatest and best of men from the Prince's broken-hearted widow. Victoria R.'

Mary Anne was so overcome she curtsied to the messenger who stuttered, 'Told to tell you, ma'am, the Queen herself has responded by return messenger.'

The numerous white Morocco leather volumes were piled high in the hallway.

'What are those dearest?' asked Disraeli.

'A thank you present from the Queen,' said Mary Anne maliciously.

Disraeli looked at her warily.

'Prince Albert's speeches,' said Mary Anne.

'All of them?' asked Disraeli.

'Every single one.'

'And she will know them word for word …' stuttered Disraeli.

'Indeed, she will dearest,' and Mary Anne handed him the top volume.

While Disraeli prepared to cope with a grieving Queen, Mary Anne wrote to Mrs Brydges Willyams to enquire after her health.

February 1862

'Do take care. It is perilous to experiment, I think, we older people have few real friends, I fear.'

Mary Anne received he following reply:

'Thank you for your enquiry Mrs Disraeli, but I have no intention of becoming weaker. Nobody need die before 100 provided they take care of themselves and avoid doctors.'

Sarah Brydges Willyams

Despite her strong words in the autumn when the Disraelis met Mrs Brydges Willyams she appeared frailer, even vulnerable. She was thinner, her skin paper-thin and she leant heavily on her stick. She rebutted any suggestion that her last bout of illness had weakened her. *'I am, of course, recovering strongly from my last bout of illness, so annoying.'*

Early in December Disraeli received a letter from Mrs Brydges Willyams's vicar, The Reverend W.G. Parks Smith, dated 3 December.

'She appears, however, very uncomfortably situated in not having any friend, nor even one servant in the house in whom she can repose any confidence and consequently requested me to recommend some trustworthy person to take care of herself and the servants ... I could obtain immediately the services of a sister of mercy but Mrs Brydges Willyams would perhaps object to have such a lady in the house. What think you?'

Despite, Mr Parks Smith's entreaties, Mrs Brydges Willyams fought death, but in 1863 death won.

The will stated *'...in testimony of my affection and in appropriation and admiration of his efforts to vindicate the race of Israel with my views respecting which he is acquainted, and which I have no doubt he will endeavour to accomplish.'*

It had been a long fight for Disraeli and with gratitude he said to Mary Anne, 'Our kind and faithful friend has never swerved from her purpose. She has freed us from most of the heavy load we have carried for so many years. We are at last comfortable. The residue of her estate somewhat exceeds £30,000.'

'Yes,' said Mary Anne. 'She has freed us.' Privately she felt with Sa gone and Mrs Brydges Willyams no more, who could he talk to, but she continued saying, 'Her memorial must be here at Hughenden. Now we can enlarge Hughenden. We need more space here to entertain, but it is too late to decorate it entirely to our taste, the world is moving on Dizzy. Today's *Times* says a railway is being built in London to carry people – underground? We are becoming old, Dizzy.'

Disraeli looked quite startled at the idea.

A day later, Disraeli received a message from Sir Philip to visit him in his offices. 'It will give us a change to visit Mr Lamb and discuss the restoration of Hughenden to its former glory,' said Mary Anne, who had numerous drawings, patterns and colour schemes, hatching in her handbag.

Unfortunately, the Disraelis had not read the will carefully enough.

'I leave my body to the care of Mr Benjamin Disraeli, to bury it inside the little church at Hughenden.'

The couple were so agitated that they pushed back their chairs and rushed to the door ignoring Sir Philip's advice.

'I wish you would consider whether some paragraph might not be advantageously put in the newspapers alluding to the bequest and the grounds for it. These things are catching and the great probability is that the example would be followed if properly known.'

In life, Mrs Brydges Willyams never visited Hughenden, in death she did. On their arrival, they found her outside the entrance, with an agitated Charles pointing to the funeral hearse, 'The undertakers say the corpse is ours.'

The new vicar, Reverend Chubb, a pedantic little man was summoned. 'The Interment Act forbids the burial of bodies inside churches, now had the dear lady died sooner …'

Mary Anne stood on one side of the hearse, Disraeli on the other. The horse remained neutral.

'I wish, Dizzy, just sometimes you would just listen to the Acts, which you are passing …'

Disraeli whispered, 'We will be buried where we can be protected against the body-snatchers.'

Mrs Brydges Willyams was laid to rest in the new Disraeli family vault under the East wing of the little church. In the spring of 1864 Mary Anne, who had visited most of the great houses of England, began restoring Hughenden and the white stucco of the building was removed from all three storeys to reveal the original red brickwork.

Disraeli hung in the Tudor styled panelled hall a Gallery of Friendship, portraits of all the men he had known and admired, Smythe, Lyndhurst, D'Orsay, and Bulwer.

Mary Anne asked, 'What is Byron doing here?'

'He was my role model, dearest.'

Mary Anne, who did not wish Disraeli's youthful infatuations, glamour and pennilessness to be remembered, hung Byron in the shadows. The kindly charcoal sketch of Sa was placed in a comfortable corner and in moments of "Dizzystress" Mary Anne gazed at the Channon's pastel, of a delightful cherub some eighteen months of age. Disraeli continually hid it in the shadows. Next to Smythe's portrait he hung a great empty mahogany frame, hanging over the drawing room fireplace. Shortly, after Mary Anne's death a copy of the miniature by Ross was placed in the frame.

'She would have no portrait of herself,' Disraeli explained.

Mary Anne, with the example of the Great Exhibition, before her eyes, Gothised the interior panelled hall and vestibule-porch lined with ferns. The drawing room became a "wonderful hideous place" its high walls covered in dark green paper dotted with fleur-de-lys – great panelled frames awaited portraits and next to it the library – Disraeli's favourite place.

But it was a house without "provenance." A place owned by two people with no background for the great frames contained no portraits of ancestors, nor busts of eminent people.

In the evenings Mary Anne worked at tapestry coverings for the public rooms. 'Perhaps,' suggested Disraeli, 'we do not need quite so many flowers, beech-leaves etc.'

'They must match the carpets, the curtains and the wall-coverings, dearest. We do like a bright house do we not?'

Disraeli shrugged. Mary Anne did not notice their illustrious guests shuddering, looking at Disraeli with embarrassment and pity.

She did not see the amused glances of her friends when she stood before the grandfather clock as it struck 10.30 and called out, 'Now I am shooing you all off to bed, an hour before midnight is worth three hours after …'

Mary Anne escorted the ladies upstairs to their beds but sometimes in the mornings champagne bottles, claret bottles and port bottles lay scattered around. The odd cigar butt still burnt away. Disraeli slept upstairs, usually rising at noon.

'I do not dare question him what goes on or doesn't go on,' Mary Anne confided to Lady Rothschild.

Visitors, were amazed to find each time they visited Hughenden, extra delights, vases from Florence planted with acanthus lilies and crimson and blue geraniums on the terraces, and hidden amongst the moss in the beech woods, violets.

'Violets,' Disraeli told his wife, 'are inseparably entwined in the scent and thought of you.'

A Japanese cherry showed its blossoms and delicately climbed against the newly restored mid-Victorian Gothic redbrick house, with battlements and a cloistered stable yard.

On 9 June Disraeli wrote to his friend Lord Beauchamp. *'We have realised a romance we have talked of for many years, for we have restored the place to what it was before the Civil War and have made a garden of terraces in which Cavaliers might wander with their lady loves.'*

In the evenings Disraeli in sugar loaf hat and black coat, wandered with his own lady love dressed in pastels, unsuitable for "a lady of her years" but they wandered like a courting couple through the grounds, hand in hand, often, stopping to talk to woodcutters or workmen.

Once walking through the woods, Disraeli asked an old man, 'Why, George you look much more content these days.'

'I am indeed, sir.'

'And why is that?'

'Well I've found the answer to a happy marriage.'

'Ah, and what is the secret?'

'The wife died sir, and I've married Bess, the barmaid, young enough to be my daughter.'

Giggling the couple returned to the house. Disraeli laid Mary Anne's pearls on the terrace, close to the pergola, and sipped sherry until nightfall, caressing his wife all the time, even before the servants. But they were to attend a wedding which did not result in a happy marriage.

25 A Royal Wedding

Out of office Disraeli and Mary Anne were going to the wedding of the century. The marriage of the Albert Edward Prince of Wales to the sea king's daughter, Princess Alexandra of Denmark, whose face Disraeli said had 'a particular repose.'

Places in St George's Chapel, Windsor, were limited. Four places remained for the Queen's personal friends, two of which were taken by the Disraelis. Mary Anne enjoyed the rage and indignation of the great world. 'The Duchess of Marlborough went into hysterics at the sight of me ... and said it was really shameful after the reception the Duke had given the Prince of Wales at Blenheim; and as for the Duchess of Manchester, who had been Mistress of the Robes in Lord Derby's administration, she positively passed me for the season without recognition.'

The young couple's joyous festival was held amongst glittering dresses, torn, filthy, blooded regimental flags, magnificent music, all deeply interesting or effective and the brooding presence of the Prince Consort was ever present, and the little Queen in her widowed garments in her Gothic cabinet, sat planning his black marble memorial, to dominate the chapel – for ever.

'Mr Disraeli is the only person to fully appreciate the Prince's great qualities...' the Queen had said, but she would not allow liberties, even from Disraeli. She caught him staring through his eyeglass at her.

'I did not venture to use my glass again, perhaps she was looking to see whether we were there ...'

When the wedding was over there was a rush for the 4.15 train to Paddington. It was remarkably small.

The Archbishop of Canterbury sat in a third class compartment, telling Mrs Archbishop, 'The meek shall inherit the earth.'

The Duchess of Westminster, wearing a million pounds worth of jewels joined them.

Several ladies of fashion wearing "balloon style crinolines" detached themselves from their husbands and found themselves in carriage No.3 with the Disraelis. When sitting, the hoops telescoped at the back, rising slightly at the sides, and as more ladies climbed into the carriage it became overcrowded and the dresses rose up to reveal under things.

Pandemonium broke out.

'Oh Lady Somerville to your right please, perhaps if the Honourable Augusta could ... Mrs Smythe Talbot ... Oh dear me ...'

Disraeli's pale face became pinker and pinker.

'Most unbecoming,' thought Mary Anne and suddenly exclaimed, 'sit Dizzy, do.'

She pulled him down on to her knee, where he perched all the way into London, looking straight ahead of him, clutching his umbrella.

26 Illness

In the late autumn 1867 the Disraelis could be seen on the train going from Windsor as it chugged its way up through the tinted mists of lowland Scotland. Here and there a wild bullock raised its head and bellowed its dislike of the approaching iron animal. An elderly gentleman poked his head out of the window and declared he still could not see Edinburgh.

The passenger travelling with them thought that the gentleman was a provincial solicitor with his wife, until the lady said in a Devonshire accent, 'I shall tell them, Dizzy, the shawl was a present from the Queen.'

The little woman pulled a brightly coloured tartan shawl around her shoulders and the elderly gentleman began to rehearse a speech. The other passenger, listening from behind *The Times*, realised his companion was journeying to Edinburgh to be offered an honorary doctorate of the University. When they steamed into the station, the carriage door swung open and the strange couple were surrounded by city elders, notable Tories, and the historian Sir William Stirling-Maxwell; velvet gloves sparkling with whiteness, shook hands with Mr and Mrs Disraeli and voices cried, 'Welcome to Scotland.'

A grand banquet, of course, must be held before such ceremonies. Most of Scottish society was keen to attend except the Duke of Buccleuch, but as Mary Anne said, 'We can manage without him.' This comment was immediately reported back to His Grace.

Mary Anne entered the University's great hall, gold banded chandeliers bearing candles hung from the timbered ceiling, solemn faces glared out from thick gilt frames, the walls were made heavy with dark oak panelling. Mary Anne tired from the journey disliked the gaunt masculinity of her surroundings, 'So different from the French Court.'

Dizzy seemed oblivious to everything and would keep saying, *England* when he should have said Great Britain.

Huge red-bearded men smiled at her. Mary Anne found

their kilts disconcerting and red knees embarrassing. She could hardly understand a word they said. Every time she glanced around her, her eye caught those of a long dead angry stag. Mary Anne's only comfort was that the other women's dresses were slightly out of date and her own bright crimson velvet tunic with Disraeli's miniature pinned high on her left breast, like a military decoration, caused no remarks.

'Oh Kok, is it you?' she asked with relief struggling to the top table, the shriek of bagpipes constantly in her ears and a drummer leading the way, throwing sticks up in the air and hopefully catching them and on a silver platter, carried with great reverence, the horrible haggis ... Oh thank goodness, dear Kok was sitting on the top table too.

A very long Presbyterian grace commenced. Disraeli looked bored. Mary Anne tried appearing devout to cover up for her husband. Later Disraeli described the occasion to the MP Sir John Skelton. He was fascinated by Disraeli describing himself as he appeared then ... "*And the potent wizard himself, with his olive complexion and coal black eyes, and the mighty dome of his forehead (no Christian temple, to be sure). The face is more like a mask than ever ... I would as soon have thought of sitting down at table with Hamlet, or Lear or the Wandering Jew.'*

As they drank "a dram" at the end of the meal Kok proposed the health, not of Disraeli, but Mary Anne saying, 'I know personally of the support and sympathy Mrs Disraeli has always given her husband regardless of herself.'

Mary Anne moved a candlestick in front of her so nobody could see the tears in her eyes. Disraeli gave a quick glance and replied for her.

His coal-black eyes looked deeply into her eyes. 'I do owe to that lady all, I think, that I have ever accomplished because she has supported me by her counsel and consoled me by the sweetness of her mind and disposition. You cannot please me more than by paying this compliment to my wife.'

On their return Norah Rooke told Hortense, to take master and mistress 'a little warm milk' She added a touch of whisky to help them sleep and recover from such a long journey.

From within the room could be heard the oddest noises.

Warily, Hortense opened the door to see master in his nightshirt jigging on the bed, while mistress danced around the room, whistling a hornpipe and waving her red nightcap in the air.

'Oh, the Scots were so kind to us, my dear,' they explained fanning the parlour maid back into life.

A few days later, Mary Anne entered the waiting rooms of the Royal Physician, Sir William Gull.

Precisely, on the stroke of eleven, a voice said. 'Sir William will see you now, madam.'

She walked into the room. Sir William, kindly, elderly, portly, pulled out a chair for her.

He sat opposite her. 'Now, my dear Mrs Disraeli, what is the trouble?'

'I am suffering from chronic dyspepsia …'

She had asked Norah Rooke for her comment, who had turned away quickly.

Now the doctor did the same.

He drummed his fingers on the desktop which got on her nerves.

'How long?'

'A year.'

The examination was over.

'The truth, Sir William.'

'I think you know it.'

'How long?'

'You have enjoyed your three score years and ten.'

'How long?'

'I cannot answer that – only God.'

Early the next morning Mary Anne fled to Hughenden and now it was Disraeli who found his wife gazing at Isaac's memorial. He saw, in the dying sunset, her rouge standing out like birthmarks, against the dying whiteness of her skin.

In that moment Disraeli understood the nature of the disease within her. He took her into his arms trying to comfort her for he understood the hurt the gods were causing her – her growing stomach carried not a new life – but a cancer taking his Mary Anne to her death.

As her pain increased Mary Anne's oddities became odder. Young society giggled behind its fans not aware how the eyes and ears of Victoria saw all, heard all.

The Queen invited Mary Anne to take luncheon with her at Windsor and looking hard at her ladies-in-waiting commanded them, 'Ladies, you will let everybody know Mrs Disraeli is a particular friend of the Queen.'

After that nobody dared mock Mary Anne.

In the House, Gladstone referred sympathetically to Mrs Disraeli's illness. The House offered its sympathy. Disraeli told Mary Anne, 'I could hardly respond I was so near to tears.'

Soon after this, Disraeli fell ill with gout. He could not visit his wife so he sent letters to her sickroom. Mary Anne wrapped them up neatly and labelled them: *'Notes from dear Dizzy during our illness when we could not leave our rooms.'*

27 Prime Minister at last

Before attending the 14th Earl of Derby's funeral Disraeli told Mary Anne, 'Rumour says it took Derby to be on his deathbed before he cracked a joke.'

'How do you feel my Lord?' enquired his doctors.

'Bored to extinction.'

As the coffin arrived, Disraeli nudged Mary Anne in the ribs, 'Bored to extinction.'

Disraeli could enjoy the joke, for Derby's last political moments were addressed to Disraeli.

Disraeli was so overcome by Derby's suggestion that he took his handkerchief to his eyes, and blew his nose loudly.

'I have never contemplated nor desired the role of Prime Minister, my Lord.'

Mary Anne, watching Disraeli, pacing the floor observed acidly, 'I hope they have not taken you at your word, Dizzy.' Luckily, they had not.

On 26 February 1868, Disraeli sat down, as a man forced by circumstance, to write to his Queen.

'Your Majesty's life has been passed in constant communion with great men, and the acknowledgement and management of important transactions. Even if your Majesty were not gifted with those great abilities, which all must now acknowledge, this rare and choice experience must give your Majesty an advantage in judgement which few living persons, and probably no living Prince, can rival.'

'The new man will do,' said the Queen.

Prior to retiring, the new Lord Derby wrote to Disraeli on 28 February:

'Let me beg of you to offer my congratulations to Mrs Disraeli upon your having attained a post your pre-eminent fitness for which she will not be inclined to dispute.'

All eyes, including Mary Anne's, were on Disraeli.

On a rainy, grey icy February 25 Mary Anne waited in a carriage outside the House listening to the crowds whispering, 'The Old Jew is going to be prime minister.'

Inside the House, the Speaker announced, 'The new Prime Minister – The Rt. Honourable Benjamin Disraeli, MP for Buckinghamshire.

The next day February 26 the Queen wrote to her daughter, Victoria, Albert's favourite child.

'It is a proud thing for a man " risen from the people" – to have obtained! And I must say – really most loyally; it is his real talent, his good temper and the way in which he managed the Reform Bill last year – which have brought this about ...'

'Dear Lennox brought me this,' said Disraeli smiling, handing Mary Anne a copy of the letter.

'How did he get it?' asked a mystified Mary Anne. 'Really, Dizzy, one day you really will go too far.'

Mr Gladstone, happily, did not know Victoria's view of Disraeli. If he had he would not have taken another piece of plum fruit cake, or put quite so much sugar into his cup when taking tea with "Dear Mrs Dizzy."

Gladstone told Mary Anne how Disraeli left the House on 27th February. 'Congratulatory cheers rang in his ears. Disraeli really is a great actor.'

He stood for a moment bareheaded and while they gathered around him he gazed out over London and then he turned to old William White, our doorkeeper, 'One day you will listen to me.'

'They did Prime Minister, oh yes, how they have.'

Lord Ashley said, 'If only your sister could see you.'

'Ah, poor Sa, she was my audience.'

'Disraeli was in a dream, ma'am. It was William White, who brought him back to reality.'

'Hurry, sir, A special boat is waiting for you, to carry you across the Solent, the Queen is waiting.'

Then Disraeli was gone into the gathering sunset, his carriage sweeping him across Westminster Bridge, passing St Thomas' hospital on to Waterloo Station. He was going away from the past into history. Disraeli boarded the Portsmouth train which pulled out immediately.

When Gladstone had left Mary Anne wrote: *'Dear Lady de Rothschild, By the time this reaches you Dizzy will be Prime Minister of England.'*

Meanwhile Disraeli was bowing low over the Royal hand.

'In loving loyalty and faith, ma'am.'

Disraeli clasped in both of his hands the tiny hand extended before him.

'Please, Mr Disraeli,' said the Queen trying to withdraw her hand.

He left the "presence" walking backwards, bowing and nodding, muttering, 'Majesty, Majesty, Majesty.'

The Queen nodded and smiled, occasionally averting her eyes left, praying, 'I do hope Mr Disraeli makes the doorway.'

The next morning Mary Anne received a hastily written note:

'It is all that I could wish and hope ... I was with the Queen an hour yesterday. Will tell all ...'

Shortly afterwards Lennox reported to Disraeli a conversation he happened to overhear between the Queen and one of her ladies-in-waiting.

'Mr Disraeli is very peculiar, but very clever and sensible and very conciliatory,' observed the Queen. 'I do hope he doesn't bow all the time. It's very disconcerting.'

On 1 March, Disraeli gave a list of his cabinet to Mary Anne which included three Dukes, Marlborough, Richmond and Buckingham and two Earls, Malmesbury and Mayo.

On 5 March Mary Anne entered the Ladies' Gallery. She stood looking down, remembering her earlier words, 'I shall not enter this place again until he is Prime Minister.' He was. Several of the gentlemen raised their hats to her and she waited ... a lone little woman, rather like the widow of Windsor waiting. At twenty minutes past four, Mary Anne saw her husband walk into the Chamber uneasily – rather like a cat on broken glass. From time to time Disraeli glanced up to Mary Anne, she nodded, to him, smiling encouragingly, like a mother would to a brilliant only son.

William White, commenting on the occasion said, 'Unlike, Mrs Gladstone, Mrs Disraeli does not come to the House often to hear her husband speak. Hers is too practical a spirit to haunt anywhere.'

There are no reports of Mary Anne's spirit returning, but the ghost of Mrs Gladstone, sits, waiting for her William to address the House. She polishes the brass rail, in front of her to such a shine that it remains in shine – even now.

At the end of March, Mary Anne marched into 10 Downing Street and marched straight out again. 'It's too dingy, Monty,' she told Disraeli's secretary.

'It is the custom, Mrs Disraeli,' Monty stuttered.

'Come along, dear do.' Mary Anne took Corry's arm and walked into King Charles Street straight into the new Foreign Office,

'Ah, Foreign Secretary, these rooms are just right for a Prime Minister's Reception.'

The Foreign Secretary burbled, 'Where do I go?'

'Anywhere, but here, sir.'

Special instructions were printed for 'regulations for carriages with company going to Mrs Disraeli's reception.'

On the evening of the reception, it rained, it hailed, it sleeted and was unbelievably cold for 25 March. Under the archway of the new Foreign Office, the hoi polloi poked fun at their betters,

'Cor, I bet you're cold, Missus.'

Dukes, duchesses, ambassadors, bishops, and even the Gladstones, alighted from carriages to jump over puddles, shivering in the barest shoulders, bare arms with diminutive puff sleeves and goose pimples covered up by diamonds.

'That way for Mrs Disraeli's reception,' said the hoi polloi warmly wrapped in numerous scarves, eating hot-chestnuts out of heavily mittened hands. They gave a special cheer for the Prince and Princess of Wales who muttered something about, 'Dear Mrs Dizzy.'

Inside Mary Anne offered hot soup, along with champagne, tables groaning with dishes and everybody forgot how cold they were.

But Bishop 'Soapy Sam Wilberforce' who constantly reminded everyone that, 'Father was the great reformer,' noted in his journal:

' It all looks to me as if England's "Mene, Mene" were written on our walls.'

Those who looked carefully saw how haggard Mary Anne had become trying to hide her appearance, 'With perhaps too generous a touch of the hare's foot, too many curls, a lavish display of new diamonds and a new organdie satin gown with layers and layers of flounces.'

During the brief time Disraeli was Prime Minister, he discussed his wonderful letters to the Queen with Mary Anne. 'Make sure, Dizzy, that your reports read like a novel, give her every bit of political news and every scrap of social gossip.'

'She is a Queen,' said Disraeli.

'She is a woman,' retorted Mary Anne.

When the Queen sent Disraeli leaves from *The Journal of our Life in the Highlands* he was sincerely touched. He thanked the Queen for her graciousness and included in his reply, *'We authors, ma'am.'*

'Before Mr Disraeli joined us I knew nothing, Mrs Disraeli,' the Queen told Mary Anne.

By late autumn the Government was in trouble over the Irish Question. Disraeli's term of Prime Minister ended in the December and the Queen faced the "stern handsome features of Mr Gladstone."

'Pet her a little,' advised his wife.

Gladstone looked at the Queen. He began to speak. Her look made him freeze. He began addressing her as a public monument. She became once more a recluse. The Buckingham Palace soirées, the inspection of troops in Hyde Park ended and Mrs Disraeli's faux pas hardly happened at all.

The Queen told her daughter Victoria, 'Mr Disraeli and Mrs Dizzy came to dinner. We discussed whiteness of skin and Mrs Dizzy said that if you want to see white skin ma'am, you should see my Dizzy in his bath. I said I would love to see Mr Disraeli in his bath. Poor Mr Disraeli looked quite shocked. I suppose Mr Gladstone would have had a heart-attack ...'

Shortly, after Disraeli resigned, James died.

Mrs Bassett whose husband had forsaken her wrote to the Disraelis saying: *I am now in desperate straits. As you know, James, was my children's father.'*

At the request of Mary Anne, Disraeli instructed Sir Philip to send Mrs Bassett money. She continued to harass Disraeli for money.

He did not reply to her letters.

28 Honoured

Mary Anne did not know for a very long time the reason she became a Viscountess. Actually, it was Gladstone who told her the full story. He was, of course a close friend of General Grey.

The General was scratching away with his quill when he heard the door open. At first he was annoyed that the entrant did not knock and then he knocked the ink over as he pushed back his chair and bowed low.

'Your Majesty,' he stuttered trying surreptitiously to wipe up the ink creeping across the table and moving towards dripping onto the carpet. Her Majesty watched. She was always aware of costs.

'I am agitated, General Grey … you have no idea how much.'

The Queen held in her pudgy little hands a letter. Her private secretary saw with dismay that the writing was Disraeli's. He read it with increasing alarm:

'...next to your Majesty there is one to whom he owes everything, and who has looked forward to this period of their long united lives as one of comparative repose and of recognized honour. Might Mr Disraeli, therefore, after 31 years of Parliamentary toil, and after having served your Majesty on more than one occasion, if not with prolonged success at least with unfaltering devotion, humbly solicit your Majesty to grant those honours to his wife which perhaps under ordinary circumstances your Majesty would have deigned to bestow on him?

It would be an entire reward to him, and would give spirit and cheerfulness to the remainder of his public life, when he should be quite content to be your Majesty's servant if not your Majesty's Minister …'

General Grey looked up at the Queen. Does one ask a Queen to sit in one's office? Her Majesty was looking around her. A pug slept in the chintz- covered armchair. There was the small gilded stool which rocked on attention and a collapsing horsehair sofa with leather patches on its arms which if one sat in it one disappeared from view.

The Queen remained standing. General Grey continued to read.

'Mr Disraeli is ashamed to trouble your Majesty on such personal matters, but he has confidence in your Majesty's gracious indulgence and in some condescending sympathy on your Majesty's part with the feelings which prompt this letter.

Mrs Disraeli has a fortune of her own adequate to any position in which your Majesty might deign to place her. Might her husband then hope that your Majesty would be graciously pleased to create her Viscountess Beaconsfield, a town with which Mr Disraeli has been long connected and which is the nearest town to his estate in Bucks which is not yet ennobled?'

Disraeli cited precedents: Baroness Chatham, wife of the elder Pitt and Baroness Stratheden, wife of John Campbell.

General Grey said quickly, 'Mr Disraeli's enemies may say to grant his request would mean, of course that Mr Disraeli could remain in the Lower House.'

The Queen's lips pursed. She had the expression of a sulky child. 'I am sure the thought has not entered into Mr Disraeli's mind.'

'Quite so, your Majesty,' murmured General Grey. 'I am sure Mr Disraeli, as always, is putting another before his own interests, but Mrs Disraeli has done no political service as such, ma'am. As you yourself have often remarked, Mrs Disraeli's oddities are becoming odder and odder.'

'Her jokes, General Grey.'

'Her clothes, ma'am.'

The Queen leant forward confidentially. He could smell lavender water.

'I must admit, between these walls only, one shudders at the thought ... Mrs Disraeli, Viscountess Beaconsfield.'

The Queen and her Private Secretary remained silent for some ten minutes, occasionally, they glanced below into the courtyard where red-coated guardsmen shouted orders at one another and horses' hooves echoed on cobblestones. The pug woke up. Castle Gate remained silent and impersonal.

'Do you think, General Grey?' the Queen asked hesitantly, 'that the dreadful story concerning the Queen, now circulating around London, could emanate from Mrs Disraeli?'

'Mr Disraeli denies it, ma'am.'

The Queen looked sharply at General Grey. He was trying to suppress a giggle.

'It has, I must admit, all the hallmarks of Mrs Disraeli's humour.'

'It is no comfort to one for the Prince of Wales to keep saying, 'Mama if it had been anyone else you would have roared with laughter …'

'Quite so, ma'am. The Queen's Majesty is offended.'

In the ale-houses and market places Her Majesty's subjects were laughing at her, but thought General Grey they laughed very kindly. His wife was a lady-in-waiting. He must remind her to tell the Queen that the people chuckled gently.

'Have you heard?' they asked one other, 'The Queen visiting up north, was greeted by a brass band.'

'What is the name of the delightful tune being played?' the old girl asked.

The bandmaster told her, 'Why it's a local melody, ma'am, been sung for years up here *Come Where The Booze Is Cheaper.*'

General Grey suppressed another giggle.

'I would not like to offend such a dear, dear friend as Mr Disraeli,' observed the Queen.

'Indeed not, ma'am. How many times has he spat out "Gratitude" when his enemies have laughed at his wife? If Mr Disraeli wished, ma'am, he would make a bad enemy.'

'Yes, as reason General you have to know. He has never forgiven you for beating him at an election … all those years ago.'

'I played it fair, Your Majesty.'

'That my dear Private Secretary was the unforgivable sin on your part.'

General Grey shuddered slightly at the sharpness of the Queen's tone and she continued speaking more gently. 'Is the decision entirely a matter for the Queen's judgement and solely her responsibility?'

General Grey nodded.

'The Queen will discuss the matter with Prince Albert. As you know the Queen has an audience with the Danish ambassador in the morning. When you bring the necessary papers for discussion the Queen will give you our answer then.'

General Grey bowed low. The pug escorted the Queen to the door.

Victoria was already in the Audience Chamber when General Grey arrived. He told Gladstone later that Mr Matthew Cotes Wyatt's pictures on the ceiling of St George slaying the dragon reminded him horribly of Mr Disraeli.

General Grey is recorded by history as a precise Civil Servant.

He bowed to the Queen.

'May I take this opportunity, ma'am, to give you this.' He wished to have on record, in case of attack by Disraeli, his recommendation to the Queen.

'On the whole though with much doubt and diffidence, I am inclined to think, your Majesty would be better to comply with his wishes than to refuse them and would venture to advise your Majesty to follow the dictates of your Majesty's own kind heart.'

'Prince Albert agrees with you,' said the Queen.

As General Grey returned to his own office he looked into the unseeing, unblinking and staring eyes of a marble bust of the Prince Consort. He saluted saying, 'Thank goodness sir. It was your decision, not mine.'

Several hours later Disraeli received a letter from Windsor Castle:

'*November 24:* '*The Queen can truly sympathise with his devotion to Mrs Disraeli, who in her turn is so deeply attached to him, and she hopes they may yet enjoy many years of happiness together.*'

Disraeli folded the paper and with a satisfied smile placed it in the secret drawer of his desk which Mary Anne read fifteen minutes later.

A few weeks later Mrs Disraeli feigned surprise when she learned she was to be Viscountess Beaconsfield and removed the smug smile from Disraeli's face with the comment, 'I think it only right and proper of the Queen.'

Disraeli removed his waistcoat from his wife's plunging needle, 'Not the dishcloths, dearest, not done in the best of society.'

Mr Rawstone, printer to the quality, since 1752, tried charging 'for the considerable efforts being made.'

'The Coat of Arms, designed by the College of Heralds,' said Mary Anne foreseeing what the man was about to say.

'It is complex, my lady, consisting of a grapevine, boars' heads, erased on a field supported by an eagle and a lion, holding pendant to an escutcheon charged with a castle ...'

'You are lucky to get the order. For a further reduction I shall recommend you to my friends ...'

'Why a castle, dearest?' enquired Disraeli placing the design behind the mantel-clock.

'For the Basevis' Spanish ancestral castle.'

Mary Anne continued to patronise the Hughenden trades people, demanding the highest standards of service, for the minutest amounts. Antonelli continued to walk shame-faced down into the village returning uneaten goods to baker, grocer, candlestick maker ... In fact the only difference a title made to Mary Anne's suppliers were orders written on coroneted paper signed Beaconsfield, even Disraeli was startled to receive notes from: '*Your Devoted Beaconsfield.*'

In the smoke room of the Falcon Inn, Mary Anne's elevation was the sole subject of conversation, but no glasses were raised to toast the Lady at the Manor to say, 'She deserves it, God bless her.'

Mary Anne overheard cook complaining, 'In my line of business, when one works for the aristocracy, one expects the trades people to nod and smile at one.'

'She's lucky to be employed at all,' Mary Anne told Disraeli in a miff.

He never noticed the servants anyway and continued to call the cook, Mrs Brown, when her name was Smith. 'You cannot give her notice. We've had her for years, dearest. She could not get another job now.'

The gossip continued downstairs.

'She even wears her coronet in bed.'

'Old Dis has pulled it off again.' He stays in the Lower House, while his peerage is worn by his Lady.'

'Don't bother with the tittle-tattle. The newspapers are kinder. It's them that carry weight,' Disraeli told his wife.

Punch wrote:

L ady of Hughenden, Punch, drawing near,
A ffably offers a homage sincere;
D eign to accept it – though playful its tone,
Y our heart will tell you it comes from his own.

B attle full oft with your Lord he has done,
E ver in fairness and often in fun,
A dding, as friends and antagonist know,
C heer, when his enemy struck a good blow.
O pportune moment he finds, nothing loth,
N ow, for a tribute more pleasant to both.
S mile on the circlet a husband prepares,
F or his Guide to the triumph she honours and shares!
I n it acknowledged what ne-er can be paid,
E arnest devotion and womanly aid.
L ong may the gems in that coronal flame,
D ecking Her brow who's more proud of his fame.

The Morning Post managed to congratulate Disraeli.

'... *while choosing to remain a Commoner, he accepts the proffered Coronet to place on the brow of his wife to whose qualities he has borne public testimony, and to whose affectionate aid he has acknowledged himself indebted for much of his success in life ...*'

Montague Corry's father, a First Lord of the Admiralty, and great admirer of Mary Anne, congratulated her at one of Lady Palmerston's tea parties, addressing her as 'Mrs Dizzy".

'I don't mind you calling me Mrs Dizzy, but I won't allow anybody else to do so.'

She had been a former little milliner, Mrs Dizzy, for too long. Now Mary Anne was a wife of a former Prime Minister, and Peeress in her own right. They may laugh at her behind her back, but before her face they would treat her with respect.

Norah Rooke, as before any great occasion, placed by Mary Anne's elbow, brandy with little water.

'It is our secret, Norah, I need it to give me courage so I can enter a great room and it keeps the pain away ... for a while.'

Rooke puffed a little more powder on to her mistress's nose. When her eyesight became poorer she placed above her right breast the miniature Mary Anne always wore of Disraeli as a young man.

Mary Anne took a deep breath and walked into society as a Peeress with head held high and covered in diamonds. Great-aunt Mary Anne's pearls could be worn with impunity.

Many of the ladies of quality were not amused. They asked amongst themselves, 'How could the Queen elevate that ridiculous, vulgar old woman?'

Lady Sumners was particularly vociferous on the point. She blamed Mary Anne for the decline of her man, Travis-Manners. He was an ex-sergeant major in the Guards, who was known throughout society for his ability to announce her ladyship's guests, in such a clear manner, that everybody in the grand ballroom heard every word he said.

That evening Travis-Manners had managed to announce: 'Your Majesty, Ladies and Gentleman, Mrs William Ewart Gladstone,' in such a way that nobody noticed her clothes were in such disarray that the shawl thrown around her shoulders hardly covered her bosom. The bodice of her dress flounced along pinned to her petticoats and Mrs Gladstone only noticed it as she stepped forward to curtsy to the Queen.

Following this incident Travis-Manners needed to gaze fixedly at The Battle of Aporto. The killing and maiming in the painting always restored him when he was a little stressed. He straightened up and beamed for coming up amongst the pineapples, swords, and flowers of the Grinling Gibbons carved stairway were the Disraelis. As they approached the Major Domono cleared his throat ready to announce. 'The Rt. Honourable Benjamin Disraeli.'

The company hovering in the ballroom drew breath and waited. Disraeli's performance was one of the sights of the season. His timing was superb. As Travis-Manners said 'Raeli' Disraeli would step forward, arms outstretched, to greet his hostess. As he did so he held everyone's attention adding much to Mr Travis-Manners' reputation.

Travis-Manners was about to announce, 'The Rt. Honourable' when he felt a light tap of a fan on his wrist. Startled, the great presence looked down to a little woman less than five tall who was looking up at him. 'Mrs Disraeli,' Travis-Manners muttered.

The company shuffled. They asked each other, 'Was this not Mrs Disraeli? What was Disraeli doing standing behind her?'

The little woman held the big man's gaze. He grew quite pink. 'Viscountess Beaconsfield and Mr Disraeli.'

Travis-Manners caught Disraeli's eye, who nodded a 'yes' with a smile.

Travis-Manners announced, 'Viscountess Beaconsfield.' He felt another tap on his wrist.

'If you please I *beckon*, I do not go on fire like a *beacon*.'

Nobody had ever criticised his announcing before. Travis Manners began again. Lady Sumners said, 'You can see the poor man shaking from here.'

Viscountess Beaconsfield, in deepest Tory blue with ruffles, with Dizzy's miniature pinned to her right breast, swept into the ballroom.

As Disraeli passed Travis-Manners he patted his shoulder. 'Never mind old man Mrs Disraeli has a heart of gold.'

Realizing what he had said he smiled at Travis-Manners in a conspiratorial manner, just like a Cheshire cat.

29 Departure

As a couple a years passed by and Mary Anne became weaker and one evening the bath chair stood alone. On its seat lay a piece of embroidery – which would never now be finished. In the centre of the terrace steps Mary Anne stood quite still, upright. Her hands clasping a gold-topped stick.

Her face puckered up. The pains in her stomach cut into her like a butcher's knife filleting out giblets. She longed to cry out but stopped because at the far end of the garden Antonelli was picking the last of the Microfolio roses. His hearing was sharp and he had been instructed to tell Disraeli when his wife was in pain.

Mary Anne straightened herself up, leaning now only with her right hand on the cane. 'Dizzy must not know how near the end is.'

The pain came sharply again. Mary Anne bit her lip tightening her grip on the stick.

Charles watching through the French windows came out of the house carrying a glass of champagne sparkling invitingly. He was followed by a boy with one of the Hepplewhites from the dining room. The lad had thrown casually over his right shoulder the Queen's shawl.

Mary Anne turned and watched as they processed towards her.

'It is cold, madam, do you really want to stay outside?'

'The wind brings with it a slight reminder of summer. I want to remember it before winter closes in.' She sat down, sitting upright as possible on the chair not allowing her back to touch the chair's back. Charles wrapped around her the heather dyed shawl. She sniffed at the Balmoral tartan. The smell of Highland peak, heathers and hazy smoked filled cottages comforted her – reminding her of Bramford Speke. She felt it was a mother hiding a daughter's disgraceful distended stomach from the world. She could hear Victoria saying again, 'Lady Beaconsfield is a particular friend of the Queen,' and knowing the mocking laughter would cease. More than ever she was grateful to Dizzy for his warmth and care.

Mary Anne's reveries were broken by Charles's voice.

'Mr Disraeli expects to be with you in an hour, madam.' He discreetly handed his mistress the note in Disraeli's handwriting.

How kind Charles is thought Mary Anne to tell me what the note says. He knows I cannot see to read it.

'I must remember to take off the shawl before Mr Disraeli sees me. It is a horrible reminder to him of long weekends with the Queen in cold rooms, eating lukewarm food and not daring to joke as he did in the other great houses. Thank goodness for something warm at last.'

'We shall remember, madam,' said Charles.

Mary Anne smiled to herself. Charles was such a tactful dear. Dizzy the great charmer. She had not been the only one to say the wrong thing. 'I like bad wine,' Dizzy had once said to the Duke of Buccleuch. 'Good wines are such a bore one knows what to expect.'

Charles saw the gentle laugh and thought it was because Mary Anne saw Antonelli was running up the terrace steps, waving the roses towards her. 'Mr Disraeli told me to give you these.'

The sight of the Italian servant reminded Mary Anne that to him nightingales whistled. It had amused Disraeli so much.

Mary Anne prayed that Dizzy would not tell her yet again that he had met so and so and told him, 'We at Hughenden have nightingales who whistle.' Her patience now was so threadbare.

The ivy around the windows began rustling, the peacocks shrieked sensing the approaching darkness and the cold hand of winter stealing forward.

The wind has a nip in it as grandma used to say, said Mary Anne to herself sipping at the champagne. It tasted like flat lemonade making her feel sick. Her throat felt rough and her mouth puckered with the sharpness. She longed for a brandy and beer, but it upset Dizzy to see her drink so commonly.

She could drink no more. 'Charles, tell Mr Disraeli I have eaten already.'

He nodded understandingly. 'I think it is time for madam to go inside.' He took his mistress gently by the arm and half leaning on her butler, Mary Anne walked into the house. As she always did.

The bath chair remained out on the lawn until quite late – long after madam had gone to bed the spirit of Mary Anne lingered in the gardens and the beech trees.

In August 1862 Mary Anne held a garden party.

She supervised the spreading of butter on to bread for eighty children. There was always the danger of Mrs Cripps being heavy with the butter. Three moulds of jelly had been prepared and in a pile in the corner were toy guns for the boys and suitable presents for the little girls.

Grown-ups were invited to a luncheon and were to be offered fillet of veal, galantine of chicken, grouse dishes, lamb cutlets and various fruits and vegetables 'all from our own gardens' apple tart or a compote of plumb and greengage.

Mary Anne was preparing for the school children's summer treat; Mrs Hussey's children arrived with their governess, if you please – uninvited.

Onlookers said she skipped and danced about with the children, not looking a day over forty – she was almost seventy. Mrs Disraeli wore a crinoline with a petticoat of fine cambric, with flounces – numerous exquisitely goffered and overall a white dress of French muslin, with purple pansies and on her head a straw with a black band – suitable for a twenty year old.

Disraeli shot the gun to start the many races and the company consumed 28 champagnes, 4 ports, 4 amontillado and 4 morellos.

Mary Anne's note in her account book ends with: *'Company took too much of everything. Mrs Cripps washed up well.'*

It was a cold March in 1872.

Mary Anne wandering around the grounds of Hughenden, enjoyed the daffodils more than she had ever enjoyed them in any spring before. She was cold and sensed this spring would be her last.

Disraeli told her, 'They want me to go to Manchester, to address a mass rally.'

She was eighty years old now and dying. Could she make just one more effort for his sake?

Easter 1872. The date that would be one of the landmarks for the Conservative party. The Disraelis arrived in Manchester Piccadilly Station, to cheers of 'Good Old Dizzy.'

'It is all well and good now,' he said in amazement to Mary Anne. 'I thought it was not my Government they disliked. It was me.'

She did not say, 'It is me they call dear Mrs Dizzy and give me posies in the street.'

He helped her out of the carriage, bowing low over her hand. It was difficult to stand tall to take the march past. Mary Anne looked at Disraeli. He stood holding his hat, just like a Royal person, as 250 Conservative Associations paraded before them.

The Queen had never received such civilian acclaim and to please her, Mary Anne wore a new Dolly Vardon, covered in "primroses" which she had to hold on to as the factory workers dashed across the street and cheered as they crowded round the carriage.

Dizzy looks so slight against Romaine Callender, thought Mary Anne. The Tory leader of the Northern Territories substantial figure greeted them coolly. He had never received such a welcome, just massed brass bands. Disraeli shook his hand firmly. 'Pleased to meet you again, old friend.'

Callender was a sound Manchester businessman and like all his sort, the centre player within a network, of influential friends and relations.

'You can't help liking the chap – odd though he is,' Mary Anne heard the leader say to his son.

As the party drove to the Free Trade Hall, they passed the Exchange, 'The largest Exchange room in Europe,' lectured Mr Callender. Disraeli pointed to a new building being erected.

'Ah,' said Callender. 'Manchester, Mr Disraeli is arriving. Mr Alfred Waterhouse, is building our new Town Hall.'

The Disraelis looked respectful. 'My cousin, Basevi, is building Belgrave Square.'

'Is that so, Mr Disraeli,' said Mr Callender, unimpressed by a mere square full of houses.

On 3 April, the Disraelis left the Callender's villa in Victoria Park, on the outskirts of Manchester. If Mr Callender had known about the Renaissance in depth he would have recognized a man of history rising to speak that afternoon, but Mr Callender did not see himself as a new Renaissance man of Manchester. Disraeli understood "this new country" and for three and a quarter hours his beautiful actor's voice echoed through that Lombardian Venetian hall.

'The programme of the Conservative party is to maintain the Constitution of the country.'

Disraeli brought his audience's attention to the powerful forces aligned against the Monarchy, the House of Lords, and the church – in fact to destroy the very constitution itself.

He finished his speech with the words, 'But the situation is still dangerous. There are occasionally earthquakes, and even and anon the dark rumbling of the sea.'

Suddenly, he stepped forward to the edge of the stage, his speech over, the audience rose en masse, cheering Disraeli to the very rooftops.

'Any moment the Doge himself will appear,' muttered Mary Anne as Disraeli bowed low to his audience, acknowledging the thunderous applause like a first night audience, but when he beckoned to Mary Anne to step on to the platform: *'the utmost deafening and enthusiastic cheers broke forth from all parts of the building,'* wrote the staid

Times. Never before had Mary Anne been a part of a political event so well stage-managed.

Mary Anne, fatigued, left Disraeli and waited at Victoria Park, Callender's home, just outside Manchester. They could hear the cheers of the crowds.

'People are spilling out into the street,' said Callender.

Mary Anne sat waiting, drained and expectant. She strained to hear horses' hooves, the noise growing louder and louder, and now the sound of carriage wheels coming up the drive and the sound of the wheels of his carriage approaching. Mary Anne, rushed out of the cold drawing room and like a girl of eighteen, flung herself into Disraeli's arms.

'Oh! Dizzy, Dizzy, it is the greatest night of all. This pays for all.'

In the empty hall, a cleaner sniffing two empty water bottles, observed, 'Funny water.'

The day before Young Corry scoured Manchester for white brandy, 'To keep the boss going.'

Finally, the only person left in the hall enjoying Disraeli's accolade was young John Gorst, Disraeli's new Central Office manager, 'Brilliantly staged managed ... coverage in all papers ... like yesterday ...'

Yawning Gorst said, 'Back to work,' setting off to smile and woo numerous newspaper editors.

Shortly, after these great achievements, Mary Anne returned to London with Disraeli – exhausted.

On May 7 against Disraeli's advice, Mary Anne went to a party at Lady Waldegrave's. 'I couldn't stay to the end but I am quite proud nobody knew I didn't feel well.'

The next day, there was a grand function at Buckingham Palace. Sir William hummed and hawed and Disraeli said, 'Definitely not, you cannot go.'

Mary Anne wandered into the State Drawing room, smiled at the Queen, nodded to various courtiers and collapsed. She made no fuss, leaving discreetly.

It is the last time, I shall ever go to the Palace, she said to herself, as the carriage drove slowly through the wrought iron gates and she heard the guard changing.

While the Disraelis remained in town, Corry managed affairs at Hughenden.

Disraeli wrote to him: *'To see her every day weaker and weaker is heartrending; to witness the gradual death of one who has shared so long and so completely my life entirely unmans me.'*

Disraeli's Manchester success was followed by a greater one at Crystal Palace, on 24th June Here Disraeli destroyed "Old Toryism" for ever, and played midwife to the New Conservatism.

'We must,' said Disraeli, 'maintain our institutions to uphold the Empire, and to elevate the condition of the people.'

Disraeli dwelt on the need for factory inspectorates, purity of food, adequate health legislation, making the pun, 'Sanitas santitatum, omnia sanitas,' summarising his speech for people to have 'air, light and water.'

The Liberal Party referred to this speech as Disraeli's policy of "sewage".

'They might scorn,' snapped Mary Anne, but rats the size of kittens played in the Paddington sewers and the Prince of Wales's recent illness could have been brought on by lack of hygiene but of course nobody thinks of that.'

Both the Disraelis were exhausted by Whitsun and went home to Hughenden. Mary Anne was now considerably weaker. In the early evening, she asked Antonelli, to push her around the grounds in a bath chair.

The public holiday over, Mary Anne insisted on returning to Grosvenor Gate with Disraeli.

'Norah, my wedding ring no longer fits.' It had to be forced off her finger. 'I feel unclean, unwed. It has not left my finger, since Dizzy placed it there.'

Mary Anne's note says: *'Dizzy's wedding ring, taken off today because my hand and finger is swolen. July 6 1872.'*

On 17 July, a carriage rumbled to Lady Loudon's. Every jolt touched every nerve in her body. 'If only this weight had once been a baby,' Mary Anne sobbed quietly to herself as she journeyed on to meet her dear friend the Duchess of Cambridge.

Mary Anne, ringless, but otherwise bejewelled, entered the drawing room. Despite the temperature being nearly a hundred the windows were firmly closed against London noise and dirt and the scent of hothouse flowers, smoke and women's perfume stank throughout the room. The room and its guests seemed to spin around Mary Anne as she fell to the floor.

'I shall be all right,' she cried out, crawling to get up and concerned not to be an inconvenience to anybody. She tried to stop Lady Loudon rushing for brandy, servants running hither and thither, but she was content to be picked up in Disraeli's arms and carried gently out of the room.

'I cannot cause such inconvenience again. I shall go out no more, Dizzy.'

Mary Anne was in immense pain and distress. Disraeli's Parliamentary commitments separated him a great deal from his dying wife, but knowing his life must continue after her own had ended she insisted he continued with his duties. Without her husband's constant presence Mary Anne became depressed.

From the House, sometimes from his office, other times from the Chamber itself, Mary Anne received loving little notes.

'I have nothing to tell you except that I love you, which, I fear, you will think rather dull ... I fear will be very late; but I hope to find you in a sweet sleep.'

Her last note said:

My own Dearest

'I miss you sadly. I feel so grateful for your constant tender love and kindness. I certainly feel better this evening ...

Your own devoted Beaconsfield'

Now, they found Mary Anne could not eat.

Lord Cairns sent pheasants from his estates, which tempted Mary Anne a little.

When Mary Anne began to haemorrhage badly a distraught Disraeli wrote to Cairns:

'We have not been separated for three and thirty years, and, during all that time, in her society I never have had a moment of dullness. It tears my heart to see such a spirit suffer, and suffer so much.'

To take her mind off things the couple resumed their exploration of the outskirts of London travelling in the new light four wheeled, two seater Victoria, bought specially for the purpose, a low step and entrance made it less painful for Mary Anne. Once she was seated, she could see about her.

Disraeli recorded the outings:

'What miles of villas! And of all sorts of architecture! What beautiful churches! What gorgeous palaces of Geneva. One day we came upon a feudal castle, with a donjon keep high in the air. It turned out to be the new City prison in Camden Road but it deserves a visit – I mean externally. Of all the kingdoms ruled over by our gracious mistress, the most remarkable is her royaume de Cockaigne, and perhaps the one the Queen has least visited. Her faithful servants in question, preparing their expeditions with a map, investigated all parts of it from Essex to Surrey, and Lady Beaconsfield calculated from the 1st of August to the end of September she travelled 220 miles.'

In October Mary Anne left London. Disraeli drove her through High Wycombe, into Bradenham country and back to Hughenden amongst glorious autumn beech trees. For a month they thought Hughenden had worked its magic. The cancer gave Mary Anne peace. She could even eat a little.

Montague Corry was so confident in Mary Anne's regained health that he organised a trip to Glasgow for Disraeli. But early in November a crisis occurred.

Mary Anne suffering dreadfully. She drank brandy Hanoverian style snapping, 'Dying is a controllable state.'

Lord Harcourt sent draughts of Trinity Ale. Dr Leggett exclaimed. 'Lady Beaconsfield, my dear lady, what quantities of ale you are consuming.'

'Doctor. You're talking to the woman who showed Wellington how to drink.'

During November Mary Anne brought her household together. 'As I have no intention of dying, just yet, from 21st to 25th November we are having a house party.'

Disraeli tried to dissuade Mary Anne. 'Such a course is far from wise, dearest.'

Doctor Legget sent messages to Sir William and Sir William sent messages back. Nevertheless, the guests arrived at Hughenden. They included John Manners, Lord Rosebery, Sir William Harcourt and Lord Ronald Gower.

Sir William Harcourt was a long time favourite flirting partner of Mary Anne. Over dinner she reminded him, 'When I was first married, I gave you Sir William, a naughty French novel to read in bed. Do you remember when I handed the book to you, I spied you looking at Dizzy's picture of naked Venus.' I said, 'You should not be looking at that picture, Sir William,' and you said, 'It is nothing to the Venus Dizzy has in his bedroom,' And you gave me such a gallant bow.'

The other guests, hidden behind the sails of Mary Anne's famous windmill, commented, 'She poor old lady has sadly altered in looks since London.'

'Shrunk and more like an anointed corpse than ever ...'

'It is so wearisome, one having to sit by and hear much of Mrs Disraeli's twaddle and little of Mr D's talk.'

Only a few days later on 5 December Disraeli wrote to Corry:

'Things have taken a bad turn here – I am most distressed.'

During the last week of Mary Anne's life, she became delirious and Disraeli scarcely left her room.

Disraeli wrote to Philip Rose: *'If anything happens I am totally unable to meet the catastrophe.'*

It was Corry who gave his boss sensible, stable, support and it was Corry who replied patiently to the Queen's endless telegrams.

Mary Anne smiled. The Queen was asking after her. The vicar suggested she prepared to meet Jesus. Mary Anne, propped up by pillows said, 'Dizzy is my Jesus and I don't want to leave him.' Wearily muttering and half-delirious, she added, 'One spends so much of one's life in bed asleep. We do not need so much sleep – until at last we must.'

The two swans on the lake remained quite still, looking up at the window third from the right. As the church clock struck noon, Disraeli closed the curtains. The swans flew up into the sun, never to return. The carol singers coming up the drive were told, 'Go away children the mistress of Hughenden is dead.'

As defined in her terms of employment, immediately Mary Anne was dead Norah Rooke laid her out and took her mistress's clothes to her own room. They were for her use, now.

While Rooke was so engaged Disraeli dealt with the practicalities of death. Dr Leggett signed the death certificate giving Mary Anne's death at seventy-six years of age. She was in fact eighty. Did Disraeli know and play the game right to the end?

Amongst his wife's belongings Disraeli found every note he had ever written to her, together with the locks of his hair she had cut over the years, neatly packaged and a letter written to him from the Continent in 1856.

My own dear Husband.

If I should depart this life before you, leave orders that we may be buried in the same grave at whatever distance you may die from England. And now God bless you my dearest, kindest. You have been a perfect husband to me. Be put by my side in the same grave. And now, farewell my dear Dizzy. Do not live alone dearest. Someone I earnestly hope you may find as attached to you as your own devoted Mary Anne.

Disraeli read in *The Times:*

'Who would have supposed, 35 years ago, that the coming history of English political life would take a direction from the unselfish affection of a woman, and a woman not marked by any unusual capacities? Society would have been as little likely to single out the widow of Mr Wyndham Lewis as destined to play an important part in life as the politicians of the day would have been inclined to see in Mr Disraeli the future leader of the Tory party. Yet the marriage which sprang from that affection was an historical event.'

EPILOGUE
Disraeli's Death

On a cold wet day, five days before Christmas, Mary Anne's tenants carried her coffin into the graveyard of Hughenden. No trades' people followed the procession, shop blinds remained up and in the inn shopkeepers toasted each other.

'The old cat is no more.'

'Earth to earth, ashes to ashes.'

For some ten minutes Disraeli stood bareheaded in the wind and the rain, looking down into the grave.

'Who'll dye is hair now?' enquired the gravedigger to the air. Receiving no reply he began filling in the grave while Disraeli turned and walked back to the Manor – *alone* and to his greatest successes.

In the nine years which remained to him: Disraeli became Prime Minister again, bought the Suez Canal, consolidated the British Empire, established the modern political system, created Victoria Empress of India, became himself the Earl of Beaconsfield.

As instructed he courted variously elderly ladies without success. He grew closer to Victoria, who later on her favourite Prime Minister's death, came herself to place primroses on his coffin. While on business Disraeli lived alone in various London hotels – for Grosvenor Gate was entailed.

And now from outside he could here the muffled sound of the clip clop of horses. 'Straw,' he muttered to himself. 'They have put down straw.'

Young Corry, no he was no longer young Corry, but a middle-aged man, had papers in his hand.

'My Lord …'

'You should have married Corry.'

'Your career is the only thing, my Lord, which has not disappointed me.'

'Who else had said that somebody … very long ago.'

He thought he was in a carriage now. The horses were galloping, a whip swished through the air. 'Go steady boys,' yelled the coachman.

He opened his eyes. He had been dreaming. It was becoming dusk.

'I hope becoming Lord Rowlandson will satisfy you, Monty.'

Corry smiled, never before had his "boss" called him by his Christian name.

Now, it was dark. They were in Mary Anne's sick room.

'Where was she? No, of course, Mary Anne was dead.'

Figures in the corner muttered to each other. One of them came towards him. It was young Corry.

'My Lord, the Queen wishes ...'

'Wishes? Not commands, not demands?'

'To be with you during your last hours.'

Disraeli manged to croak.

'No, no she will only ask me to take a message to Albert.'

From somewhere came a silvery laugh.

'Oh Dizzy really.'

Unseen fingers closed Disraeli's eyes.

The voice whispered:

'Welcome home my dearest husband, welcome home.'